D1474275

THE PACT

Charles D. Richardson

Published by JamaRPublisher, LLC

Interior Book Design by www.integrativeink.com
Cover Design by Angie Shearstone, Shearstone Creatives

Library of Congress Control Number: 2006935899
ISBN–13: 978-0-9789510-0-9
ISBN–10: 0-9789510-0-X
Printed in the USA by Lightning Source, Inc. on acid free paper.

"It is a double pleasure to deceive the deceiver."
– Proverb –

"Some are born great, some achieve greatness,
and some have greatness thrust upon 'em."
– William Shakespeare –
Twelfth Night

"The fox barks not when he would steal the lamb."
– William Shakespeare –
Henry VI

"Power tends to corrupt; absolute power corrupts absolutely."
– Lord Acton –

"Nuclear war, like the Cosmos, is beyond human
comprehension."
– Charles D. Richardson –

ACKNOWLEDGMENTS

To John R. Kent, Joint Strike Fighter Media Relations; Lockheed Martin, who provided me with invaluable information about the F-35 program; my brother Bobby Richardson, an F-117 expert; Stephanee Killen, Integrative Ink; Tony Martini, former Air Force F-4 jock and Air Traffic Controller; and Paul Hoover, former A-4 Navy Airdale and Air Traffic Controller.

Last, but not least, to my encourager, author, idea maker, and my loving wife, Jama.

THE PACT

PROLOGUE

August 2011
Atlantic Ocean

The sleek F-35C Snake, officially known by the US Navy as the Lightning II, shudders each time a gust of wind howls across the tossing deck of the *USS Harry S. Truman*. Commander Scott Wallace occasionally glances outside as he scans the checklist on the Panoramic Cockpit Display (PCD). The wind-driven rain beats against his canopy like a jackhammer. The colored-coded jerseys and helmets of the catapult team are barely visible. Hampered by the violent weather, they struggle valiantly in the partial darkness preparing the Snake for launch. Using close coordination with Scott, the catapult team coaxes the Snake forward and into launch position. Finally, the tow bar locks into the shuttle and the holdback mechanism is connected. The Snake is now attached to a two-piston, steam-powered catapult located underneath the deck, which will literally sling it into the air. Commander Wallace inserts the lat/long of KNHK, the international identifier for Patuxent River Naval Air Station, into the INS/GPS.

After verifying that the Snake is attached to the catapult and the jet blast deflector is up, the catapult officer, known as the shooter, advises Scott to throttle up. The F135 turbofan engine quickly spools up, straining against the holdback mechanism that keeps the Snake in place until the launch button is pushed. Flight controls, engine instruments, electrical systems, and hydraulics are all go. The Air Boss' radio crackles in Scott's helmet.

"Rifle 1, Dragonfly, we're steaming at twenty-two knots, wind is from 120 at 30 knots, gusting to 45 knots. Altimeter 2882. Radar indicates the eye of Hurricane Esther is forty miles southwest of our position."

He flips a switch, turns the island superstructure green light on, and transmits, "Rifle 1, you're cleared to launch at your discretion. Good luck and fly safely."

Scott thumbs the transmit button and replies, "Roger that, Dragonfly," as he enters the altimeter setting.

When the bow sinks to its lowest point and starts to rise, Scott presses his helmet against the head restraint and salutes. The catapult officer glances to make sure both green launch lights are on and the launch crew is in position, pauses a second until the bow rises to an optimum position, then hits the red launch button. The catapult and the 40,000 pounds of thrust from the jet engine hurls the F-35C with such force that within two seconds the indicated airspeed zooms from 48 knots to 150 knots. Five seconds later, the Snake enters thick, churning clouds. Bright lightning dances in all quadrants. He reduces power, punches gear and flaps up on the PCD, and begins zigzagging around the heaviest areas of precipitation. The turbulent air of Esther heaves Scott's Snake in all directions, as if it was nothing more to contend with than a mere gnat.

Moments later, he breaks out on top of the weather at 47,000 feet. He had been too preoccupied by the extreme weather to communicate by radio. Clear of the weather, he contacts the Carrier Air Traffic Control Center (CATCC) which has been monitoring his flight on radar and radio since launch. He continues climbing until reaching 58,000 feet, then levels off and adjusts the power for cruise flight. It's an amazingly beautiful moonlit night, with smooth air and almost continuous lightning in the clouds several thousand feet below. The eye of the gigantic hurricane is clearly visible on the PCD. This is the final phase of the Navy F-35C Operational Test and Evaluation Program. Exceedingly trying. Exceedingly dangerous. But necessary. The Snake must prove over and over that it's got the stuff to operate in adverse conditions. Only a handful of naval aviators were selected to complete the grueling test pilot program. Later, they will write the operational manuals for future airdales to follow.

As expected, the Snake has performed flawlessly in weather conditions exceeding the minimum requirements for the test. He touches the auto-pilot button on the PCD. This is the first time in several hours he could let his brain rewind. He sucks his lungs full of oxygen and relaxes.

Wow! That was much worse than I anticipated. Glad it's over.

Probably need four or five days at Pax River to complete the paperwork and debrief the Admiral. Then detour by Norfolk on my way to Fort Worth NAS and spend some time with the family. Over the past year, I've been absent way too much. Now that we've finished, maybe things will change. Maybe I'll get a desk job at Norfolk and work eight to five. Ha. Who am I kidding? I'd go crazy without driving one of these babies. And making sure those young airdales who will push these Snakes through their paces know what they're doing. Admiral hinted I might be assigned as liaison to the SAID project. Hope not. I want an air-wing of my own. Do some real flying.

A time clock in his brain breaks his chain of thought. Time to take care of business. After mentally calculating fuel burn, and current position, he makes a comparison with the onboard computer. The computer is relatively close to being within conformance. He adjusts his facemask and smiles. All is well. He'd check in with the New York Air Route Traffic Control Center (Center) in approximately thirty minutes for an IFR clearance. Only one aircraft moves across his PCD screen, and it is fifty miles' distance and several thousand feet below, maintaining a constant flight level.

Probably stop and refuel at Knoxville on my way back to Fort Worth from Norfolk. Stay overnight with my parents. Haven't seen them in…almost two years. Man, where's the time go? It flies…

At this very instant, Scott's best friend, Major Vance R. McGruder, diligently guides a smart bomb toward a target in Esfahan, Iran. This event will forever change both of their lives in a dramatic and chilling manner.

Like to see Grandpa, too. What a great man. Funny. Wish I could tell a joke like he does. Great timing and never forgets the punch line. Keeps everyone in stitches at parties. Loves genealogy and telling stories about his ancestors. After he retired from his ranch, he spent several years rummaging through attics, UT archives, closets, and any place else rumored to have family historical documents or photographs. Some of them were handed down and carefully preserved through several generations, as far back as the Revolutionary War. Unknown to the family he published a book containing this assorted historical data and presented a copy to each family member as his Christmas gift. I pretended that I was really impressed. But a fourteen-year-old kid has other things on his mind than family genealogy. I remember very vividly the first time I did become interested in his book. I was home during spring break cleaning out my closet, and there it was. Removed the dust with a towel, sat down cross-legged in the middle of my room, and thumbed through every page. I was intrigued when I discovered that my ancestor, who fought in the Revolutionary War, had my identical name. Then I recalled Mom telling me about him when I was very young and that she had named me after him. Didn't think much of it at the time. There were no photographs of him or his family, but his powerful, descriptive words were almost as good as a picture. He kept a detailed journal with many intriguing stories, describing events in great detail. My favorite was and still is the exploits of my ancestor, Major Scott Wallace.

1

Holston Mountain, NC
September 19, 1780

Scott Wallace looked up from weeding his garden when Bronco, his coon dog, peeked through the split-rail fence and began barking. Well below Scott's vantage point, a horse galloped through a creek, splashing water that formed a small rainbow. He removed his wide brimmed hat and wiped sweat from his brow for a better look. It was mid-September, but the sun was beating down unmercifully hot on the southern slope of four-thousand-foot Mount Holston. Perspiration turned his homespun shirt dark across his chest and back.

The rider spurred his fatigued horse, driving it straight up the steep ridge and directly toward Scott. Keeping his eyes on the intruder, he slowly picked up Lucy from her resting place. Lucy was his long-rifle, named after his mother Lucille. He felt for his knife, verifying that it was in its deerskin sheath, then checked Lucy to make sure she was ready for action. She was.

As the rider approached up the steep embankment, his horse slinging dirt and small rocks into the air, Scott recognized him as William McCullough, a member of the Watauga Association. Cautious relief settled over him as he expelled air from his lungs. Scott had chatted with him on several occasions at the Watauga meetings and occasionally at church.

Scott eyed the heavy rifle in his hand for a moment. She'd been manufactured somewhere in Pennsylvania in 1776. Sporting a .50 caliber, 48-inch barrel with rifling, she was unbelievably reliable up to an incredible 300 yards—and deadly under 200 yards. He carefully leaned Lucy against a spot where two rails converged in the split rail fence.

The fatigued horse came to an abrupt halt, its nose only inches from the split rail fence, breathing rapidly. White foam dripped from its mouth, and its nostrils changed in size and shape with each deep breath. McCullough threw one leg over his lathered horse, leaped onto the fence, and then to the ground while Scott constrained Bronco. The two young men approached each other as McCullough removed his wide-brimmed hat and extended his hand.

"Morning, Scott."

"Howdy. Where you off to in such a hurry?" Scott replied, surprised that McCullough remembered his first name.

"I'm helping recruit a militia. We might be in big trouble with the Redcoats."

"Redcoats?"

"You know, the British, and of course them turncoats in the Carolinas that are fighting fer them. They been fighting up North for almost four years, I reckon, and now they plan to invade our mountain country 'less we buckle under to the king and his dogs. That's 'less we stop 'em. The people of the Carolinas who are fighting the British and their Loyalists are steadily losing. Last spring they captured Savannah and Charleston."

Scott's face paled. He had not heard from his parents in almost a year. Their home was in Charleston. He wiped perspiration from the back of his neck with a piece of homespun and replied, "Do you know any details, if Charleston was destroyed or how many were killed during the siege?"

"I only know the city was bombarded considerably. I don't know about civilian casualties. The Continentals protecting Charleston surrendered after suffering a great loss."

Scott stared off into the distant mountains and said wistfully, "My parents live in Charleston."

"Oh…real sorry to hear that. Hope they're okay."

"Me too. I'm acquainted with Charleston. Lived there for almost a year when I was a boy. Big houses built right on the ocean's edge. Pretty place. Always big ships coming and going. At times, the streets were clogged with British soldiers. Strutting around half drunk in their bright uniforms as if they owned everything and everybody. Too many people live close to each other, and most of the time they're in a big hurry to get somewhere. And it has a bad odor. Not like up here in these mountains where everything's clean. But my parents love

Charleston. They own, or did own, a small inn."

McCullough noticed Scott's change in demeanor. His face was ashen. McCullough tried to cheer him up. He thought for a moment, then said, "I've heard Charleston is called 'the place of the four m's.'"

"The four m's?"

"Yep. Mud, men, mosquitoes, and manure."

McCullough let that thought soak in for a second, then began laughing heartily. Scott didn't. He only managed a thin smile as he stared at a distant peak. His mind was absorbed with the dreadful thought that his parents were probably in great peril.

After a short pause, McCullough continued. "Anyhow, in July, Colonel Shelby and Major Robinson took about four hundred men, including me, across the mountains to help confuse and kill a few Brits and their weak-kneed Loyalist turncoats. We were involved in some relatively small hit-and-run clashes against detachments of a smart aleck British Major named Ferguson."

A big grin came over McCullough's face. "But at a place called Musgrove's Mill, we really made 'em bite the dust, killing a passel, and took about seventy prisoners. We were preparing to hit 'em again at a fort further south called Ninety-Six when a courier arrived with word that a large battle had been won by the British and Loyalists at a place further south called Camden."

"Camden?" queried Scott. "I've heard of Camden, but I don't know exactly where it's located."

"Me neither. But must be fairly close to where we were

at the time. We were advised to get our butts out of there due to the overwhelming force in the area. We immediately split up with some of the men heading south fer Georgia, and others took the prisoners and went east. Some of Ferguson's men chased us 'til we escaped into our refuge, here in our mountains. Reckon it was enough to get Ferguson's ire up."

"How far into the mountains did Ferguson pursue you?"

"Stopped at the foothills. 'Bout this same time, a man from up Sapling Grove was visiting his aging parents who live—er, *did* live—in the North Carolina flatlands. While he was there, this Redcoat feller Ferguson and a band of thieves and turncoats burned his parents' home and barn to the ground—murdered his parents before his eyes while trying to get information that they didn't have. They beat him real bad and were ready to string him up when they found out he was one of us."

McCullough cupped his left hand over his mouth as if he were in pain.

"Knocked his front teeth out and let him go only after he swore he would deliver Ferguson's ultimatum to people in these parts. Of course, he would have gladly delivered the message voluntarily considering the seriousness of the threats, but I guess Ferguson don't think like us."

"Not at all. That's barbaric. Those Brits are supposed to be civilized," replied Scott.

Scott stepped over to the fence and gently patted the nose of McCullough's horse. He turned toward McCullough and said, "What did this Ferguson feller say?"

"He demanded in writing that all weapons be turned in

to a place to be designated by him, meetings couldn't take place without his express permission, and each family would pay a tax with food, horses, or anything of value as determined by Major Ferguson. All manufacturing of ammunition must either cease or be under his control. He also demanded that we take a loyalty oath to the king and sign papers to that affect. We would become slaves to him."

Scott lowered his head in deep thought and interjected, "I couldn't accept any of those absurd demands. I doubt if many of us would."

"Same here. I'd rather be dead."

Scott leaned over and picked two late-season tomatoes, wiped the dust off, and offered one to McCullough.

McCullough took the tomato and bit into it. He nodded his head in satisfaction, paused while he swallowed, and continued. "If we don't meet his demands, he threatens to invade our country in the spring. He probably wouldn't take any male prisoners and would burn and destroy any property that wasn't useful to him. He didn't mention our wives and children, but they have suffered greatly in the Carolinas, and we could probably expect worse."

While considering the obvious seriousness of the situation, Scott felt his pulse quicken and found it difficult to swallow as he digested the provoking news.

"We have discussed this many times at the general store, and at Mr. Sevier's house. Not everyone believes Ferguson could survive in these parts. But most of us agreed that we shouldn't take a chance—that we should go after him. Do our fighting somewhere else and not jeopardize our way of life. Anyhow, that's what brings me up here. Shelby and Sevier are forming a militia. All able-bodied men are strongly urged to muster at Sycamore Shoals between now and September 25 for selection and processing. We already have 'bout three hundred volunteers, but we know that not all of these will be acceptable. Riding ability, toughness, condition of your horse, and accuracy with a long-rifle are important matters to be considered. We are pleading for the help of every able-bodied man in these here parts."

"Almost three hundred volunteers? This place is growing mighty fast," Scott interjected.

"It's amazing ain't it?" drawled McCullough. He removed a deerskin tobacco pouch from his shirt and offered Scott a chew.

Scott shook his head. "Don't chew. Never liked the stuff. Hear it's not good for your system. Another bad Indian habit I don't need."

McCullough smiled, revealing his stained teeth. "Smart man. Wish I could stop."

McCullough momentarily stopped talking while he used his hunting knife to cut a chunk off of the twisted roll of tobacco. Then he continued, pausing occasionally to turn his head and spit.

"If you should decide to join us, report with your rifle, horse, and as much powder and lead as you can spare. I expect you'll be needing extra clothing and a blanket. Everything else will be supplied by Shelby and Sevier and several other big landowners in the valley. The men not selected to attack Ferguson will be assigned to help the families left behind and keep a watchful eye on the Cherokees. Two men will visit each family frequently and assist in killing hogs, gathering the winter's food supply, and making necessary repairs. Some fear an Indian uprising if the Indians discover that so many men are absent. That's a possibility, of course, but most of us believe that trouble with them is unlikely, especially now that winter is fast approaching."

Scott reached beneath a bush and pulled out a wooden bucket of cold water from his nearby spring, dipped a gourd dipper in the water, filled it, and began to drink, keeping his visitor in view. He swallowed most of the water, sloshed the remainder a few times to wash the gourd, and then tossed the water out. After refilling it, he handed it to McCullough. McCullough thoughtfully flipped the cud of tobacco out of his jaw with an index finger as he reached for the dipper.

Turning his head as McCullough drank, Scott noticed his wife Rebekka and their two young children, James and Melanie, peering out of their log cabin's rustic front door. Melanie grasped her mother's long skirt and remained out of the stranger's vision.

The cabin had been built four years earlier by Scott and his two neighbors, Edward McGruder and Thomas O'Neill. It was located on a relatively level location on top of a spur 1,400 feet above the valley and 3,900 feet above sea level. Visitors were rare and kindled a strong curiosity, especially in the children.

Scott cleared his throat and looked away from the cabin.

"As you can see, I have a young family to care for. You

said they would receive help. How can I be sure that my family would be treated well?"

"A fair question. A committee headed by Mr. Shelby will choose only men known to be trustworthy. Even so, they will be sent out in pairs and rotated on a weekly basis. We don't want men to worry 'bout their families. By the way, my wife and I have two young girls, and I have volunteered again."

Scott nodded. "Sounds reasonable. I'll discuss all of this with my family and make a decision."

McCullough offered another handshake as he said, "Fair enough. You look like the type of person that would greatly assist us. We'll pray fer Charleston. Hope to see you soon."

McCullough turned, scampered over the fence, and straddled his horse, which had not moved except to flush flies away by shaking its skin and whisking its tail. He waved at Scott's family with his hat, turned, and scrambled his horse down the steep slope in the direction of Scott's two neighbors.

Scott picked up Lucy and walked toward their cabin as James and Melanie scampered toward him. He wiped the distraught look from his face. The children must not know the awful truth.

"Who was that man, Daddy?" Melanie asked, hugging Scott's leg, obviously relieved that the stranger had left.

Scott knelt down, smiled, and said, "He's a friend from across the valley. Attends church with us."

"Oh, okay."

Rebekka remained on the small front porch holding a cupped hand above her eyes to shield the glare. Her long red hair glistened in the sun. As Scott and the children approached, he could see the concerned look on her face.

They sat down on the log steps leading up to the porch. Bronco yawned and lay down in a shady spot. Lucy lay on the porch, her long barrel pointing away from the family.

"Rebekka, that was William McCullough from across

the valley. He's a member of the Watauga Association and our church."

"I recognized him. What brings him up here?" Rebekka asked cautiously.

"Needs our help. Seems the British have brought their war to our neighbors across the mountains in the Carolinas. Some of the men from our community have been assisting the Carolinians in their struggle. Now the British are threatening to retaliate and destroy us for helping. Shelby, Sevier, and some others are forming an army and plan to go across the mountains to help. They want me to go with 'em." He didn't mention Charleston or his parents. Perhaps later.

Rebekka clasped her hand across her mouth and looked away, suppressing the tears that sprang up in her large brown eyes.

Scott stood up and reached for Rebekka's hand, grasping it tightly. James and Melanie watched their parents intently. Rebekka felt the rough calluses on the palm of his large, strong hands.

He wrapped his other arm around her waist and whispered, "We have a few days to decide. Let's talk about it some more at supper time."

She nodded, glanced down at the children, and then looked up into Scott's blue eyes. He gently kissed her as a breeze unfurled a strand of her hair, caressing his face. He held her tightly for a short time, picked up Lucy, and walked toward the garden, with Bronco and James trailing a few steps behind. Scott's mind was racing ahead, thinking about what must be done around the homestead if he should go.

In a way, he had already made up his mind.

That evening at dinner, an unusual quiet hung over the Wallace family. The normal chatter about the day's activities, and the rough and noisy but friendly play of the children were absent. Although he tried not to reveal it, Scott was deeply troubled because of the decision he and Rebekka must make. His normal robust appetite fled, and he had only consumed a small amount of ice-cold milk from the springhouse. Normally he would have downed two full cups. Finally, Rebekka broke the silence.

"The children and I talked for a long time this afternoon. They seem to understand that you may have to go away for a while."

Scott noticed a slight quiver in her voice.

"We have decided that you know best about these matters, and we'll support whatever you think best."

He was surprised at such a quick decision.

"Then I'll think it over for a while and decide. I thank all of you for making this easier for me. If I do go, I know things will be harder for you. I definitely won't go if our two neighbors go also. It might be an invitation for the Indians to enter these parts if all three of us leave at once. Shelby and Sevier will leave some men here to help, but they might not visit up here very often, especially if the winter is harsh. On the other hand, we have wood that will last till spring. Our sweet and irish potatoes are in the cellar. Our corn is shocked and should be plentiful for your horse and the two cows to eat this winter. I could bring in what is left of our garden before I leave, and James and Melanie can gather the apples and store them in the cellar. But the hogs must not be slaughtered until the first heavy frost."

James and Melanie looked at each other and grinned, proud that they had, for the first time, been included in tasks that would help ensure the family's survival through the winter.

"Tomorrow we should all gather more walnuts and chestnuts," Scott continued. "But for now, let's cheer this group up."

James, the oldest at six, and Melanie, four, nodded and began eating.

"And besides, if I should decide to go, I'll probably be back before you know it."

This announcement was greeted by a round of giggles from the children as their eyes brightened and thoughts ran through their heads of wondrous things Daddy might bring them when he returned from a strange land.

Shadows stretched and darkness came quickly after the sun dropped below the ridges to the west. Rebekka used the fireplace to light a tallow candle and placed it on the rustic walnut table, which had been hewn by Scott during the previous winter. It brightened the gloomy room considerably as the flame danced to and fro, delighting and at the same time intriguing the children by casting mysterious shadows throughout the room.

"Tell you what," Scott told the children, "later tonight, let's pop some corn and maybe your mom will tell us another story."

The children grinned, nodded their heads in agreement, and promptly forgot about the possibility that their dad might be leaving them.

Sunday, September 24, 1780
Sycamore Shoals, NC

While Scott debated whether he should join the other Over-mountain Men, Major Patrick Ferguson was leisurely camped at a small hamlet called Gilbert Town, located in the shadows of the Blue Ridge Mountains. There he dispersed bands of Loyalists in all directions. Their mission was recruiting, training new recruits, and destroying the property of un-submitting Patriots. A special team of troops scoured the countryside looking for Loyalist deserters. A five-minute trial and a hanging tree awaited those unfortunate enough to be caught in their snare. Ferguson's confidence was at a very high level; he believed the so-called revolt was all but over.

In a few short weeks, Scott was destined to encounter this well-known and up-and-coming British leader at a small ridge located on the North and South Carolina line called Kings Mountain.

Saturday had been a busy day as final preparations for the trip to Sycamore Shoals unfolded. Scott had struggled several days with the pros and cons of whether he should join his neighbors in their struggle against the British. Concern for his parents and his own family tipped the scale.

At the first flicker of daylight, the four mounted their two horses and started on a journey of approximately five treacherous miles westward and 1,400 feet below their cabin. Scott's horse, Spurt—named for his quickness and prowess—barely provided sufficient room to carry him and James. Extra equipment not normally taken when traveling to the valley took up a considerable amount of space. This included a blanket and an extra pair of deerskin clothing to be worn over Scott's summer homespun should the weather dictate. He also carried a knife, a shot-bag, a pouch full of parched corn and assorted nuts, maple sugar, a powder horn, and Lucy, his long-rifle.

The plan was to travel nonstop to Sycamore Shoals so as to arrive in time for the eleven o'clock church services. Some parts of the route were so steep and unforgiving that a prudent rider would dismount and lead his horse along the narrow paths, which the Wallaces were cautious to do. One careless misstep or a loose rock could send them careening down a rocky slope for hundreds of feet.

After three hours of nonstop traveling, they reached the valley floor. Hugging the north shore of the Watauga River for some distance, they forded the river near Sycamore Shoals, pausing momentarily to give their thirsty horses a well-deserved drink from the cold and sparkling stream.

When Spurt pounded his front hoof into the water, trout darted in all directions, to the children's delight.

As they rode around the last bend in the Watauga before Sycamore Shoals, the horses were brought to a standstill. The children craned their necks for a better look. In a relatively level field adjacent to the river, many tents of varying sizes and colors had been pitched in perfectly aligned rows. Several plumes of smoke drifted into the air. Faint commands could be heard as the mountain men practiced ground maneuvers. A group of men charged their horses to a staging area, quickly dismounted, and ran to a mound of rocks and trees. Puffs of smoke emitted from the area and a second or so later, the distinctive sound of long-rifles filled the autumn air.

After several rounds were fired, a man wielding a glistening sword commanded a retreat. The men mounted and galloped away as quickly as they had appeared. The tactics of taking cover behind natural objects, striking, and then vanishing worked well when combating the Cherokee. And indeed they would work equally well when fighting the British, who, for the most part, still insisted on fighting a gentleman's war by lining up in neat rows face-to-face with the enemy.

A large white tent sat on a small mound overlooking the staging camp. A flag adopted by the Colonies and another by the Watauga Association hung from staffs placed on either side of the tent door. Men hurried in and out of the tent carrying documents. This was the headquarters of Colonel Isaac Shelby and his counterpart, Lieutenant Colonel John Sevier. Scott was well acquainted with Sevier through his position in the Watauga Association. Although Scott was an officer, he did not hold a position on the Court as Sevier did. Nevertheless, Sevier had sought his opinion on several important issues. During the past two years, they'd developed a mutual respect for each other.

Scott and his family were arriving near the end of a frantic effort to increase the amount of lead mined from the hillside near the Nolichucky River. Others were helping in the tedious and dangerous job of mixing the saltpeter, sulfur, and charcoal to make gunpowder. Volunteers kept two looms spinning to make clothing of various sizes for the men. Never before had the people joined in a common cause to such an extent. The two blacksmith shops were overwhelmed because the majority of horses arrived in need of new shoes. Scott was stunned to learn of the enormous effort that had been under way for several weeks and felt somewhat guilty that he had not reported sooner.

4

The bell of the small white church rang as Scott and his family neared. It was evident that only a small portion of the crowd would be able to assemble inside. So all men were asked to stay outside, allowing the women and children to remain inside, but there was still a great overflowing. Finally, a decision was made to hold services outside where everyone could attend.

After the sermon, which touched on the tribulations of Moses, comparing them to the similarities of the upcoming campaign, and after asking for divine guidance, the dinner announcement was made. Almost immediately, men began unloading tables from wagons and lining them up under several large sycamore and oak trees. Women swarmed around the tables immediately, covering them with pots of food containing fresh vegetables from late gardens and pies made from apples, pumpkins, and other fruits. At this time, the church bell rang thirteen times. This was the signal for the beef, venison, and pork to be delivered. Three wagons arrived from the camp loaded with the meat, which had been roasting over green hickory logs since the previous afternoon.

Reverend Abraham McConnell climbed upon a table, held his hands high, and motioned for the crowd's attention. As grace was said, only an occasional whinnying horse, the honking of a flight of geese flying south, and the faint sounds of men giving orders in the distant camp were audible. Then it was time for the feast. Many families, like the Wallaces, had traveled since dawn with only snacks for breakfast, so the food was a welcome sight.

As Scott and his family ate and mingled, they met their close friend and neighbor Edward McGruder, his wife Margaret, and their son Craig. The boys hadn't seen each other for several weeks and scampered off to play.

"How long have you been here?" Rebekka inquired.

"Since yesterday," Margaret replied. I'm amazed at all this activity. And I've seen people that I had almost forgotten. I'm so proud of Ed. He's joined Lieutenant Colonel Sevier's regiment. But at the same time, I'm worried stiff. Those awful British have sure upset our apple cart."

Rebekka interjected, "I'm worried, too. But, like Scott said, 'if we don't cut the snake's head off now, it might bite us later.' Scott hasn't made his mind up completely. Not yet anyway. It's his decision to make."

Rebekka looked admiringly at Scott, winked, and added, "He's a very good husband and father, and I'll fully support whatever he chooses to do."

Scott blushed. The McGruders giggled.

"Have you talked to Thomas O'Neill lately?" inquired Edward.

"No, I haven't," Scott replied. "In fact, it's been quite a while."

"Thomas won't be going with us. Lot of pressure from his wife, I understand. Scott, sure hope you join us. We need leaders like you. A leader that can ride and shoot with the best."

"Thanks, Ed. I'll decide after talking to Sevier. I want assurance from him that our families will be safe and looked after properly while we're gone. The fact that Thomas is staying helps considerably. But I want more than that."

This was good news for Scott. His decision-making process as to whether he would join the Militia of the Over-mountain Men had just become easier. After almost an hour of eating and fellowship, Major Robinson climbed upon one of the wagons and rang a cowbell to get everyone's attention. Then he began to speak in a voice that carried a great distance.

"Thank you and good afternoon, ladies and gentlemen. My name is William Robinson, and I'm a major under Lieutenant Colonel Sevier."

The crowd gave him a great ovation of clapping and whistling.

"Thank you again for allowing me to speak to you on this glorious day. First, thanks to everyone involved in preparing this wonderful food."

More applause.

"After tomorrow this will only be a memory because we

will travel light and won't carry a lot of food and unnecessary items with us. We must move quickly and cannot be burdened with a heavy load of provisions. I want to congratulate these fine men that have already been selected to ride with us. Tomorrow we will complete our selection. We estimate that another five or six hundred will be selected, and the remainder will stay here for security from the Indians and to help those families in need. Men, please don't feel dejected if you're not selected because we need good men to remain here that are equal in every respect to those going."

The crowd gave a nod of approval.

"As for you that are here with your families, rest assured they will be properly fed and have adequate sleeping quarters until we leave early Tuesday morning. We have several available tents, houses, and the church for this purpose. Food will be served here three times daily. In the event of rain, we will eat in tents at the camp. For those who need assistance, please contact me after this announcement.

"We have entertainment planned for you this afternoon—everything from horse racing, to shooting competitions, and wrestling. This evening after dinner there'll be music and dancing."

The major was once again interrupted by boisterous yelling, whistling, and clapping.

He smiled and held his hands up for quiet. "This will take place in the large field north of our camp. If you're not a participant, please remain behind the markers and watch your children because some of these activities can be dangerous." He paused to allow these words to sink in.

"Tomorrow will be a day of business. All able-bodied men should report to the main entrance to the camp with your horse and rifle immediately after breakfast. As for those with families, don't worry—we have plans to keep them entertained during the day."

Rebekka squeezed Scott's hand, looked up at him, and smiled.

"For those selected, you will remain in the camp for orientation. We will gather information about you such as your name, the names of your family members, and where you live. We will provide training in maneuvers and working together under command. We will also introduce you to your leaders. That's all I have. Thanks for your patience. Anyone needing shelter, please form a line in front of the wagons."

Rebekka and James encouraged Scott to participate in the afternoon competition. One event that interested Scott was the rifle competition. Winning the riding and shooting contest would boost any man's stature in the community for years.

The simple rules stated that a pumpkin approximately the size of a man's head would be strung from a tree halfway along a track one half mile long. The objective was to place a bullet in the center of the pumpkin while riding a horse. A marker would be placed fifty yards perpendicular to the pumpkin. The participant must not ride closer to the pumpkin than the marker. Participants could, if they wished, pause and fire at the pumpkin; however, a combination of time and accuracy would determine the winner.

A total of ten participants entered the contest. Scott pulled the number seven from a hat and would be the seventh participant to display his skills, or possibly fail, before the large gathering and his family.

The first contestant almost stopped his horse, fired, and then galloped off, adding seconds to his overall time. Analyzing the crowd's reaction, Scott surmised that only two of the first six participants had scored a hit. Finally, it was his turn, and the throng of yelling and waving spectators peered anxiously in his direction. Several boys clung precariously from a sapling for a better view.

He checked Lucy and then patted a well-fed and rested Spurt. Now it was his chance for fame, or failure.

An official at the other end of the field called out his name and lowered a white flag, signifying the start of his run. Scott gently squeezed his knees against Spurt's sides, loosened the bridle rein, slapped him lightly with his hat, and then tossed it to the ground. Spurt lunged forward as if he had been fired from a catapult. Despite the warnings, a boy jumped from behind the ropes and scooped up Scott's hat.

Scott leaned forward, head down to reduce wind resistance, and spoke to Spurt. He thundered down the open field, ears laid back, slinging dirt and grass as his hoofs dug in. As he approached the half-way mark, Scott stood up slightly in his stirrups for a smoother ride, raised Lucy, aimed, caressed her trigger, and felt her powerful recoil on his shoulder. Through his peripheral vision, he saw the pumpkin swaying back and forth, its insides spilling out. A hit! Another encouraging word in his ear, and Spurt flashed past the finish line.

He slowed and headed back to the judges' table. The crowd showed its appreciation for his fine display of riding skills and marksmanship. Although the cheering and yelling had begun when his bullet struck its mark, he hadn't heard any of it. His pumpkin was examined by three judges. The bullet failed to penetrate the center of the pumpkin, but his time of 45 seconds for the half-mile run had been the fastest thus far and placed him at the top of the scoreboard.

The next two participants missed the pumpkin and were disqualified. With only one participant left, Scott felt fairly secure in his position. But he was also very knowledgeable concerning the skills of the final contestant, his neighbor and friend, Edward R. McGruder.

Scott and Edward had been on two expeditionary trips together, scouting for Indians as far southwest as Chota, the Cherokee capital. Edward had demonstrated his skills and bravery in several small skirmishes with the Cherokee. The two men had formed a special bond, deep respect, and confidence in each other. It was with this respect that Scott now turned to watch Edward ride.

When the flag dropped, Edward's horse sped toward the target. He fired without slowing and encouraged his horse to go faster, whipping him with a leather strap. It was to no avail. His horse seemed startled and confused by the screaming and waving crowd, boltered sideways, and lost vital seconds. Edward's time lagged Scott's by eight seconds, but his bullet struck one half inch closer to center than Scott's had.

The judges finally announced a tie as the two young men

shook hands and bowed before the cheering crowd. This was the most important event of the competition, and both wives and children came forward and proudly stood nearby as Lieutenant Colonel Sevier congratulated them with a short speech. The young boy presented Scott with his hat. Scott shook his hand. This pleased the crowd who was in a festive mood, and they showed their appreciation with a thunderous roar of clapping hands, whistling, and Indian war-whoops. There would be no awards given, and none was expected. The admiration from the people was more than enough.

Afterward, during a casual conversation, Sevier said, "Great demonstration of your superior riding and shooting skills. Both of you are potential leaders. We desperately need men of your caliber. So, have you joined us?"

Edward responded, "I've joined your regiment."

Sevier looked at Scott and said, "And what about you, Scott?"

Scott shook his head. "I have not joined. I am concerned about the welfare of my family. Will you give my family reasonable protection and assistance?"

Sevier glanced at Rebekka and said, "I assure all of you that we will provide safety for your families. We will visit each home at least once a week. That includes families that live at higher elevations like yours."

Through his experience working with Sevier in the Watauga Association and on an Indian expedition, Scott held him in high esteem. His word was as good as a written contract.

Reassured, Scott turned toward Rebekka for her final

thoughts. A smile and nod from her was all he needed. Lieutenant Colonel Sevier welcomed both men to his regiment and wished them well.

September 26, 1780
Base Camp
Sycamore Shoals, NC

A cool breeze stirred the American and Watauga Association flags to life. Colonel Isaac Shelby rose from his chair on the makeshift podium to address the audience. He planned to be very short and to the point. Jittery men were ready to ride into the unknown and wouldn't tolerate extensive posturing or political talk. Some of the younger men had never been east of the mountains and had only their imaginations to picture what it would look like.

The militia was positioned before the podium on Shelby's left. They were in two separate regiments representing Shelby and Sevier. They stood proudly beside their horses holding their long-rifles with their right hands. It was a rather loose but definitely military formation, with nearly half of them wearing coonskin hats and the rest either bare-headed or wearing a large-brimmed hat. Their families, friends, and on-lookers were gathered on the right. Many of the young wives wiped tears from their eyes as they gazed at their husbands, wondering if they would see them again.

The speakers consisted of Lieutenant Colonel John Sevier, Colonel Isaac Shelby, and Reverend Isaiah Davidson. It was a solemn occasion, very unlike the party atmosphere of the past two days.

Scott's pulse beat faster than normal, making a rhythmic sound in his temples. His palms became clammy, and his mouth felt as if it had been lined with cotton as he listened intently to Shelby's comments. For the first time, he realized the remarkable difference between the militia he had joined and the Indian expeditions. The Indian scouting parties usually consisted of small groups of men who knew and trusted each other. This group consisted of many strangers—strangers who might come to hold his life in their hands.

His neighbor Edward stood next to him with a sober expression on his face. They were already close friends, but their friendship would weld stronger during the next few days as destiny awaited them both.

"Good morning, ladies and gentlemen," Shelby began, in his commanding voice. He had been commissioned Colonel of the Militia of the newly created Sullivan County earlier in the year.

"Today we embark on a journey to help preserve our way of life—the one we all cherish so much. We are free to do as we please provided it doesn't harm our neighbors. The

British want to take our freedom from us. Looking at these fine men standing before us convinces me the British are in for a huge surprise."

A loud roar went up from the crowd standing on the right, startling some of the horses, but the militia members only stood a bit taller.

"I have observed some of you in action and personally know many of you and your families."

Turning his head toward the guests, he continued. "Some of these men fought bravely with me and Colonel McDowell and others this past July at the Musgrove's Mill battle. This is the same area to which we are now returning. Their experience, knowledge of the area, and leadership will help immensely. I have full confidence that all of these young men will be brave when the time comes to make Ferguson eat his words. And now I would like to introduce my good friend and neighbor Lieutenant Colonel Sevier, who has some important words for you."

Lieutenant Colonel Sevier quickly stood to address the crowd, sensing that valuable time was fleeing. At the same time, he recognized the advantage of building support for the effort. After the polite hand clapping subsided, Sevier began.

"Thank you, Colonel Shelby, for those fine and fitting words." The thirty-six-year-old's voice carried to the crowd in a way that would one day help elect him as the first governor of the state of Tennessee.

"I have great admiration for this outstanding and upright group of volunteers that are ready to contribute the ultimate sacrifice for their beloved homeland, their families, and for the cherished way of life that we all have come to love. The British and the turncoats that are helping them will, if unchallenged, completely change our way of life forever. They have captured two prime cities in the South—Charleston and Savannah."

Rebekka clasped her hand over her mouth and looked in the direction of Scott when she heard Sevier mention the capture of Charleston. She didn't want to reveal her added anxiety, which would further upset her children. So she reached down, held their hands tightly, and threw her shoulders back in a brave and confident manner.

Sevier continued. "Recently they won some other important battles in that region. The stronger they get, the more American citizens in the Carolinas join the British cause—out of fear, greed, or both. It's similar to consumption, it just keeps devouring until all is lost. We must alter this reckless and destructive course led by the so-called Lord Cornwallis but chiefly engineered and executed by Major Patrick Ferguson. We have held the Cherokees at bay, and we intend to repel the British Redcoats and their cowardly turncoats as well. We have the desire and motive to win. We will persevere." Sevier nodded in the direction of the Virginia militia and continued. "And let's not forget our fine friends from Virginia. I heartily welcome them."

He did not mention that Colonel William Campbell from Virginia, McDowell, and others would join them en route with additional men. Such information, if delivered to Ferguson through a spy, could adversely affect their mission. Nor did he mention the recent devastating defeat of General Gates by

Cornwallis near Camden, with a loss of over two thousand men—killed, wounded, or captured, and all ammunition and baggage wagons captured. Instead, he closed with, "Good hunting and Godspeed. And now Reverend Davidson."

As Reverend Davidson stood, the crowd, including the militia, whistled and clapped until Reverend Davidson held his Bible high in his right hand. All the men removed their large-brimmed or coonskin hats.

"Good morning, ladies, and all you fine men ready to defend our cause. I will now read from Psalms. 'Rescue me from the cruel sword, and deliver me from the hand of aliens, whose mouths speak lies, and whose right hand is a right hand of falsehood.' Let us bow our heads and pray. Oh God, our merciful maker, leader, redeemer, and judge of all mankind, bestow your kindness and un-measurable love and wisdom upon our sons and husbands as they endeavor to uphold your word. Watch over them and return them safely to us, we ask in your holy name. Amen."

Some of those hearing these words—those familiar with their foe, Major Patrick Ferguson—wondered if Reverend Davidson was referring to him. Ferguson carried a remarkable heirloom sword, was considered an alien, and his right arm had been shattered by a bullet at the battle of Brandywine some three years earlier.

6

Colonel Shelby, who had temporary overall command, rose, replacing his large-brimmed hat. After shaking hands with the other two speakers, he gave the order for the men to mount their horses. Lieutenant Colonel Sevier, Colonel Shelby, and four of their officers mounted their horses at the head of their respective regiments. Shelby pulled his pistol, held it high, and fired a volley that signaled their departure. In slightly less than five minutes from the beginning of the speeches, they were on their way. It was a glorious sight as 680 horses galloped toward the rugged and beautiful mountains, flags fluttering in the mounting wind.

A hint of fall colors glinted in the early morning sun at the higher elevations. The weather would change for the worse during the day as the first cold front of the season approached. Their target, Ferguson, was still camped at Gilbert Town some sixty-six miles south-southeast—but that was on a direct course. It was more than double that distance along the winding trails through the rugged Appalachian Mountains.

Scott nervously looked over his shoulder hoping for one last glimpse of his family. He wondered if he would ever see them again. Wondered if they would make the trip home safely with Rebekka and the two children riding on one horse. This was the first time these thoughts had entered his consciousness but it would not be the last.

By lunch, they had traveled almost twelve miles and gained a thousand feet in elevation. They stopped near the Doe River to eat and rest. The Fork Mountain was in full view to the north and the sixty-two hundred-foot Roan Mountain stood majestically a short distance to the south. Her top was obscured with clouds forming ahead of the approaching cold front.

After a short rest, the men moved on, although at a somewhat slower pace. The rugged terrain and thinning air tested the stamina of their horses. The wind was gusting considerably and getting colder as the elevation increased and the cold front neared.

Scott turned in his saddle and stared one last time toward Sycamore Shoals and the surrounding hills and ridges.

Have I made the right decision to leave my family with winter approaching? Sevier sounded so confident. Said his safety committee was top notch. I believe him…but what if he's wrong? Will their food be adequate if I'm not back in a month or so?

Many other thoughts, mostly negative, gravitated through his brain. He thought of his parents in Charleston and how the war may have affected them. Scotts's parents were proud and intelligent, but poor. They'd emigrated from an area near Inverness in the Highland of Scotland to

Virginia in 1767 when he was only thirteen years old. Inverness is an area of great beauty because of the rugged, mountainous terrain, but it offered very little hope to a young family who owned no land and few possessions. Thus, his parents set sail for America, his father having sold his services for five years to pay for their passage. Memories of his former homeland and their similarities were probably why Scott settled his family in the Holstons.

The plan was to rendezvous at a pre-selected campsite known as the Resting Place. Several men driving a slow herd of cattle had departed Sycamore Shoals the previous day. If all went as planned, the Over-mountain Men would feast on fresh beef for supper.

The small army arrived at dusk and set about establishing a campsite. Every man rushed to set up the camp before the fast approaching storm arrived. It was a daunting task for those in charge, providing direction to 680 men—even men who were knowledgeable about living off the land, as these men were. Food for man and beast had to be obtained and prepared, and a reasonable amount of protection from the elements must be arranged to protect from the approaching storm. The men set about using their outdoor skill and knowledge of nature. First, a skeleton was built similar to but flatter and smaller than a typical wigwam. Thick cedar branches were cut and interwoven over the skeleton, their tips pointing downward. Next, a thick layer of leaves was placed over the cedars. Several inches of dry leaves served as a bed. With two men working together, a snug and almost waterproof shelter quickly emerged. Staging areas were designated for cooking and corralling horses. A tent used for headquarters was erected in the middle of the camp. Sufficient guards were immediately posted in strategic locations and rotated every two hours to enhance alertness. Last, but not least, were the ten unlucky men designated to dig a latrine and then cover it with dirt before breaking camp the following morning.

After a discussion at headquarters, they decided to butcher part of the herd and return the remainder to Sycamore Shoals. Coaxing stubborn animals to keep up with the horses would be futile and consequently slow the progress of the entire army. The meat would be usable for approximately two days while in the cold air, but any remaining would be discarded as the army descended the eastern mountains into a warmer climate.

7

Wednesday, September 27, 1780

The men awakened at daybreak. The aroma of fresh bread, beef, and coffee filled the morning air. During the night, bitter cold rain had turned to snow. Approximately two inches covered everything that had not moved after the storm moved through. Scott and Edward shared their temporary cedar shelter, which had kept them reasonably dry and comfortable during the storm. They were fortunate in that neither was tasked for picket duty. Within an hour, the camp had broken and commands were given to proceed.

After a ride of approximately four miles, they emerged from the forest into an open area called the Bald of the Roan. It was a breathtaking sight. The early morning sun glistened off the distant, snow-covered peaks. Sevier and Shelby sat on their horses in an elevated area to address the militia while it enjoyed the early morning sunrays.

"Gentlemen, we made good progress yesterday,"

Lieutenant Colonel Sevier began, rubbing his stomach. "I believe everyone has a full belly this morning."

This evoked laughter and some cheering from the men.

"However," he continued, clearing his throat as he surveyed the two regiments, "I have a bit of disheartening news. During the night, two men from my regiment left our camp."

A loud groan emitted from the regiments, echoing down the canyons.

"Their horse's hoof-prints indicate they headed southeast toward the Carolinas. We must assume the worst. They're probably headed straight for our enemy, to give, or more likely sell, intelligence about our size, firepower, intentions, and travel plans. Our staff discussed this earlier in the morning and at first decided to return to Sycamore Shoals. We also considered traveling along a different route that would be more dangerous and would take longer. Neither option is feasible because of our rendezvous plans with Colonels Campbell and McDowell. If we change our course to any extent, we could miss them altogether. We must have their support in order to overcome Ferguson. Therefore, we will continue as planned with two exceptions. Four men from my regiment—men who have traveled this area extensively—will act as scouts. They will ride several miles ahead of us and check out areas most likely to be used for an ambush. Additionally, I request that each one of you maintain a vigilant outlook at all times. This will become more important as we start down the eastern slopes. Hopefully, by then, Colonel McDowell will have joined us with word of Ferguson's location and strength. Keep the faith, and don't be overly concerned. If these men have indeed committed such a despicable act as we suspect, I guarantee you that they will regret their actions. Commanders, form your regiments for movement."

The terrain for the next several miles descended approximately a thousand feet. All horses were dismounted for the slick and treacherous descent along narrow paths with deep gorges just inches away. Unfortunately, two pack horses slipped on the slick mixture of mud and melting snow. Everyone watched in dismay as the horses tumbled down the steep gorge. The packs were recovered, but the horses had to be shot due to their severe injuries. This unfortunate incident, coupled with the two suspected deserters, seemed to cast a demoralizing mood throughout the ranks.

The small army solemnly inched approximately two more miles through rough and slick terrain, where it camped earlier than planned near Roaring Creek. Numerous bonfires were started to cheer the men up and allow those with damp clothes to dry them for the first time in almost twenty-four hours.

The following day, while the militia was having lunch, Colonel Campbell from Virginia arrived on schedule with another two hundred men and assumed command of his regiment. Shortly thereafter, Colonel McDowell rode into camp, somewhat earlier than expected. His scouts had observed Ferguson camped at Gilbert Town early Wednesday, the twenty-seventh, with an estimated eleven to twelve hundred men and several wagons. No artillery was observed. Some of his men were dressed in the standard red and white British uniform. While McDowell was briefing the officers on this latest intelligence, Ferguson broke camp and marched south toward Pilots Mountain, his next camp site.

The Over-mountain Men marched to the homes of Colonel Elliot McDowell and his younger brother, Major Joseph McDowell, at Quaker Meadows, situated near the head of the Catawba River. Setting up camp had become routine and was done quickly after it was announced that several fine steers were on the menu, compliments of the McDowells. That evening, singing and laughter were heard throughout the camp as many campfires flickered, fed from rail fences, also compliments of the McDowells. Later in the evening, Colonel Cleveland from North Carolina arrived with three hundred and fifty men and was greeted by cheers from the Over-mountain Men that echoed down the mountainsides. Incredibly, fate must have intervened because Cleveland's regiment passed undetected only four miles east of Pilot's Mountain where Ferguson was setting up camp.

While these dramatic and morale-building events unfolded, a demoralizing message was being delivered to Ferguson. The two deserters from Sevier's regiment finally made contact with Ferguson. After some intensive interrogation to ensure, to the extent possible, the reliability of the two, they were welcomed and fed. Afterward, Ferguson listened intently to their interesting story. He doubted their authenticity, so he divided the two deserters and thoroughly cross-examined them. Their stories held up under skillful questioning by Ferguson and two of his Loyalist officers.

Ferguson was jarred into reality. He realized he was in imminent danger, but he cleverly disguised his concern. His countenance may have belied his deep concern, but his actions did not. Despite his earlier threats, down deep he wanted no part of a sizeable army of screaming and fearless fighters who could easily overtake his slow moving wagons. He immediately sent expresses south to Lieutenant Colonel Kruger, Commanding Officer of Fort Ninety-Six, and east to Lord Cornwallis at Charlotte. But he downplayed his concern in his carefully worded request for reinforcements. He dispatched scouts in all directions in a desperate attempt to locate and retrieve the several hundred Loyalists recently released on home leave. Another troubling issue that now befuddled Ferguson was his shortsighted decision to dispatch seventy-five men to search for the elusive Colonel Clarke.

On Saturday, September 30, the Over-mountain Men and their southern counterparts marched south toward Pilots Mountain while Ferguson was breaking camp. Scouts rode in all directions searching for Ferguson but did not make contact. Likewise, Ferguson's scouts were searching for the Over-mountain Men. Their blind movements resembled a gigantic chess game.

Major Ferguson, out of desperation, initiated a plan of deception. He would eventually march eastward toward the safety of General Cornwallis. But initially he issued orders to march south to Fort Ninety-Six without disclosing his real plan to anyone, including his officers. Intelligence was intentionally leaked to the locals who were suspected of being loyal to the Over-mountain Men. If the Over-mountain Men received this intelligence, they would, hopefully, go on a wild goose chase to the south while he escaped eastward.

Ferguson marched four miles south toward Ninety-Six, deliberately making sure he was observed by two families that would almost certainly report his maneuvers to his antagonists. He entered the Broad River and proceeded in the riverbed for approximately three miles, then departed the river on its north bank and turned east toward Charlotte.

A detachment of men were ordered to camouflage the army's movement beginning at the riverbank and extending approximately two miles. All horse and wagon tracks were filled with dirt and sand. Horse manure was buried. Large tree limbs were dragged back and forth to further destroy the evidence. A scattering of grass and leaves were added, which completely evaporated any sign of the passage of Ferguson's army. Ferguson schemed to build up his army. He issued a proclamation, designed to shame more Loyalists into joining his militia and encourage those on home leave to return. However, the proclamation was a huge mistake because it backfired and served another unintended purpose—it infuriated the proud Over-mountain Men and their southern counterparts.

Pilots Mountain, NC
Monday October 2, 1780

The ever sly and devious Ferguson ordered his scouts to post copies of the proclamation along a route toward Ninety-Six. An Over-mountain scout found a copy posted on a tree and immediately delivered it to Colonel Campbell, who was still camped near Pilots Mountain. This unusual delay was due in part to haggling among the colonels over who should become the overall commander. Finally, Colonel Campbell was selected as temporary Commanding Officer until such time as a General Officer could be appointed by the Southern command. Colonel McDowell was selected by the other officers to undertake this important mission. He departed immediately to confer with General Horatio Gates at Hillsboro, North Carolina. His younger brother, Major Joseph McDowell, became commander of his regiment.

Colonel Campbell was awestruck with the undignified wording of the proclamation. He seethed with anger but at the same time recognized the psychological value of reading it to his men. If it infuriated him, he believed it would affect his men in like fashion. He gathered all the regiments together for that purpose and the thirty-five-year-old redheaded colonel slowly rode among the men, speaking loudly so all could hear.

"Gentlemen, one of our alert scouts found an important document written by Major Ferguson. I believe this is a vain attempt by him to recruit more Carolinians through fear and intimidation. Listen carefully to this insulting propaganda.

"'Deneards Ford, Broad River, Tryon County, October 1, 1780. To the inhabitants of North Carolina. Gentlemen, unless you wish to be eat up by an inundation of barbarians, who have begun by murdering an unarmed son before an aged father, and afterwards lopped off his arms, and who by their shocking cruelties and irregularities, give the best proof of their cowardice and want of discipline; I say, if you wish to be pinioned, robbed, and murdered, and see your wives and daughters, in four days, abused by the dregs of mankind—in short, if you wish or deserve to live and bear the name of men—grasp your arms in a moment and run to camp.'"

Campbell paused, stood in his stirrups, and continued.

"'The Backwater men have crossed the mountains; McDowell, Hampton, Shelby, and Cleveland are at their head, so that you know what you have to depend upon, if you choose to be pissed upon forever and ever by a set of mongrels, say so at once and let your women turn their backs upon you, and look out for real men to protect them. Pat Ferguson, Major Seventy First Regiment.'"

Campbell smiled to himself and realized that the message was a godsend. Hearing themselves referred to as barbarians, murderers, dregs, rapists, and mongrels motivated these formidable men more than anyone or any other act could have done. He seized the opportunity and continued. "Apparently, the major is not so smart after all. He doesn't even know who's chasing him! The men thrust their long-rifles upwards and yelled an Indian war chant in unison.

"He's nearby, and we'll catch up with him soon. When we do, let's make him eat the words of his proclamation!"

These words brought on an even louder and thunderous roar from the men. They were pumped up and ready for action.

By Tuesday, October 3, no reinforcements were in sight. So the bewildered Ferguson broke camp at 4 AM and marched eastward on his way toward Charlotte. He traveled an incredible twenty miles and set up camp at Tate's Plantation, located near the Broad River.

While Ferguson was settling in at Tate's, he was visited by an elderly gentleman purporting to be a strong supporter of King George. Ferguson apparently didn't suspect the imposter, and after two glasses of fine French wine, openly discussed his intelligence assessment and probable intentions. He also disclosed, almost bragging, that expresses were en route to Lord Cornwallis at Charlotte and to Lieutenant Colonel Kruger at Ninety-Six, requesting reinforcements. Of course, this disclosure to a stranger could have been nothing more than a ploy designed by the clever Ferguson to spread fear among Campbell's men, but Ferguson's statement would have to be taken as factual. If in fact Ferguson had sent for additional forces, this in itself indicated that his plans were to stand and fight.

After making a complete visual survey of Ferguson's army and supplies, the spy bade goodnight to Ferguson and his officers. He arrived at Flint Hill the next morning, October 5, totally exhausted. He quickly briefed the Carolinians on what he had learned during his brief chat with Ferguson.

Immediately after the briefing, Colonel Lacey and his aid rode westward with the vital intelligence toward what he hoped would be Campbell's camp. Unknown to Lacey, Campbell had moved further south and was now camped at Alexander's Ford on the Green River.

On the evening of Thursday, October 5, Colonel Campbell convened a meeting with the other colonels and senior officers. They crowded around a small table in his tent.

"Gentlemen, I wish to voice my concern with you about the poor condition of some of the men and their horses. I estimate half of them are having trouble maintaining the necessary stamina and speed needed to overtake Ferguson. I suggest the best men and horses be culled immediately with the remainder to follow as expediently as possible."

His suggestion was discussed for a short time, then unanimously accepted. The selection process began.

Due to the uncertainty of Ferguson's true location and intentions, Campbell maintained continuous scout excursions within approximately five miles of his camp, emanating outward like an omni. As providence would have it, Lacey and his aide encountered one of these scouts shortly after darkness fell. At first, Lacey was not believed by the suspicious and trigger happy scout, but after answering several questions correctly and stressing the urgency to move quickly, the scout reluctantly agreed to escort the colonel and his aid to Alexander's Ford, minus the ball and gunpowder in their weapons. When Lacey arrived at Campbell's camp at Alexander's Ford, he was viewed with deep skepticism. After some tense moments of interrogation, Lacey mentioned a recent meeting he'd attended with Colonel McDowell and presented credentials that convinced Campbell and the other officers of his true identity. Campbell escorted Lacey to the operations tent, where a map of the area was unrolled and laid on a small, portable table.

Lacey pointed at a spot on the map and said, "This is the approximate location of Tate's Plantation, where Ferguson was camped yesterday evening."

Campbell was awe-struck, confused. He had taken Ferguson's bait and assumed Ferguson was headed south for Ninety-Six. Lacey continued. "Ferguson's force consists of approximately one thousand well-equipped men and several supply wagons."

Campbell rubbed his chin, then looked around at his officers, as if to apologize for the error in judgment, and said, "Gentlemen, Ferguson has somehow bamboozled me. Perhaps, it was best. Perhaps it was meant to be. Regardless, before pursuing Ferguson, we must first proceed southward to the Cowpens. Our scouts observed much beef and grain horded there by the Loyalists. Even our best men and horses are fatigued and hungry, and not in any condition for an encounter with Ferguson. Therefore, I consider it imperative to feed and rest our men and horses, before striking out for Ferguson."

Immediately after the briefing, Colonel Lacey departed for his regiment at Flint Hill. He would gather his three hundred men and await Campbell at Ray's Ferry on the Broad River.

At daybreak, October 6, Campbell broke camp with seven hundred select men and thundered south toward the Cowpens. Scott Wallace and Edward McGruder rode with this elite group. The remainder of the force followed behind at a slower pace.

After a hard day's ride, with only three short breaks, Campbell and his regiment arrived at the Cowpens as the sun was setting in a red October sky. Soon cattle were being slaughtered, and a nearby cornfield was raided. A mouth-watering aroma spread over the camp as the beef was roasted over the open campfires. Horses were fed, watered, and their saddles removed to provide maximum benefit from the short rest period. Each man checked the condition of their horses' hoofs and had new shoes installed as needed. Although not necessary, word was passed to inspect their long-rifles, and to replenish powder and lead balls if needed.

While Campbell was en route to the Cowpens, Ferguson

neared a knoll known as Kings Mountain. A scout reported to him that the knoll contained a clearing on top large enough for an encampment. Ferguson rode immediately to the crest. He inspected the bald ridge and made a snap decision to make camp on the apex.

He ordered his soldiers to build a makeshift road up the southwest side of the ridge. The men felled trees and moved large boulders where necessary. As darkness fell, the winding outline of a primitive road emerged along the rugged hillside. One by one, all seventeen baggage wagons were laboriously pushed and pulled up the serpentine shaped road to the top of the knoll.

Ferguson ordered them parked in a defensive circle in the northeastern and largest portion of the knoll. He believed that controlling the high ground would give his army such an advantage that he decided to forgo the standard operating procedure of building a breast-works, although tree trunks, soil, and rocks of all sizes were readily available. A formidable defensive structure could have been constructed in a short time.

This serious mistake of not building a wall for protection was highly unusual for an experienced and heretofore cautious officer like Ferguson. This was followed by another costly mistake that weakened his position even more: he ordered almost ninety men to go on a foraging party, searching for food and intelligence.

Meanwhile at the Cowpens, after eating a hearty meal of roast beef, corn, and steamed applesauce, the men tried to rest but most were either too tired or too anxious to fall asleep. Campbell knew it was imperative to proceed toward Ferguson's last known position as expeditiously as possible. He suspected Ferguson had moved several miles further east; or worse, Lord Cornwallis may have received Ferguson's plea for help and acted on it. In the event that an overwhelming force of British troops or Loyalists arrived in time to assist Ferguson, Campbell would probably be forced to cancel the planned attack.

A few moments before departure, word was passed to gather around Campbell for a briefing on what was to follow. Campbell stood on a tree stump. Light from the campfires reflected off his face. He removed his large hat, clasped his hands behind his back, and began.

"Gentlemen, I hope everyone has had plenty to eat. I realize we had a very short rest period and that you need more time. But, if we tarry, Ferguson could slip through our fingers again. He tricked us once. We aren't going to let that happen again. We'll depart shortly, riding all night with only an occasional brief rest for you and your mounts. This would be a difficult ride even with a full moon. The darkness will challenge all of us."

Yeah, it's dark as the soot in my chimney, Scott thought.

"Keep eye contact with others near you. We don't want to lose a single man. That person could be the lucky one that shoots Ferguson."

The men laughed, shook their fists in unison, then screamed an Indian war whoop. That was what Campbell wanted. He knew this elite group was doggedly tired and needed their morale propped up.

Scott carefully observed Campbell's mannerisms, his speech, and the way he enthused other men with words. Without realizing it, he was formatting his own leadership skills, which would serve him well in the coming years.

Campbell continued to speak. "Our guides are local men who are familiar with this area, but their skills will be tested to the utmost. It looks like rain will start soon, so please keep your powder dry." He concluded with, "I'm greatly honored to ride with such an outstanding group of men."

At 9 PM, the small army mounted and rode eastward, paralleling the state border between North and South Carolina. A light, cold drizzle began falling, threatening to dampen gunpowder as well as spirits. Scott pulled his deerskin clothing from his saddlebag and wrapped it around Lucy. She was more important to keep dry than himself.

As the militia rode at a fast trot, Scott's mind drifted back to what seemed ages ago. How Rebekka had carefully rolled and tied the extra deerskin clothing and blanket into tight bundles for ease of transporting. How concerned she was about his health and the clever manner in which she'd avoided any discussion of injury, or worse. Scott was glad the subject had not come up. Severe fatigue, imminence of battle, unfamiliar surroundings, and fear of the unknown can play tricks on the human mind. Scott's raced back and forth between reality, his family back in the mountains, and his parents in Charleston. He was sure he could smell Rebekka's freshly washed hair and feel her silky smooth skin against his cheek. A smile appeared on his face for the first time in several days. Sometimes he was not sure if all this was real or if he was hallucinating. Images swirled in his mind of his family asleep in their mountain cabin, a small fire flickering in the fireplace to ward off the October chill.

As he had done several times before, he began to analyze the wisdom of volunteering to fight the British and Loyalists. But, then he would remember the threats made by Ferguson and somehow it all seemed reasonable and the right thing to do. He was fighting for the future of his country, family, and his parents.

He thought about how he would react if he were required to shoot a man up close. Close enough for eye contact. He had killed Indians in self-defense, but it had always left him with a guilty conscience. White men were encroaching onto land the Indians had occupied for thousands of years.

He shook his head and slapped his face to bring himself out of his stupor and back to reality. His head bobbed up and down, half asleep, as the long line of men plodded forward. They had been riding for approximately four hours in soggy, sandy soil when Campbell ordered a brief rest period at 1 AM. The date was Saturday, October 7.

Scott slowly dismounted and leaned against Spurt for support and warmth, shivering from the dampness and cold. Spurt turned his head and nuzzled Scott as if to reassure him. Most of the men had slept little for over forty hours, and fatigue was starting to show in their swollen, puffy faces and red eyes as they huddled in the cold, damp night.

All the men knew the importance of keeping their rifles and powder dry and in firing condition. But, due to their fatigued condition, Campbell ordered each of his captains to remind their men of this important duty. Campbell's plan was to achieve the advantage through a stealthy surprise attack. To help achieve this advantage, he issued orders banning the test firing of rifles and talking above a whisper. All metal objects, except their weapons, were wrapped to muffle their clattering against each other.

After a thirty-minute rest period, orders were quietly issued to remount. Scott didn't fully realize how tired and sore he was until he tried to swing his right leg over Spurt's back, a skill that was normally executed almost without effort. His heel caught on the saddle and although he struggled with all his might, gravity forced him back to the ground. Stalling momentarily while he caught his breath, he awkwardly climbed belly first onto the saddle, balancing Lucy who seemed to weigh a ton. He noticed some other men having the same problem. His head ached, and the thought occurred to him that if the rest of the volunteers were as tired as he, they may not be very effective against a rested and well-fed enemy.

They were all mounted and ready to ride when a scout returned with news that Ray's Ferry lay approximately a mile ahead, and Colonel Lacey was waiting there with two hundred mounted men. As the news quickly but quietly spread, spirits were greatly uplifted. Some of the men had to restrain themselves to keep from yelling a war-whoop. The addition of Lacey's troops brought the force to nine hundred highly motivated and capable men, just slightly less than Ferguson's forces.

Ferguson commanded a force that consisted of one hundred well-trained and motivated Provincial Rangers from New York and New Jersey. These troops wore the red British uniform and were highly disciplined and capable. The remainder were Loyalists from the Carolinas, some of whose loyalty might be in question if given the right opportunity. Intelligence revealed that several of the Loyalists were close relatives of Colonel Lacey's men.

As Campbell approached Ray's Ferry, he halted his single file regiment and ordered the men to dismount and rest. While Campbell and Lacey conferred, the drizzle stopped, and the moon temporarily showed itself before darting back behind the thinning clouds. Large patches of ground fog formed in low-lying areas. Lacey told Campbell that two of his scouts, who were from the area, visited a Patriot neighbor during the night and were told that Ferguson was camped on top of Kings Mountain. It was about a four-hour ride from Ray's Ferry. Realizing the significance of this information, Campbell ordered a rest period until 9 AM. This would give the weary riders and their horses almost five hours to rest and prepare for battle.

Scott quickly gathered some grass for Spurt, removed the saddle, and tied his rein to a nearby rail fence. Cold, hungry, and fatigued, he wrapped his blanket around his body, placed his head on the warm saddle, and fell asleep almost immediately with Lucy cradled in his arms.

Saturday Oct 7, 1780
Near Kings Mountain, SC

At 8 AM, Campbell's men were awakened and informed to prepare for movement in one hour. Fires were not allowed. Breakfast would be eaten cold. Some of the men had squirreled away a few morsels and unselfishly shared with those who had none. This generous sharing may have been just that, or perhaps it was done with a thought in mind that this could be their last meal together. At any rate, it further welded these tough men together.

The next hurdle facing Campbell's men was crossing the Broad River. Scott was very concerned. He knew from experience that crossing such a wide river would be very dangerous. It would put them in a vulnerable position. The danger would increase exponentially as the size of the formation increased. Fortunately, the river was at its lowest crest, which would help make for a hasty crossing.

By 10 AM, the regiments were safely on the east side of the Broad. The river had not presented a real problem, with water no higher than a horse's belly. Only one rider fell during the crossing, when his horse slipped, but he managed to keep his long-rifle out of the water.

At 1 PM, a sharp-eyed scout captured one of Ferguson's young and very scared couriers. The courier initially denied his identity and lied about his mission; however, when he was searched, the scout found Ferguson's terse but frank message to Cornwallis requesting reinforcements. This was his second request and was triggered by a message he'd received earlier that morning from the commander of Fort Ninety-Six advising him that the fort was in a weakened condition and could not afford to lose a single man to aid him.

During the interrogation, it was confirmed that Ferguson was still camped atop Kings Mountain. The courier volunteered that Ferguson was wearing a checkered shirt to protect his uniform. Ironically, the youngster was apparently either disoriented or deserting because he was traveling westward instead of eastward toward Cornwallis's headquarters at Charlotte.

Colonel Campbell and his officers were immediately briefed on the intelligence and a war council was called.

Campbell addressed the council. "Gentleman, I believe the odds have finally tilted towards us for a favorable outcome. Perhaps it is divine guidance. In any case we must take advantage of the situation and mount a stealthy, vigorous surprise attack." Campbell occasionally turned his head so as to make direct eye contact with all his officers.

"To reduce noise and enhance our stealth," he added, "the men will leave their horses here and march to Kings Mountain. Regimental commanders will ride. From the intelligence we have gleaned, it's my opinion that Ferguson has created himself a problem. As we all know, higher ground normally has a military advantage. But in this case, I believe it will work in the reverse for Ferguson. His primary protection is his wagons and they're not very effective against a determined aggressor with long-rifles."

Some of the officers chuckled at this comment.

"Nevertheless, we should not let a perceived advantage lessen our will to win. In fact, it should increase that desire. Now, I'll take any of your suggestions and comments."

A young major suggested the word *Buford* as the countersign to reduce friendly fire casualties. Another officer suggested priming their rifles with dry powder and the removal of uncomfortable clothing due to the warmer climate. A recommendation was made for the captains to choose some of the most fatigued men of their commands to be responsible for horses and personal effects that would be left behind. The suggestions were quickly approved.

Campbell pulled his knife from its sheath, knelt down, and said, "This is how we'll attack." Using his knife blade, he carved a map of the knoll in the sand. "Split the men into two divisions, or columns, with Major Chronicle leading the left. The left column will consist of Chronicle, Cleveland, Williams, and Sevier in that order. The right column will be lead by Major Winston and followed by McDowell, myself, then Shelby." Campbell pointed at the northern portion of the knoll and emphasized, "The two leading columns will meet here."

If successful, Campbell would completely surround and trap Major Ferguson, reminiscent of Joshua's charge into Jericho.

"Instruct your men to hold their fire until the Indian war-whoop is yelled by my men. If the situation allows, each commander will attack with approximately half of their men, then fall back. If the Loyalists commit a bayonet charge, the reserves will fire over the heads of our retreating men."

Campbell stood, removed his hat, and slowly turned to make eye contact with all the officers huddled around him. "Gentlemen," he said, "this is our greatest and shining hour. I predict Ferguson will either surrender today, or die. Die today … like this." Simultaneous with his last statement, he slammed his knife into the heart of the map. He ended with a short prayer asking for God's divine help and guidance.

Scott noticed the concern on the faces of some of the men, including his buddy, Edward. He reckoned that his concern was also evident to others within the regiment. Scott tapped Edward on the shoulder and whispered, "How you doing, neighbor?"

"Fine." He shook his head a moment later. "No, actually I'm…I'm a bit nervous right now. Been thinking about my family and who would take care of 'em if one of those bastards should get lucky."

"Me, too, and all the other men I'm sure," Scott responded. Taking his hat off and running his fingers through his hair, he added, "You and I have been in a similar fix several times before and managed to survive by looking out for each other's hind parts. Let's do the same today." Edward responded with a nod and thin smile.

11

By 2:15 PM, the battle was imminent. Commanders had completed briefing their men and formed them into two loose formations, two men abreast in each column. A strange sensation draped itself around every man, testing their manhood, their courage, and their fears. They marched briskly toward Kings Mountain, now clearly visible in the distance. Scott and Edward managed to fit into Sevier's formation side by side.

At approximately 2:45 PM, Major Chronicle and Major Winston neared their designated area at the northeastern segment of Kings Mountain. A picket lazing in the warm afternoon sun with his Brown Bess Musket leaning against a pine tree glimpsed some unusual movement through the partially de-foliated trees. He jumped to his feet and immediately recognized their clothing and long rifles. The dreaded, screaming Over-mountain Men and their southern companions had arrived. Too bewildered to yell, he nervously aimed his Brown Bess Musket and fired the first lead ball of the battle. Ferguson heard the shot, bolted out of his tent blowing his silver whistle and shouting orders to his subordinate officers.

Scott heard the shot ring out in the distance, and shortly thereafter more shots echoed, with increasing frequency. He would describe the sounds many years later as analogous to popcorn shortly after being dumped into a hot skillet of grease. Fortunately, only two balls from the inaccurate muskets found their mark, and they were nearly spent when they hit two men in Major McDowell's regiment. Although the men had been instructed to refrain from firing back if attacked prior to hearing the Indian war-whoop, young Major McDowell's leadership was tested to the ultimate in keeping that pledge.

Meanwhile, Sevier rode among his regiment, encouraging them to move as fast as possible to their assigned area. Scott heard the British officers yelling commands. A shrill whistle emanated from the knoll as drums rolled louder and louder. Colonel Shelby and Colonel Campbell's regiment received withering fire from Ferguson's men, who were quickly mustered in the narrow southwest portion of the ridge. Colonel Campbell finally saw and heard enough. He ordered his regiment to scream the Indian war-whoop and charge. Scott and Edward screamed so hard the veins in their necks bulged. As the yelling and screaming quickly spread, the knoll virtually shook, and the British drums were temporarily silenced. They ducked behind trees, boulders, and other natural objects as they worked their way up the wet, slippery slopes, firing only when a hit was assured.

Scott's heart beat rapidly; his temples pounded as blood surged through his veins, delivering extra oxygen to his demanding body. The deafening sounds of rifles, men yelling, and the incessant British drums tested his courage to its limit. The battle had begun. He joined the other screaming men and charged forward, clutching Lucy in his right hand.

Just as Major Chronicle stopped his horse and waved his hand to encourage his men forward, a lead ball from a Brown Bess struck him in the neck, tearing through both jugular veins. The ball almost knocked him from his saddle, but he managed to upright himself momentarily before tumbling to the ground, dead. Lieutenant Colonel Hambright saw him fall and immediately took command.

When the first round of firing into the regiments of Campbell and Shelby subsided, Ferguson ordered the first bayonet assault. This portion of the ridge was very rugged, littered with large rock outcroppings and deep ravines. The first charge down the eastern slope was led by Ferguson's trusted Lieutenant Craig Allaire.

Most of the first wave of Campbell's men were two-thirds of the way up the craggy slopes when they saw the charge begin. Campbell's men fired their rifles with deadly accuracy despite the bothersome afternoon sun rays flickering through the thinning trees. But, there was not sufficient time to re-load their rifles, and without bayonets, they began a hasty retreat.

Campbell had kept about one hundred men in reserve, rifles ready. He patiently waited until Allaire's men neared the bottom of the ridge, stabbing or clubbing any unfortunate man that tarried or stood to fight. Then it was Campbell's time for revenge. He ordered his reserve unit to attack. The Loyalist, realizing their predicament, wheeled and began clawing their way up the steep, slippery embankments. Many dropped or threw down their muskets. They were perfect targets for the sharpshooters who took careful aim and emptied their long-rifles into their antagonists, then fell back to reload. What remained of the bewildered Loyalist finally disappeared into underbrush and smoke, leaving their dead and wounded behind.

As Campbell prepared his men for the second attack, directly across the ridge, Sevier was successfully using the same tactics. He directed half of his men to charge up the southwestern part of the ridge, leaving the remainder for a counter attack.

Scott was assigned to the second assault force and watched as Edward charged up the steep embankments, dodging back and forth among the trees and rocks. Edward momentarily saw several silhouettes moving at the crest of the ridge, rested his long-rifle on a rock, aimed carefully, squeezed the trigger softly, and saw his quarry fall. He initially considered withdrawing to reload but decided he had sufficient time before being overrun. His overconfidence was a huge mistake. His trembling hands took longer to reload than normal, and by the time he took aim, several red-coated Provincials were within fifty yards of his position. He brought down one of the redcoats, turned, and scampered down the makeshift road. In his haste to escape, he deviated from his normal procedure of using the trees, ravines, and other natural objects to evade the onslaught. He hadn't run very far before a withering stream of balls zipped over his head like a swarm of bees, and then he was hit in his back and right leg. He fell to the ground in agonizing pain. His long-rifle skidded down a rut made by Ferguson's wagon wheels.

He lay on his back, frightened and unable to move, as the white puffs of clouds slowly turned gray. Then blackness enveloped all the light.

Forthright, Sevier ordered the second assault. Scott scampered up the steep incline, ducking behind anything that would offer protection and bamboozle his arrogant enemy. At the sight of charging men, a few shots rang out, but the balls whizzed by well above their intended target. Then Ferguson ordered another bayonet charge.

Scott crept up to a huge pine tree and rested Lucy against its trunk. Keeping as much of his body protected as possible, he took aim and gently squeezed her trigger. As Lucy recoiled against his shoulder, he saw another red-coated Provincial twirl, fall backward, and slide down a steep embankment head first. A young man slipped, tumbled, and lay somewhat dazed, staring up through a canopy of large pines. Before Scott was able to assist, one of Ferguson's Loyalists charged and thrust his homemade bayonet into the unfortunate man's chest. Lucy was un-loaded and his hunting knife was no match for the well-trained Loyalists and their bayonets. It was time for Scott to re-group at the bottom of the ridge and fight the enemy on the terms of the Over-mountain Men.

As Scott hastily descended the ridge, dodging and

weaving, his many years of experience fighting Indians quickly put yards between him and his oppressors. As he neared the bottom of the ridge, his path took him near Ferguson's wagon road. By this time, the remainder of the British charge was working their way back up to the top of the ridge. Scott was temporarily out of harm's way.

In the distance, he saw a man lying in the road dressed in clothing worn by the Over-mountain Men. Scott ran toward him, still wary to expose himself in the open road. As he came closer, he noted the grotesque manner in which the wounded man's right leg was bent backwards above his knee. He froze when he recognized Edward. Looking around for enemy activity, and seeing none, he leaned Lucy against a tree. Bent over, he grabbed Edward's shirt and gently shook him. His eyelids fluttered, then opened.

"Ed, it's Scott. You're going to be fine. I'm going to straighten your leg, then pull you out of this road."

Barley audible, Edward whispered, "Scott, I'm hurt real bad. Promise me you'll look after my family."

"You're going to do it yourself," Scott said. He broke a small limb from a tree and inserted a piece of it between Edward's teeth. "Bite hard. I'm going to straighten your leg." The twig fell from his sagging mouth.

After Scott extended Edward's leg, he grabbed his arms, pulled him head first out of the road, and propped him up against a pine tree. He slit the leg on Edward's trouser, then folded and moved the cloth out of the way. He gasped when he saw the large femur protruding through the flesh and the substantial amount of clotted blood around the large wound.

When he pulled hard on Edward's leg, it emitted a sucking sound as the bone disappeared back into its normal location. A blooded lead ball, one side flattened, emerged from the wound and fell to the ground. Scott picked it up and put it in his pocket. He removed the handkerchief from Edward's head and tied it snugly around his wounded leg. Scott didn't notice the blood oozing from the wound in Edward's back. In a desperate effort to console his buddy, Scott said, "Ed, I'll be back in a few minutes. I've reloaded your rifle. Keep alert and stay awake."

Edward's eyelids quivered as he slowly gasped, "Keep my family with you."

Believing he could do no more for Edward, Scott reloaded Lucy and dashed back toward his regiment, hoping to secure medical help for his wounded buddy. But just as he arrived, Sevier yelled the command, "Charge to the top, men," and another battle cry echoed along the ridge. As they determinedly charged up the steep hillside, the pungent smell of gunpowder filled the air. The embankments were littered with the dead and dying. Many were still in the same contorted position assumed where they'd fallen. But the determined Over-mountain Men and their southern brethren were undaunted and gallantly pressed forward.

This time they reached the summit with little resistance and were greeted by the remnants of Campbell and Shelby's regiments. The three regiments joined and continued fighting tree by tree, and stone by stone, inching ever closer to Ferguson's fragile, ineffectual fortress, his circle of wagons. The battle had been raging for almost an hour when a Loyalist jumped onto the hub of a wagon wheel and waved a white handkerchief, only to be cut down by a furious Ferguson. The Patriots approached from every direction, firing at will with deadly accuracy, squeezing the noose around Ferguson's neck tighter and tighter.

Realizing that all was lost and hoping to eliminate needless casualties, Captain DePeyster suggested to Major Ferguson that an honorable surrender was in order. Major Ferguson angrily replied that he would never surrender to a bunch of mongrels. He agonized over his losses, watching in disbelief as his supposedly well-trained troops missed their targets over and over with their inaccurate muskets.

If my bull-headed and ignorant superiors hadn't rejected my advanced breech-loaded rifle, I would be on the offensive. But now all is lost.

He jumped on his white horse, held his sword high with his left hand, and motioned for the Provincials to follow him. Six did. He turned to a southwesterly direction and rode defiantly straight into the heart of Lieutenant Colonel Sevier's regiment, slashing at any man in his path. Ferguson would have been a very distinctive target even without his checkered shirt and white horse.

A cry went out through the woods that Ferguson was

escaping. Ferguson darted from behind a small rock outcropping, turned his horse, and cut through a rifleman's arm with his sword before he could fire. Several shots rang out, and Ferguson dropped his precious family sword when his left arm collapsed. With both arms dangling uselessly, Ferguson lost control of his horse. It snorted and veered left toward Scott, who had taken a position on a small knoll. He placed his right knee on the ground, rested his left elbow on his left knee, took careful aim, and squeezed Lucy's trigger. Ferguson was not more than thirty yards distance when the shot rang out. Scott's lead ball ripped through Ferguson's aorta.

Ferguson tumbled from his saddle, his horse still at a full gate. As he fell, his left foot lodged in its stirrup, and his lifeless body was dragged down the ridge in an unceremonious fashion for several yards before his horse was stopped. One of his followers also lay dead, and the others promptly surrendered.

Scott re-loaded Lucy and ran northeastward toward the occasional firing near Ferguson's headquarters. As he neared the bald summit, he saw several Loyalists waving white flags and handkerchiefs in surrender. Colonels Campbell and Shelby rode among them, accepting the surrendering officer's swords and ordering the frightened and demoralized Loyalists to lay down their rifles and other weapons and form a tight circle. Realizing the battle was virtually over and that medical help was not to be, Scott darted back down the slope toward Edward.

Near the bottom of the ridge, Scott noticed a small

stream of water and began filling his empty pouch. Then the most nauseous feeling that he could recall erupted over him. The accumulation of all the hideous carnage he had witnessed that afternoon came to a head and revolted. A severed hand with only two fingers lay almost hidden in the pool. A heavy blow from a sword had taken its toll. As he fell to his knees, the last bit of food left in his system ejected from his parched mouth. Several moments later, he staggered to his feet and soon found another small pocket of water further upstream. He splashed some of the cool water onto his face, refilled his leather pouch, and drank. Using the last bit of energy left in his depleted body, he hurried in the direction of Edward.

As he drew near, he realized Edward was probably dead. He lay slumped on his side, his eyes open and lifeless. Blood slowly oozed from one corner of his open mouth. Several green flies swarmed around his face and leg. Scott collapsed onto his knees and began sobbing. Mangled bodies and dying men lay throughout the woods, but this was different. He inched closer and held his friend's lifeless hand. No pulse. He gently straightened Edward's body and closed his eyelids and mouth. Next he removed his handkerchief, dipped it into the pouch, and cleaned Edward's face and hands. When he was finished, he placed the handkerchief over Edward's face and reverently crossed his arms across his chest before saying a short prayer.

As he turned and slowly walked away, he swore he would never forget this appalling sight, and he promised Edward he would carry out his dying wish.

As he climbed up the steep incline, the noxious odor of human waste, blood, and gunpowder hung in the late afternoon air. For the first time since the battle began, he became aware of his throbbing shoulder—the result of Lucy's powerful re-coil. Then he heard a single shot ring out from the direction of Ferguson's camp. It was followed shortly thereafter by rapid fire and shouts to desist. Ferguson's foraging party had returned.

Sensing what had taken place, one of the surprised Loyalists fired into the Over-mountain Men. Confusion ran amuck. Some of the men thought the shot signaled the expected arrival of the notorious and hated Major Banastre Tarleton. The Over-mountain Men and their southern friends started firing almost point blank into the prisoners. Dozens were killed. By the time Scott ran to the prisoner of war holding area, the foraging party had surrendered and order had been somewhat restored.

Colonel Campbell instructed his commanders to determine casualties, organize aid to their wounded, and prepare a decent burial for their dead. Lieutenant Colonel Sevier reported to Colonel Campbell that his fortunate regiment only sustained two killed and three wounded. When all commanders finally reported their losses, the total was truly remarkable. Only twenty-eight killed and sixty-two wounded, substantially less than the British casualties.

By 6 PM, all wounded Patriots had been recovered and were under the care of Major Ferguson's physician, who had miraculously withstood the battle without a scratch. Then the most difficult and unpleasant task of recovering the twenty-eight slain began in earnest.

Sevier assigned Scott the responsibility to assemble a group of men who would tear down some of the tents and cover the fallen Over-mountain Men. Twenty-eight honor guards kept watch throughout the night. Campbell ordered his men to build numerous campfires to ward off animals, make escape more difficult for the prisoners, and to prevent a surprise attack by Tarleton.

The break of day was welcomed by Scott, as the eastern sky turned bright orange and signaled the end of the most dreadful night of his life. The constant moaning and screaming of the wounded and dying had echoed throughout the night. The body stench mixed with smoke from the fires made breathing difficult. Many of the men had tied a handkerchief or piece of cloth over their nostrils.

Horse litters were being built to carry the wounded Over-mountain Men. Each litter consisted of two poles with a piece of tent cloth or a blanket attached to each pole. The two poles would be attached to either side of a horse, making a relatively comfortable and efficient means to transport a wounded man.

Colonel Campbell ordered Captain DePeyster to attend to his wounded and bury his dead as quickly as possible. Captain DePeyster protested that he could not properly bury over a hundred and fifty bodies, even if he had the entire day. Colonel Campbell advised DePeyster that the order stood. He would not delay his departure for any reason. Campbell believed Cornwallis's troops could arrive at any moment. Campbell's men were low on gunpowder and lead balls. And Campbell sensed the Over-mountain Men were in no condition, mentally or physically, for another tough fight.

The commanders reluctantly agreed to destroy all the well-made wagons, which would have brought a large sum back home. Colonel Campbell ordered the wagons searched for food or any other valuables, then burned. Ferguson's prized printing press was destroyed, but his fine china and silverware was divided among the men assigned to carry out the order.

An Over-mountain Man yanked on a blanket covering an odd shaped object in one of the wagons. As it fell away, two dirty, scared, and sheepish looking scoundrels sat up with their hands in the air pleading for mercy. They were immediately identified by several men in Sevier's regiment as the two deserters. After a round of butt kicking and shoving, the situation quickly deteriorated. Two ropes were tossed over an oak limb. Colonel Sevier was quickly summoned by a sensible thinker, positively identified the two, and called for order. He immediately charged the two with treason, ordered their hands and feet securely tethered, and posted around-the-clock guards. He advised them they would be tried under North Carolina law for treason.

At 9 AM, the Over-mountain Men conducted a quick but fitting military funeral for their fallen heroes. All men were present except those guarding the prisoners and assigned picket duty.

The fallen men were laid in a common grave in a perfectly straight line, their bodies then covered with cloth from Ferguson's tents. Colonel Campbell eulogized his gallant and brave men in a short but emotional speech. He then asked the men to remove their headgear and observe a moment of silence.

As the grave was being covered, twenty-eight volunteers, including Scott, fired a volley over their friends and fellow soldiers as a fitting goodbye.

The Loyalists quickly buried their dead in two shallow pits. Ferguson was awarded a certain amount of honor and dignity. His officers buried him in a shallow but unmarked grave near the apex of the knoll and covered the grave with a layer of stone.

All wounded Loyalist prisoners declared unable to march by both their doctor and a Patriot officer would remain on the battlefield. Almost six hundred Loyalist prisoners were ordered to form a single file line. Most able-bodied Loyalists were ordered to carry two muskets, minus their flintlocks. Campbell ordered the barrels bent on the remainder of the muskets. All horses and the militia's personal effects were brought up to the camp and distributed to their owners.

It was difficult to tell who was happier, Scott or Spurt, when they were reunited. At 10 AM, the long journey back home began. Scott was overwhelmed with joy to be sitting in Spurt's saddle again and heading home.

After traveling a short distance, the men breathed fresh air for the first time in several hours. Scott took one last look eastward. A pall of smoke from the campfires and burning wagons slowly rose and drifted eastward toward Charlotte and Lord Cornwallis. Scott saluted his friend Edward, turned, and never looked back again. His thoughts turned to his family on the Holston.

The march back home was agonizingly slow mainly because of the prisoners, who were in no mood to hurry toward an unknown destination, and the wounded, who needed special care. Late that afternoon the remainder of Campbell's Over-mountain Men were located and rejoined their original regiments. Along the way, some of the wounded Patriots died and were properly buried.

When they reached the foothills and safety, some of the men demanded a trial for the Loyalists who had allegedly committed crimes, including murder, as well as the two deserters from Sevier's regiment. Campbell called a meeting of his officers to discuss the legality of such a trial. He finally ruled that a military trial met the North Carolina Code. If two or more witnesses confirmed allegations of murder or other atrocities, the accused could be pronounced guilty and sentenced to death by hanging. Campbell authorized the trials to begin.

After the two deserters and seven Loyalists were strung up, the men's appetite for revenge was nearly satisfied. Their shouting gradually ceased except for a handful of diehards. Campbell gave the remainder of those convicted an offer to sign a statement giving allegiance to the Patriots, or die. They all gladly gave their allegiance.

The following evening, Lieutenant Colonel Sevier conducted a briefing concerning a recently passed law by the North Carolina Legislature that captured Scott's imagination. A tract of land bounded by the Holston River, Powell River, and the Virginia state line had been set aside as bounty land for officers and soldiers in the Continental Line. Warrants would be issued to those remaining in service until hostilities ceased or to the next of kin for those soldiers killed in action. The number of acres decreed would be determined by rank and number of months served. Some of the land contained rich river bottom soil, soil that Scott had tread upon and sifted through his fingers.

On Sunday October 15, 1780, Scott entered the clearing where his cabin was located. He stopped Spurt in the middle of the small stream, taking in the moment as the sun disappeared behind the ridges. Then his heart almost stopped. Rebekka and their two children emerged from the springhouse. Bronco was the first to notice Scott and Spurt. When he recognized them, he howled and ran in their direction. Rebekka screamed Scott's name, dropped the wooden bucket filled with water, and ran down the slope, both children and the tumbling bucket closely behind. Scott jumped off Spurt and grabbed all three in a bear hug that seemed to last forever. Then he looked into Rebekka's beautiful eyes and kissed her softly. They strolled up the hill to the cabin, with Spurt and Bronco closely behind.

After dinner, he told stories about his travels, and the battle at Kings Mountain, but he excluded the horrors he'd witnessed there. He waited until the excited children were asleep to tell Rebekka about Edward's death.

The next day, the family visited the McGruder residence and broke the sad news. Scott and Rebekka attempted to console Margaret and Craig, but their grief was almost too much to bear.

After several days at home, Scott discussed the act passed by North Carolina setting aside bounty land for service in the Continental Line. When Scott indicated he might join the Continental Line, Rebekka was distraught inside but as always fully supported his decisions.

In late November, Scott rode to Hillsboro with Sevier, Shelby, and five hundred mounted sharp shooters. The lure of owning a substantial tract of prime land and fighting for liberty at the same time was sufficient motivation. He would be fighting not only for a noble cause—a new country free of the British—but also for his own family and his parents. His children would greatly benefit through a chance for a better education and other opportunities. It was an opportunity that he could not neglect.

The morale and confidence level of the men was very high. The Battle of Kings Mountain had proven that the so-called elite British army was not invincible. Scott and most of the other Over-mountain Men joined Major General Nathaniel Greene's Southern Continental Army and were assigned to the Fourth Regiment.

On January 17, 1781, he returned to the Cowpens under General Daniel Morgan and acted heroically in the defeat of Tarleton. For his acts of bravery and leadership during this battle, Colonel Sevier promoted him to Lieutenant.

Over the next several months, Scott led his squad of snipers in battles at Guilford Courthouse, Fort Ninety-Six, and Eutaw Springs. He rose through the ranks quickly and General Greene promoted him to Major after the battle of Fort Ninety-Six. After this battle, he went home on leave. One evening, while visiting with Colonel Sevier, he described some beautiful bottom land known to him and situated on the south side of the Clinch River approximately forty miles northeast of Knoxville. He requested Colonel Sevier set aside a portion of this land for him to claim when hostilities ceased. Keeping his promise to Edward, he requested Colonel Sevier posthumously promote him to sergeant and set aside a thousand acres in the same general area for Edward's wife Margaret.

While stationed at Hillsboro, he learned that his parents were well and had reopened their inn. Scott was discharged at Hillsboro in October of 1783, when the Continental Line was disbanded. He received some cash and a book of pay vouchers good for money at some later date, presumably when the state treasury would be more stabilized. But the two most important documents ever issued to Scott were from the North Carolina Secretary of State. His read as follows:

> Land Office, Military WARRANT, No. 1305
> To the principal surveyors of the Land set apart for the officers and
> Soldiers of the State of North Carolina.
> This shall be your WARRANT to survey and lay
> Off in one or more surveys, for Scott D. Wallace
> His Heirs or Assigns, the Quantity of Four Thousand
> Eight Hundred Acres of Land, due unto the said Scott D. Wallace

In consideration for his services for three years as a Major
in the North Carolina Continental Line.
Agreeable to a Certificate from the Governour and Council received into the Land Office. GIVEN under my Hand, and the Seal of the said Office, This 5th Day of November in the Year One Thousand Seven Hundred and 83.

A similar warrant was issued to Margaret McGruder for a tract of land containing a thousand acres adjacent to Scott's.

Scott's lifetime dream had come true.

Commander Wallace selected a UHF frequency for the New York Center on his PCD. After receiving an IFR clearance, he continued reminiscing. *My second most favorite ancestor was Richard. He was a man with high principles and integrity. Always fought for the underdog. The little guy. I like that idea. Did well until he took on the TVA, and lost. Grandpa's book was filled with highlights of his adventurous and dramatic life...*

August 1934
Vicinity of Loyston, TN

The late afternoon sun reflected off the abundantly chromed, jet-black Buick of the Richard Wallace family as it rumbled up the steep incline, leaving a trail of dust that slowly settled back to the ground. As they neared the school, the deputy directing traffic motioned for Richard to park in a reserved spot near the entrance. He disliked preferential treatment, but in order to smooth the flow of traffic he parked as directed. The local communities had been looking forward to this meeting with the Tennessee Valley Authority for days. Rumors had spread throughout the region with the speed of wildfire. Some rumors held good news, but most of them harbored dreadful things to come.

As thirty-one-year-old Richard and his family entered the auditorium, they were escorted to seats near the front. Richard had been taught since childhood never to be pretentious or overbearing toward those who were less fortunate. This method of dealing with people was handed down from his fifth great-grandfather, who settled on the estate in 1783. The Wallaces were well known for their fairness and generosity. Their five tenants lived in better homes than most landowners. As a result, the farm was maintained in an immaculate condition, producing bountiful crops and cattle of such high quality that their steaks were sought by the better restaurants in Knoxville and surrounding cities. Their farm was one of only a handful in the region that had managed to keep all of its original acreage intact and in the same family.

It was sweltering inside the auditorium with standing room only. Many of the ladies used hand-held fans to stir the muggy air. A large map of the area stood on an easel at the front, with various colors designating actions envisioned by the TVA. Three men dressed in suits sat on a bench at the front, facing the audience. At intervals, corresponding to their overweight condition, they wiped perspiration from their foreheads and necks.

At the appointed time of 7 PM, TVA representative Albert Lilenthal stood and approached the lectern. He smiled broadly while surveying the audience, then he shuffled his notes, cleared his throat, and began.

"Good evening, ladies and gentlemen. My name is Albert Lilenthal. My job with the Tennessee Valley Authority is land acquisition. The TVA plans to build a dam at Norris. I want to thank you, on behalf of the TVA and my two associates, for your presence. Your attendance on this unusually warm evening indicates to me that you have a great interest in our project."

A slight rustling in the crowd, accompanied by smothered laughter, distracted Lilienthal. He reached for his handkerchief to wipe the perspiration from his forehead. A large moth buzzed around his head. As he ducked and swatted, his notes fluttered to the floor like September leaves. The crowd erupted in laughter. Embarrassed and caught off guard, he removed his coat, loosened his tie, and re-grouped his papers. Another low mumble emanated from the crowd as they chatted with each other and shook their heads.

Trying to ignore the disturbance, he stepped near the map and pointed to an area on either side of the Clinch River depicted in bright red.

"This area is projected to be under water at its highest level, usually in the spring."

Some of the people near the front leaned forward for a better look. An elderly woman pointed her gnarled finger at Lilienthal and yelled, "That's my farm in the middle of that water. Who are you to decide such a matter?"

Control of the meeting was nearly lost when several other people began protesting, yelling loudly that they would never leave their homes under any circumstances. Recognizing the hostility of the group, Lilienthal wisely waited patiently while the crowd vented its anger. Finally, he cautiously held up his hands, trying to quiet the room.

"I want to assure all of you that we, or rather the TVA, will pay a fair price for your property. We have experts in real estate who will determine the fair market price of each parcel of land. They will contact you and make an appointment to assess the value of your farms. We hope members of your family will accompany the representative when your property is appraised."

Lilienthal pointed at a green area on the map adjacent to the red area labeled "Taking Line."

"A band of land on either side of the lake must also be purchased. We will use it to protect the lake from erosion and perhaps for future recreational purposes."

An angry young man stood up, shook his fist at Lilienthal, and yelled, "So you big shots are taking our land to make a lake so your big shot buddies can have parties on their cabin cruisers."

After shouts of agreement from the crowd subsided, Lilienthal responded.

"Sir, I appreciate your concern, but President Roosevelt wants a better life for all of you. This area needs electricity in order for industry to move in and provide jobs for you and for future generations. I invite each of you to study the map after the meeting. We will remain here to answer all questions you may have."

An obviously relieved Lilienthal wiped his face and neck

with his damp handkerchief as he introduced the next speaker, Hanover Morrison.

Morrison had closely observed the assembly during Lilienthal's presentation and had become annoyed but also somewhat nervous. As he rose from his seat, an elderly woman in the front row dropped her fan. Recognizing a chance to seize the moment, he quickly picked it up, smiled, and presented it to the woman, hoping he would gain some leniency from the unruly crowd. She accepted the fan without any comment or sign of emotion.

"I also want to thank you for your attendance and patience under such adverse conditions." Morrison's hands shook slightly, and his voice was an octave or so higher than normal. He loosened his collar and continued. "My official job title with the TVA is Population Relocation. In other words, we will assist you in purchasing and moving to a new location chosen by you. We are training a staff of fine people at the university located at Knoxville who will assist you in this endeavor. After their initial training, they will develop a list of properties for sale within approximately one hundred miles of Knoxville. This will include property in cities, small villages, and farms. Our goal is to make sure you obtain property as good or better than your current farm. Several of our agents are locals and know the difference in value between fertile bottom lands as opposed to hilly or red clay soil covered with large outcroppings of limestone rocks. And of course you will be compensated accordingly."

He held up a form. "To help us locate and work with you, please fill out a form TVA 1935 before you leave tonight." Morrison had several other topics to discuss but cut his session short. "Are there any questions?"

No one in the audience spoke. Most gazed back at Morrison with narrowed eyes that spoke more than any words could convey.

"If there are no questions, then I am honored to introduce our next speaker, Mr. Tip Morrison."

In his haste to return to the safety of his seat, Hanover bumped into Tip's arm, knocking his notes from his hand. He quickly retrieved the papers while some in the audience sniggered. Moving to the lectern, he hoped to obtain a semblance of acceptance using some dry humor. His presentation would probably be the straw that broke the camel's back. Pointing to Hanover Morrison he said, "This fellow may have the same last name as me, but let me assure you we are not related." Some people in the audience chuckled. He needed it. He would accept any help he could find. He cleared his throat and began.

"Good evening, ladies and gentlemen. It's my great pleasure to be here and to represent the Tennessee Valley Authority. My job is to ensure that cemeteries, which will be covered by water or otherwise become inaccessible, are removed to another location. This will be done in the most respectful and dignified manner possible."

A hush ensued over the audience. Fans abruptly stopped and mouths and eyes opened wide as people stared at each other in disbelief. Apparently, most of those present had not contemplated moving themselves, much less disturbing their buried ancestors. Some of the cemeteries were over a hundred years old. Several contained the remains of important families, as well as veterans of the Revolutionary War, Civil War, and World War One. Cemeteries were usually clustered around churches and treated with a spiritual reverence and respect. To disturb the final resting places of these proud and viciously independent people would strike at their very soul.

Morrison seemed oblivious to their shock. "We are planning a national cemetery for the re-interment of your loved ones. This cemetery would be beautifully landscaped and perpetually maintained by the TVA. Of course, anyone wishing to use another cemetery will be reimbursed twenty dollars by the TVA for each re-interment. If any of you prefer, the graves will not be disturbed. But some of them will be covered with water. The National Cemetery would only be used for the purpose of re-interment, and space would not be provided for future burials." He looked over the crowd and smiled. "I will be happy to try to answer any questions."

The crowd was silent. Finally, an elderly gentleman arose to speak, supporting his trembling legs with a cane. He cleared his throat and then wiped his mouth with his red handkerchief before stuffing it back in the pocket of his bib overalls. The audience turned their heads and locked their eyes on the speaker.

"Mister, I have lived in these here parts all my life. Most of these people here have, too. Some of our youngsters went up north over the years looking for work, but most of them eventually returned to our beautiful hills and rivers. Most of us men have willingly supported the government, beginning with the revolution. Many have paid the ultimate sacrifice. Why would this government now turn on us as if we were insects to squash? You promise us a better life. Who asked for a better life? We love the way we live here, with neighbors that will always help when needed. I understand that we live longer than most folks—take me for instance." The crowd laughed, but it was nervous laughter. A cool breeze from the nearby Clinch began pouring through the open windows.

"So we must be doing a few things the way it was intended. You can tell the President that my place is not for sale at any price, and I don't want to be buried in his fancy national cemetery or any other one 'cept my own."

He held on to the back of the bench in front of him for support and slowly sat down as the crowd erupted with applause, which lasted for several minutes. Then the crowd began chanting and clapping their hands in unison: "We want Wallace, we want Wallace."

People turned and stared. Some of those setting behind Richard encouraged him by patting him on the back. Finally he stood, looked over his shoulder at the crowd, and walked toward the front. The crowd clapped and yelled louder. As he approached the lectern, the room became quiet again. Tip Morrison held his hand up, as if to stop Richard, but a deputy sheriff motioned for Morrison to back away.

"I'm sorry, sir, but our format does not include unscheduled speakers from the audience," Lilienthal interjected.

"I believe the crowd has just changed your rules,"

Richard countered, as he moved behind the lectern.

Tip Morrison wiped the perspiration from his face and glanced at Lilienthal. Lacking support, he quietly sat down.

Richard surveyed the crowd. The room was slowly cooling down. The light summer breeze carried a pleasant aroma of freshly mown hay mixed with honeysuckle blossoms. Outside, millions of lightning bugs lit the countryside as they lazily ascended and descended in unchoreographed acrobatics, while bullfrogs on the banks of a nearby creek kept cadence with their throaty croaking.

"I didn't attend this meeting with the intent to debate this issue. However, like most of you, I didn't realize the extent of the planned encroachment upon our community." Richard turned and addressed the three TVA representatives.

"This is a very alarming and shocking revelation. I took a few notes during your presentations. You did not adequately disclose some significant issues." Richard pulled a piece of paper from his pocket and placed it on the lectern. "If you indeed have the authority to seize our community, and I'm not saying you do, tell this audience what that authority is."

Lilienthal stood and said, "Congress passed the TVA Act, and it was signed by the President in May 1933. The Act provides for flood control, improved navigation on the Tennessee River, as well as agriculture and industrial development for this area. As a spin-off, just think of how many locals will earn good wages as they help construct the dam."

"Perhaps so. To my knowledge, not one person,

including our own representatives, coordinated this matter with us," Richard replied, shaking his head. "This catastrophic change was cast upon us as if the TVA somehow knows what is best for us, what we desire. If your map is correct, the 'taking line' will include most of my farm. At least all the premium soil will either be covered with water or confiscated by the TVA for alleged improvement of our lot." Richard glanced at his notes. "You also failed to address the cost of moving. As farmers move to other locations, available land will decrease, meaning prices will most likely escalate to meet the demand. Will you take this burden into consideration?"

"I don't recall addressing supply and demand of property," Lilienthal replied in a low tone. "I believe in a free market."

"And we believe in a free country," Richard shot back. "Free of government over-reach."

The crowd jumped to its feet and applauded. After a short time, Richard motioned for them to sit down.

"And what have you planned for the many tenant farmers? They don't own land. Where will they go and what will they do?"

Lilienthal struggled for an answer. "Actually, we haven't addressed the tenant issue yet."

"Does that mean you will?" Richard asked.

"Certainly, certainly," Lilienthal said, nodding his head. "Of course we will provide some sort of relief for these tenant farmers."

"The hour is late, but please remain for a few moments

after these gentlemen leave. We have some issues to discuss." Looking at the TVA representatives, Richard added, "I would appreciate it very much if you would leave the map so that we can study it in more detail."

This was a polite signal for the three to leave. For their safety, a deputy sheriff escorted them to their government vehicle and watched until it disappeared over a ridge.

Richard addressed the crowd. "Obviously we can't physically fight the TVA and win. They have the backing of the entire U.S. government. However, there is a slim chance that we could prevail in the courts. If any of you are interested in filing a law suit against the TVA, raise your hand."

The entire crowd held their hands high.

"Excellent. I will contact my attorney in Nashville first thing in the morning. In the meantime, I recommend that each of you attempt to determine the true value of your property. Before you leave, please locate your property on this map and decide how the dam will affect it. Good night, and thanks for your confidence in me."

The crowd stood and applauded until Richard and his family exited the building.

The Wallace family sadly watched as movers loaded a van with their possessions. The date was January 10, 1936. A dusting of snow had fallen two nights before and stubbornly remained in shaded areas.

Their two-story brick Georgian, designed by Rebekka Wallace, had stood majestically overlooking the hills and the scenic Clinch River for nearly one hundred and thirty years. The windows seemed saddened and bewildered as the last piece of furniture was removed. The stately home was scheduled to be demolished the following day.

A half-mile away, a Model A Ford struggled along the frozen gravel road carrying all the meager possessions of a tenant family. A young man riding a horse at full gallop turned into the winding road leading up to the Wallace residence. Richard recognized the boy as Ronald, the son of William McGruder, a close friend who lived on a farm adjacent to his own.

"Mr. Wallace, come quickly! Papa hung himself!" Ronald

yelled, hysterical. "He's at the barn, but I was afraid to cut him down. Mother fainted when she found him."

"Get off that horse," Richard demanded, moving quickly to help the boy down. "We'll drive over there. Quick, get in the car."

Richard drove to the back of McGruder's house and parked near the barn. He was stunned by the grizzly sight. William McGruder's limp body swung lazily back and forth in the light breeze. His crumpled hat lay on the ground nearby. White foam oozed from his drooping mouth and nostrils. His eyes were dilated and unusually large and his face was pale because of the blocked carotid artery in his neck. He was dressed in a black suit, which he often wore as principal of the county school.

Richard suggested that Ronald go inside the house, but he refused.

"Okay, you stay here and I'll go up in the loft and lower him to the ground," Richard whispered and gave the distraught boy a hug.

Richard scrambled up a ladder leading to the loft. He found a rope used to winch hay up into the barn loft. William McGruder had secured the rope to a supporting beam, tied it around his neck, walked to the opening at the end of the barn, and jumped. He was probably dead on impact as the full weight of his six-foot body snapped the rope around his neck.

Richard partially untied the rope while bracing one of his feet against the beam. He leaned backward and gradually reduced tension on the rope until it slowly moved, lowering

William's body gently to the ground. When the rope went limp, Richard ran to the opening at the end of the barn. Below, young Ronald sat on the ground holding his father's crumpled body in his arms.

While Richard climbed down the ladder, three neighbors arrived and removed the rope. Richard and the other three men struggled as they carried McGruder's body to his house where it would be prepared for burial.

Along the way, a piece of folded parchment fell from McGruder's coat pocket. Ronald picked it up, read the first two lines, and then quickly tucked it into his coat pocket. It was the document his father had read to him at the dinner table the previous evening in the presence of the entire family. It was a solemn occasion, with candle light flickering upon Ronald's face as he held up his right hand and took a solemn oath to uphold The Pact. To consummate and seal the oath, Ronald had cut a small incision in his right thumb, drawing blood, and placed his bloodied thumbprint next to his name.

Saturday June 26, 2010
The White House

President Brian Whitby, Vice President Walter Browning, and Chief of Staff Joe Peterson walked briskly down the hall from the Oval Office to the Cabinet Room. They had been conferring with two congressional leaders about a very controversial matter since early morning. As President Whitby entered the door, cabinet members, military officers, and sixteen members from the intelligence community rose to their feet. He was dressed immaculately in a tailored blue suit with matching tie, white shirt, black plain-toe shoes and cuff links bearing the presidential seal. He stopped behind his chair at the head of the large, oval-shaped table, which had been carved from the trunk of a California redwood and bore the presidential seal. Glancing around the room, he nodded his head and said, "Please," signaling for everyone to be seated.

Paintings of various American presidents and dignitaries decorated the walls. Leather backed note pads containing a pen with the presidential seal lay on the table in front of each cabinet member. A gold inlayed chandelier, a gift of France, gave the room a touch of elegance. The colors were displayed near a wall to the president's right. June sunshine streamed through the windows. President Whitby looked around the room again and smiled. "Good morning, ladies and gentlemen," he said. "I apologize for interrupting your plans on this beautiful Saturday morning. What a day for golf."

Some of the cabinet members chuckled and nodded their heads in agreement.

"However, certain crucial events, some of which you are already grievously aware, warrant our immediate attention. Several months ago, the Chinese government sent a shock wave throughout the world when they unveiled their mighty submarine, the Cockroach. How they managed to design and build this very dangerous submarine without our knowledge is baffling. Nevertheless, that is not the subject of our meeting this morning. This troubling matter of our intelligence lapse will be investigated at a more desirable time and through normal channels. I want all of our energy focused on the task at hand—that is, how do we counteract this threat. To further this effort, Mr. Albert Counce, DNI, and his staff have developed a comprehensive NIE. Mr. Counce."

"Thank you, Mr. President. Ladies and gentlemen of the cabinet, officers, and staff, we have worked tirelessly to produce this NIE in a very short time frame, yet we have ensured its accuracy to the extent humanly possible. We judge with high confidence that the Commission on Science, Technology, and Industry for National Defense under the overall command of the Peoples Liberation Army (PLA) managed to secretly develop, test, and commission several nuclear powered submarines into service.

"We estimate with moderate confidence that in 2000, the PLA selected a site to develop a large, stealthy submarine. They chose the site at Wuhan near the Yangtze River in the Province of Hubei."

Counce turned toward a Navy Captain, who quickly unfolded and displayed a satellite photograph of the area near the Hubei Province. The map was marked *TOP SECRET* in large red letters. Counce pointed a laser at the manufacturing site.

"The giant Three Georges Dam, under construction since 1993, harnesses the Yangtze and prevents frequent flooding, which could destroy such an expensive project. The location is perfect. It fits like a glove. We assess with high confidence that China's mission was to develop a submarine that would allow Beijing to be on an even or superior footing with America. The following year, the PLA amassed a highly sophisticated group from the China State Shipbuilding enterprise to initiate the project. Some of the institutions selected were the Shipbuilding Technology Research Institute, the Hangzhou Applied Acoustics Research Institute, the China Ship Research and Development Academy, the Shipbuilding Technology Research Institute, and the Wuhan Maritime Communications Research Institute.

"We assess with great certainty that in 2005, Beijing, the Kremlin, and several other smaller satellite neighbors formed the Shanghai Cooperation Organization or SCO. This was a significant step between two nuclear powers, who had long viewed each other with suspicion and at times contempt. That same year, Russia and China began military exercises in the Yellow Sea. The Shanghai Cooperation Organization brazenly ordered the U.S. to move its military bases from Uzbekistan and Kyrgyzstan.

We assess with moderate confidence that only eight years later, in 2008, the first submarine, code-named Cockroach, was launched and preceded down the Yangtze into the East China Sea for testing. Coincidently, the US Navy commissioned their latest Virginia-class submarine in 2007. But at a maximum speed of 32 knots and dives restricted below one thousand feet, this small submarine has been judged by some analysts as a 'sitting sub' should a Cockroach encounter occur.

"We judge with high confidence that the Chinese economy is and has been exploding, and demand for oil is enormous. China's growing appetite for energy is only equaled by the U.S. Although Beijing dominates the Sudan, Kazakhstan, Turkmenistan, and Venezuelan oil production, the U.S. controls most of OPEC and the Gulf of Guinea. We assess with high confidence that China desires a larger bite of the African oil primarily to keep it from flowing to the U.S., and that she is now willing to flex her muscles. She is ready to call America's bluff.

"We assess with moderate confidence that a distinct

advantage weighs in China's favor as she gains a toehold in the Gulf of Guinea. Al-Qaeda attacks the American oil companies relentlessly with car bombs, small arms, and RPGs, inflicting damage to refineries and pipelines that can take weeks to repair. Al-Qaeda doesn't clash with China as they do the U.S. For the most part, China has somehow managed to avoid direct confrontation with the Muslims. In hopes of countering this threat, the U.S. formed the U.S. Africa Command in 2007. We assess with certainty that the new command does not have a clear objective; has not been accepted by all African nations; has inadequate organization, equipment, and personnel; and is ineffective in the overall scheme of things in Africa.

"We judge with moderate-to-high confidence that in 2007, China deliberately tightened the screws and created a big headache for the Pentagon. She substantially tilted the balance of power, demonstrating her resolve and technological prowess by destroying one of her orbiting satellites with a medium-range ballistic missile. In late 2007, U.S./China relations soured further after the U.S. awarded the Dalai Lama with a Congressional Gold Medal. China accused the U.S. of 'blatant interference in her internal affairs.' We judge with high confidence that China's global expansion will continue, and almost certainly they will expand their dangerous cat-and-mouse tactics of probing our defenses by operating very close to NATO and U.S. airspace. However, the USDI assesses these estimates with only moderate confidence.

"In March 2009, a commissioned squadron of

Cockroaches sailed from their homeport in Shanghai and proceeded south. Their destination was the Formosa Strait, which divides the mainland of China from Taiwan."

A map of Taiwan and a large photograph of the Cockroaches were displayed. "Once inside the strait, the submarines surfaced for Taiwan and the entire world to see. A red flag was hoisted on the mast of each submarine, and those crewmen not on duty stood at parade rest on the sub deck in their impressive dress uniforms.

"Apparently for extra impact, a tight formation of five Chinese Sukhoi SU-34MK Morays screamed by, making a low pass over their Cockroaches." A large photograph of this dramatic event was displayed. "They made a tight turn and flew by at slow speed, dipped their wings, engaged afterburners, and accelerated almost straight up. Reaching fifty thousand feet, they leveled and returned to base. Taiwan Air Defense detected the jets on their early warning radar and scrambled a flight of F-22s. But little intelligence exists on the Moray's performance and capabilities. Taiwan's air force cautiously stayed clear of the intruders. The Cockroaches maneuvered around the entire island, then disappeared back into the East China Sea.

"We judge with only low confidence that the Cockroach is capable of launching several Ju Lang 4 intercontinental ballistic missiles tipped with nuclear warheads as some have suggested. We judge with high confidence that this capability will be achieved within two years. We judge with high confidence that the Cockroach can evade, outrun, and dive deeper than any other submarine known to exist or planned.

It is very quiet, making it difficult to locate and track by the US Navy. They have developed procedures to loiter undetected for weeks at extreme depths. US Navy Intelligence determined with high certainty that a camera found floating in the Pacific with a severed fifty-foot nylon cable once belonged to a Cockroach. It's a simple but effective device. The sensitive digital camera, capable of a three hundred and sixty degree scan, can take detailed photographs at distances heretofore unknown. A wooden arm with a rubber-coated lead weight attached to the bottom of the camera acts as a simplified gyro. The gyro keeps the camera level by counteracting the ocean wave action. There are virtually no mechanical parts inside the mechanism to make noise or break. To ensure stealth, the camera is deployed and recovered using a crank turned by sailors inside the submarine. It is very likely that the Chinese use this camera to spy on and photograph key ports and other strategic targets of interest.

"After displaying themselves in the Formosa Strait, the Chinese began a program of deception that perplexed our intelligence community for almost two years. They kept most of their Cockroaches deployed around the world but made it appear that only one particular submarine was operational at a specific naval installation. Very likely, the idea was to fool the world into believing that the Cockroaches were having difficulties and only a handful were operational, perhaps for testing or training. This feat was accomplished in a similar, uncomplicated manner used to develop the Cockroaches in complete secrecy. Each submarine based at a particular naval installation was issued the same exterior serial numbers. The real serial numbers were displayed inside the submarines where spy satellites could not see. The fake serial numbers were prominently displayed on the decks in full view of spy satellites. The submarine movements were coordinated so that only one Cockroach would be in a particular port at any given time. The U.S. satellites would observe what appeared to be the same submarine returning after a two- or three-day cruise.

"We assess with certainty that a Cockroach had a serious mechanical problem at sea and returned to base earlier than planned. Due to a coordination error, a departing Cockroach and the arriving Cockroach with the emergency passed each other near the base before the departing Cockroach submerged. Their ruse was finally discovered weeks later by a sharp-eyed NSA specialist in a routine review of the satellite photographs when she noted both serial numbers were the same. This revelation was very troubling. For the first time, the U.S Navy Intelligence concluded with high confidence that many Cockroaches had been and are today traveling the oceans virtually undetected."

Counce paused to let this information sink in. Some of the members were awestruck.

"Everyone is reminded that all information in the NIE is classified and is to be used or discussed with only appropriately cleared people on a need-to-know basis," Counce added. "At this time, I suggest we have a discussion on how to proceed with a counter to the Cockroach. Mr. President, that concludes my NIE on the Cockroach."

"Thank you, Mr. Counce, for your most detailed analysis and historical review of the Cockroach. I believe it's obvious to all of us in this room that our country has lost its edge in world military dominance. I personally feel that we are naked, vulnerable to the whims of the Chinese. Therefore, I think it is incumbent on me as the President of our great country to request Congress to pass legislation authorizing necessary funds for the Department of Defense to proceed smartly with the development of a counter to the Cockroach."

At that time, Secretary of Defense Joseph McNamara jumped to his feet and began clapping. Within seconds, the entire room had joined him.

After the clapping subsided and everyone was seated, President Whitby continued. "Thank you very much for your overwhelming support. I will contact key congressional leaders, hopefully today, and apprise them of the Cockroach threat and ask for their support in expediting the authorization bill."

Everyone rose until the President and his entourage exited the room.

The following month, a bewildered Congress authorized a spending bill for the Department of Defense to expend necessary funds to develop, as expeditiously as humanly possible, a counter to this formidable threat to world peace and stability. Within days, the Pentagon developed the basic framework for an offensive weapon dubbed SAID

If measured on a scale, the SAID project would easily compare to the Manhattan Project in scope, size, and cost.

17

April 11, 2014
Knoxville, TN

Exiting the terminal at McGhee Tyson Airport, Major Vance McGruder flagged a taxi and directed the driver to downtown Knoxville. He would have preferred to obtain a rental car and drive himself, but auto rental companies become skittish when customers want to pay in cash instead of using a credit card. His credit card was stamped with his real name and address, and would leave a trail when used, something he wished to avoid at any cost.

He dressed casually, with a floppy hat to cover his Marine Corps haircut and a pair of dark sunglasses to cover his eyes. He was traveling light, carrying an attaché case and a round trip ticket.

"Where to, sir?"

"Bank of America."

"Which one?"

"The branch on West Main," McGruder replied.

The taxi driver punched the destination into his GPS and headed for the Alcoa highway.

"Beautiful day. You from 'round here?"

When McGruder ignored the driver, he added, "Be 'bout thirty minute drive ta downtown Knoxville. Heavy traffic this morning."

Arriving at the Bank of America, he handed a hundred dollar bill to the driver and instructed him to wait.

McGruder closed all his various accounts, totaling almost $285,000—all in one hundred dollar bills—and stuffed the money into his attaché case. Re-entering the cab, McGruder instructed the driver to proceed to the nearest FedEx store where he obtained a FedEx Large Box and a U.S. Airbill form. He returned to the cab, removed the money from his attaché case, and dropped it into the FedEx box, making sure the driver could not observe the transfer. Instructions on the box clearly prohibited sending items such as cash or cash equivalents. McGruder ignored the instructions. He filled out the U.S. Airbill using fake names for the sender and recipient. Under special handling, he checked the box to hold the shipment at a FedEx store near MCAS Beaufort until the following Wednesday.

He paid the shipping charges by cash, returned to the cab, and instructed the driver to proceed north on Interstate 75 to Norris Dam. He told the inquisitive driver that his great-great-grandfather helped design the dam and that he wanted to visit, photograph, and take a look at his work.

The driver was familiar with the area and drove directly

to the overlook at the dam site. McGruder removed a set of binoculars from the attaché case and scanned the dam and surrounding terrain. His main interests were the location and type of Homeland Security cameras, armed guards, water level, and the terrain surrounding the dam. He pulled a small camera from his shirt pocket and took several pictures. He took a close-up of a metal sign giving the details of the dam, including its height of 1,080 feet above the ocean.

Returning to the cab, he instructed the driver to proceed over the dam. He snapped several photos as they drove across the dam on route 441. Then he instructed the driver to rejoin the interstate and drive south toward Knoxville, stopping at the first large shopping center with a MegaMart.

The puzzled driver reminded McGruder of the cost involved in renting his cab for an extended time. McGruder handed him another hundred-dollar bill and told him to wait. The driver grinned from ear to ear and said, "Yes, sir. Betcha bottom dollar I'll wait."

Inside the cavernous store, McGruder grabbed a cart and strode to the hardware department. He selected a red roll and a white roll of duct-tape, scissors, and a pre-paid, disposable cell phone. The phone would serve no purpose other than to confuse and waste the time of investigators if such an effort should occur at some future date. He picked up a dozen red roses at the flower shop, then joined the long line of Saturday morning shoppers at the checkout area.

A destitute appearing family with three unkempt kids shuffled along in the line ahead of him. The man was dressed in overalls, hadn't shaved in days, and was obviously chewing tobacco. His wife was dressed in very worn jeans, an oversized man's undershirt, and shower clogs. She grasped a cigarette lighter and pack of cigarettes in one hand and somehow managed to hold a sleeping infant in her arm as she unloaded the cart while her husband gazed around the store, undaunted. The two older boys appeared undernourished, placid, and remained quiet as they stared at McGruder. At first, he looked at the family with contempt, but then he studied them more intently as the line moved forward.

Let's see, they're buying bologna, chips, bread, cookies, candy, and soft drinks. The beer's not for the kids, I hope. No milk, no fruit or vegetables. Maybe they have a garden…really none of my business. Besides, they're probably happy, oblivious to the carnage inflicted upon people and the environment in many parts of the world by our great and wonderful leaders. Maybe ignorance does bring bliss. Actually, down deep I guess I'm somewhat jealous. I can't believe I'm at this inglorious point in my life, but I would probably change places with him right now if I had the chance. If I only had my family back again…I wouldn't have lost them if our asinine civilian deciders, deceivers, in Washington had learned a simple lesson from our adventures in Vietnam, Somalia, Afghanistan, Iraq, Iran, Venezuela…There never was any real threat from these people. We've made them a threat, a resolve to get even, to hurt our soft underside. My own government built a case against them, convinced the average Joe here in this country that we either invade and conquer them, or they'll broil our kids and eat 'em. What a farce. Unbelievable propaganda and deceit courtesy of John Q. Public. But the public, with very short memories, fall for it over and over again, and the perpetrators and manufacturers of all those killing machines get filthy rich.

Ah, at one time I was a believer also, part of a moronic war machine. Yeah, I'm responsible for murdering those five Iranian kids. I'm guilty. Period. Collateral damage…Fog of war…shock and awe. Nothing but stupid bureaucratic lingo designed to soften a horrible tragedy. The fact that I was given erroneous lat/long by a hysterical eighteen-year-old kid doesn't relieve me of my responsibilities. I dropped that smart bomb…If only I hadn't volunteered for that mission…if only I hadn't seen those torn bodies…

"Morning, sir. Looks like you're fixing to fix some things up."

"Yeah, work around the house is never finished."

All right, clown, mind your own business so I can get outta here.

As he swiped the items, the clerk gazed at McGruder's attaché case.

McGruder observed his stare and said, in an agitated voice, "Problem?" He definitely didn't want a rent-a-cop filching through his case. And it would be difficult to explain to the local authorities why he was carrying such a large amount of cash.

"No, sir. I know it's yours. We don't sell items made of expensive leather. Just like the way it looks. Wouldn't mind owning one of them thangs myself. No, sir, I surely wouldn't."

McGruder rolled his eyes in disgust, thought about dressing the man down, but realized that he hadn't really said anything out of the ordinary. Only made a complimentary remark. He reminded himself of the necessity to keep his temper under control and fit in to whatever environment came his way. McGruder handed the clerk a crisp one hundred dollar bill.

"Yes, sir, we take cash, too. Just as good as money."

I wish I could tell him he shouldn't quit his day job, but I better not.

He forced himself to say good morning to the clerk, walked briskly to his waiting cab, and directed his driver to Smoky Mountain Aviation at the Knoxville Downtown Island Airport. The newly purchased items were stuffed in his attaché case.

Arriving at the airport, he gave the driver a wad of money and instructed him to be back at 3 PM.

18

The operations manager greeted McGruder, "Afternoon, sir. How may I help you?"

"Afternoon. Kevin Holston. I have a reservation for a one-fifty-two."

McGruder had researched the FAA database for Cessna 152s rented by Smoky Mountain Aviation noting their color and aircraft identification. He decided N321BE was perfect.

"Yes sir, Mr. Holston. Recall talking to you. She's re-fueled and ready to go. Could I see your pilot, driver's license, and a major credit card please?"

McGruder handed him a very authentic looking pilot license and Tennessee driver's license.

"Don't use credit cards anymore. Got in over my head once—three cards almost maxed out, paying outrageous interest. Never again. Now it's cash or checks."

"Yeah, the news is full of stories like that," the manager said, nodding his head. "Something's gotta give, and soon."

Glancing up at the overhead weather display, the man

droned on while McGruder fidgeted inside.

"Excellent weather east of the Mississippi. Just returned from a sight-seeing trip around the Smokies with two customers. It's an annual outing with them you know. The dogwoods and redbuds are in full bloom in the lower elevations. Beautiful creation of God. Unusually smooth air, too.

"Holston…By chance is the Holston River named after one of your ancestors?"

"Well, who knows? Actually, I'm not into genealogy. Could be. My ancestors settled somewhere in what is now northeast Tennessee just before the Revolutionary War."

"Is that a fact? Very interesting. Were they involved in that war?"

"Very much so."

Shouda kept my mouth shut. Be careful blabber-mouth.

"Mind if I ask where you're heading?"

Not at all, buddy. I'll just explain my entire life to you. No problem.

"Just some pleasure flying and a need to keep current, you know. Probably fly by the Smokies if it's smooth like you say."

"Sounds good. Sir, we require a VFR flight plan be filed and a weather brief even for local flights. Insurance requirements, you know. It's no big deal. Just show the route as a fifty-mile radius of Knoxville." He pointed toward a red phone hanging on the wall next to a green aeronautical chart. "You can file your flight plan with the Flight Service. We keep all our aircraft data on file with the FAA so it's not necessary to include that information in your flight plan. As requested, your aircraft is N321BE. She's the white one with red markings in the number four slot to your left leaving the back door."

"Yep. Nice aircraft. Or at least it was the last time I rented her."

"You've rented from us before? Funny, I couldn't find your name in our database. Must have been purged. How long ago has it been?"

McGruder chided himself. *You're talking way too much blabber-mouth. Watch yourself, Marine.*

"Oh, several years ago. Computer probably drops inactive accounts."

"It does. But rest assured I'll make the entries immediately. Good customers are what makes our business. That will be four hundred and fifty dollars please, sir. After you return, we'll top 'er off, charge you for fuel used, plus Hobbs meter time. We'll refund any overpayments of course." He paused. "Sure you don't want to upgrade to one of our newer models with a glass cockpit?"

"Nope. Guess I'm just old fashioned. A VOR or ADF will do just fine."

And a GPS in those glass cockpits leave a trail of where you've been and when you were there. No thanks.

"Understand. I'm sorta like that myself. Just old fashioned I guess." He gave McGruder a document with several lines of very small print and said, "Sir, this is our standard rental agreement. Feel free to review it then sign at the bottom."

McGruder pretended to scan over the agreement and

then signed with his left hand, although he normally wrote right-handed. He laid five one hundred dollar bills on the counter. The ops manager closely examined each bill by holding them above his head toward the ceiling lights, then marked the corner of each bill with a unique character.

"Have a safe and enjoyable flight," he said, once his inspection was complete.

"Thanks." McGruder filed his flight plan and proceeded to the flight line.

After a very thorough pre-flight, McGruder climbed into the cockpit. He fastened his shoulder harness and completed a pre-taxi checklist, then started the engine. After ensuring oil pressure and other instruments were functioning normally, he taxied eastbound, pulled a World Aeronautical Chart, CG-21, from his attaché case, and placed it in the right seat. Next, he tuned one radio to the common traffic advisory frequency of 126.6 and the other radio to 122.2 for Flight Service. A Cessna 172 was on final for runway 26, and the pilot announced she would make multiple touch-and-goes.

McGruder glanced at his aircraft's identification displayed on the instrument panel, keyed his radio mike, and announced he was departing runway 26 behind the 172 for a south departure. Scanning the pre-departure checklist, he skipped the item about activating the transponder on the appropriate code.

Let's see what Knoxville Approach can see on their primary radar.

After engine run-up, trim set and flight controls checked for takeoff, McGruder checked for traffic on final, keyed his mike, and transmitted:

"November 321BE departing runway 26 at Downtown Island."

He added a slight amount of power and taxied to the runway centerline, added takeoff power, and lifted off about halfway down the runway. Runway heading was held for a short distance, skirting along the south bank of the Tennessee River to avoid a noise sensitive area of houses south of the airport. Turning left, he threaded his way through an antenna farm situated on top of a small ridge. Leaving 1,400 feet, he called Flight Service and advised, "November 321BE departed Knoxville Downtown Island at 1830 for three-hour local flight."

After acknowledgment from Flight Service, he switched his number one radio to Knoxville Approach Control and transmitted:

"Knoxville Approach November 321BE, over Volunteer, southeast bound at 2,300 feet, request radar service in local area."

Shortly afterward Knoxville approach responded:

"November 321BE, radar contact, squawk VFR."

McGruder acknowledged the instruction but took no action.

In approximately two minutes, Knoxville approach transmitted:

"November 321BE not receiving transponder; reset on code 1200 normal and ident. Traffic is a Boeing 717 two o'clock five miles on right base for runway 23 right. Say altitude."

"November 321BE, traffic in sight. We're still at 2,300

feet. I'll track outbound on the one-five-o radial to avoid the service area."

When McGruder's distance measuring equipment indicated fifteen miles southeast of the Volunteer VORTAC, a local FAA navigational aid, Knoxville approach control advised:

"November 321BE radar contact lost due to clutter from the mountains. Say intentions."

About what I figured, thought McGruder, and replied, "November 321BE roger. I'll turn southwest bound and do some sight seeing. I'll also have the transponder repaired. Thanks for your help."

Instead of making a right turn to the southwest, he made a sharp left turn. Pushing the power control knob full forward, he started a climb to avoid the rising terrain. He had no intention of proceeding to the southwest. Instead, he hugged the side of the Smokies to mask his aircraft from the prying eyes of Knoxville Approach's radar. The controller couldn't care less about McGruder's intentions, but his flight might become important to others in the government in the near future. McGruder knew that his flight would be recorded by an FAA computer if their radar were tracking his aircraft. He would leave no trail to be followed by inquisitive investigators.

Twenty minutes later, the city of Newport slid beneath his left wing. Forty-five miles further to the northeast in the shadow of the Smokies lay the sleepy but beautiful city of Elizabethton, TN, originally known as Sycamore Shoals. An FAA navigational aid appropriately named Holston

Mountain was located near the home-site of McGruder's ancestors. But McGruder had no plans to visit this area.

After twenty minutes, he considered himself well outside Knoxville's radar coverage and turned left to a heading of 300 degrees. Twelve minutes later, he was overhead the More Murrell Airport at Morristown. He landed and taxied to an area of the airport that would provide maximum privacy.

There was little activity at the airport for a Saturday afternoon, which is what he had hoped for, and he began transforming the aircraft registration number N321BE to N821BL. McGruder's research had confirmed N821BL did not exist in the FAA's registration database. He carefully trimmed a piece of red duct tape and set about converting the number 3 to a perfect number 8. Using the same technique with a piece of white duct tape, he modified the red letter E to a red letter L. Then he quickly but carefully altered the identification on the opposite side of the fuselage. Twenty minutes later, the transformation was complete.

He was certain that no one had observed his unusual activities. No aircraft or vehicles had stirred on the airport since his arrival.

He removed a camera holder from his briefcase and attached it to the magnetic compass. It was a simple contraption made from a metal coat hanger and two rubber bands. The camera was set to automatically take a picture every five seconds. Then it was inserted into its fabricated holder and secured by a large rubber band.

He removed a black ski mask and placed it on the right

seat cushion. Last, he removed a small GPS receiver and attached it to the yoke on the passenger side. McGruder had previously entered the latitude and longitude of 361905 degrees north and 834701 degrees west into the GPS, the location of his ancestor's watery grave.

He departed and turned to a heading of 295. He maintained an altitude approximately 1,000 feet above the terrain, descending into the valleys before climbing, skimming over the ridges. This was terrain that his ancestors had originally settled after the Revolutionary War.

Ten minutes after departing, he was over what had once been the beautiful Clinch River. He eased the power back, trimmed the nose slightly down, and began descent. He pulled the ski mask over his head.

Numerous boats…wonder how many were bought with blood money from manufacturing all sorts of killing machines and bombs? Nukes? No doubt…

They'll probably call the FAA on their cell and complain about a low flying aircraft. Bet I'm interfering with their afternoon cocktails. Too bad. I'll be long gone before any action can be taken.

He descended to 1,000 feet mean sea level. Twisting and turning, he followed along the path of the original river as much as possible. Due to the serpentine-shaped lake, he was occasionally forced to pull up steeply to miss the rising terrain and rejoin the lake further downstream.

Two miles from the location of the former cemetery, he lowered the flaps to forty degrees. When the aircraft slowed to minimum maneuvering speed, he opened the window and discarded the materials used to convert the aircraft identification followed by the phone. Over the unseen cemetery where William McGruder, author of the Pact, was buried, he saluted and dropped the roses. They spread apart and fluttered downward to the glistening water. He circled the spot again, pulled a damaged lead ball from his shirt pocket, stuck his arm out the window, and dropped the ball. In a quavering voice, he said to no one, "The sun will shine on you again." He raised the flaps, turned the camera on, and continued on his mission.

Nearing the Norris Dam on a heading of 170, he made a very tight right turn to a heading of 270, avoiding the rising terrain east of the dam. He added full power and started his final run. Because of the higher terrain and his low altitude, the dam was not yet visible. With full power on in level flight, the little Cessna shuddered and its engine whined as the RPM indicator passed the red line. The next and final turn would be the most difficult, and the most crucial. He banked approximately sixty degrees, making a perfectly coordinated left turn to a heading of 170 degrees. The dam lay straight ahead and only a quarter mile away.

McGruder's fearless military flying skills showed as he maintained altitude to the very last second. Close-up photographs of the dam were a crucial step in his plan. Several people on nearby boats gasped and pointed at the small aircraft, which appeared to be on a suicide mission. Just yards north of the dam, McGruder pulled the yoke back almost to his chest to clear the 1,100-foot dam. The Cessna's nose pitched up to a precarious attitude. As the airspeed rapidly decreased, the stall warning horn began screaming. He pushed the nose over, felt a slight bump as he flew over the dam, and headed down the Clinch.

Turning west, he ducked under the power lines stretched over the river, then turned right and followed Interstate 75. In approximately five miles, he added power and started climbing to a higher altitude, then proceeded direct to the Jacksboro airport. Five miles south of the airport, he checked in on the Jacksboro common traffic advisory frequency, using the fake aircraft identification of N821BL.

After landing, he parked and shut down the Cessna. The airport was quiet, with only one other aircraft taxiing for takeoff. He placed the camera, mask, and GPS in his attaché case and proceeded to the ops room. After cajoling a package of peanuts from an uncooperative machine, he walked across the room to a large table covered with an aeronautical chart. He opened his attaché case and pretended to make a measurement on the chart, all the while making mental notes of those present. The attendant and his small contingent of assistants were huddled around a small TV immersed in the Masters Golf Tournament. They hardly noticed McGruder's presence.

He proceeded back to the aircraft confident that he was not being observed by anyone, yanked the duct tape from both sides of the fuselage, and stuck it in his pocket. Thirty minutes later, he entered the traffic pattern at the Knoxville Downtown Airport and landed. The driver was waiting as instructed with visions of more Franklin notes. McGruder was on a high, and the driver would not be disappointed.

McGruder arrived early at the McGhee Tyson airport for

his flight back to Savannah and decided to kill some time in the airport bar. He was feeling great after his successful mission.

Straddling a stool cowboy style, he ordered his favorite drink. A local TV station went live with a breaking news story. It concerned a complaint from a young woman. Several reporters and their camera crew jostled around the attractive blond. Her white SUV stood in the background sporting a large scrape along its side. She began, "I was traveling across Norris Dam this afternoon. My SUV was struck by a low flying aircraft." She turned and pointed toward the SUV.

McGruder twirled the stool toward the TV and said to the bartender, "Turn the volume up."

She paused for dramatic effect. "An instant before I was struck, I saw something in my peripheral vision. I instinctively swerved and side swapped a car. That vehicle didn't stop. I did." She waved a piece of paper and continued. "I was issued this ticket for reckless driving, which I don't think I deserve."

A camera operator standing on a stepladder zoomed in on a crescent shaped, black rubber smear on top of her SUV, then switched back to the woman.

McGruder looked up at the ceiling and mused, *I remember a slight bump when I crossed that dam. That's my mark. That was a very, very close call…*

"I think somebody should find out who was flying so recklessly and take action against that crazy pilot instead of me. It could have been much worse. I'm saddled with an expensive ticket and a bent car. I filed a complaint, but I don't think they're taking me seriously." Several questions were hurled at her simultaneously. She answered one.

"No, I couldn't see the pilot or any numbers on the plane. It happened too fast. All I know for sure is that it was a small, white plane. I saw the underside, the wheels, and wings an instant before it struck my car. Its motor made lot's of noise."

The commentator looked into the camera, shrugged, and said, "Well, there you have it, folks. A bizarre story indeed. A representative for Homeland Security and the FAA told us they would try to identify the mysterious aircraft. The FAA emphasized that their regulations do not allow pilots to legally fly aircraft as low as this pilot allegedly did. We'll have an update at ten. Back to our studios."

McGruder sipped his drink and concurred with the bartender that the idiot flying that airplane was living dangerously and was to blame. He glanced at his reflection in the large mirror mounted behind the bar and lifted his glass for a toast. A devious, almost mystical smile slowly changed to a devilish grin.

I bet a flurry of frustrating activity is taking place inside the ivory halls of the FAA. They're vainly searching their computer files for an aircraft that, according to their computer, doesn't exist. But Homeland security will provide them with a perfectly clear photograph of an aircraft that does *exist. Soon the finger pointing and tail wagging will begin as the bureaucrats of each agency defend their turf. The FAA will spend endless hours searching their database for all white Cessna 152s. Once that's done, they'll scour the records for all 152 rentals within the fuel range, VFR flight plans, and fuel sold to 152s. That will take days, more likely weeks. Ha. Have fun boys.*

He tipped the waiter, emptied his glass and headed for the long security line.

An hour later, McGruder was on a flight en route to Savannah via Atlanta. During the flight, he clutched his attaché case, as if it contained all the world's top secrets.

February 7, 2015
Freeport, Bahamas

As the huge Frugal A380 Airbus circled to land on runway 24 at the Freeport International Airport, Major Vance McGruder stared intently out his window, making mental notes of the highway leading to an oil refinery located on the southeastern end of the Grand Bahama Island. The refinery itself was not visible through the puffy clouds hanging lazily over the island, but he recognized the roads, terrain, and prominent objects leading east from the airport. He had studied a map of the island and was familiar with the main highways, airports, cities, ports, marinas, and the oil refineries.

In an effort to look inconspicuous and blend in with the other tourists, he wore jeans, a white pullover shirt, sneakers, and dark wrap-around sunglasses. He had been on military leave for the previous five days and let his heavy black beard grow. Most likely, a close friend wouldn't recognize him. A retired couple sat next to him on the flight from Atlanta. After extolling their life history to McGruder, they apparently expected him to do the same, but he faked dozing and later read the *Atlanta Constitution* in an effort to discourage their inquisitive questions.

Exiting the aircraft, he was herded into a large room where customs agents went through their routine of simulating a luggage search and stamped his fake passport while he filled out a standard declarations form. His carry on luggage and attaché case didn't set off any alarms with the customs folks. The obviously bored agent asked McGruder three simple questions.

"State your reason for visiting the Bahamas."

"Real estate transaction."

"How long will you remain with us?"

"Possibly a week. Depends when my work is completed."

"And where is your lodging."

"Sandollar."

"Very nice place. Thank you, sir, and have a nice stay."

McGruder proceeded directly to the men's restroom. He closed the stall door and pretended to use the toilet by flushing it and shuffling around. He changed his shirt to a more colorful one. A wig to camouflage his Marine Corps haircut dramatically changed his appearance.

Exiting the terminal, he kept his distance from the crowded arrival and departure area and hailed a cab. As soon as the taxi started moving toward the Queens

Highway McGruder said, "Sandollar."

"Yes, sir, the Sandollar, a fabulous place. You staying with us very long?"

"A few days. Depends how things go."

"Sounds like a business trip."

"I guess you could call it that."

Twenty minutes later, the driver pulled into the brick driveway adorned with elaborate landscaping and stopped under the portico. A bellhop opened the door and reached for McGruder's attaché case. McGruder whacked his hand and said, "Do I look feeble or something?"

The elaborate lobby of the Sandollar was decorated with a huge chandelier, marble flooring, and mahogany woodwork. McGruder approached the receptionist and barked "Goodwin."

The smiling, young female replied in a courteous tone, "Yes, sir, Mr. Goodwin, and welcome to the Sandollar."

She put on her glasses, which had been dangling from a chain around her neck, and zapped some data into a keyboard.

"Oh, I see you're staying in our Executive Club. It's beautiful. A great selection. Great view and accommodations. May I see a major credit card, Mr. Goodwin?"

"Negative, er… no. I don't carry credit cards. Cash only. You take U.S. dollars?"

"Of course, sir. But…this is highly irregular. I may have to get approval from my supervisor. Just a moment, please."

As she started to pick up the phone, McGruder threw seven one hundred dollar bills on the marble counter and shot back in a strong Marine Corps voice, "You said you accepted American dollars. Young lady, I'm in a bit of a rush. Either take this cash or let me speak to the hotel manager."

Her eyes seemed glued to his large, hairy hands. She pondered the situation, then looked up at McGruder. He narrowed his eyes and stared at her. She weighed the odds of getting into trouble with management, or him, then said, "Of course, sir. If it's okay, you may pay the balance on departure. Oh, I almost forgot, sir. I have a package for you." She punched some numbers and letters into the keyboard, opened a large safe, and handed a FedEx box to McGruder. He grunted, winked at her, and said, "Thanks," as he laid a hundred dollar bill on the counter.

McGruder signed the registration card left handed as Arnold Goodwin, shoved the plastic key for room 813 into his pocket, and headed for the elevator. He checked out the opulent room and its elaborate furnishings. After removing $2,000 from the FedEx package, he opened the room safe, stuffed the package inside, and spun the dial.

He knew he was near the casino when the smell of cigarette smoke first entered his nostrils and the sound of bells and whistles rattled his ears. He ignored the machines and headed to the blackjack tables. He wasn't particularly interested in winning money. He was interested in finding someone that would perform a task for him. Or recommend someone for a broker's fee. He studied the traits, language, and other mannerisms of the players. Deciding on one of the three players at table five, he joined the group.

McGruder's selectee was well dressed, brassy, and familiar

enough with the waiters and dealers to call them by their first name, which meant he spent a lot of time in the casino.

After dropping almost a thousand dollars, McGruder struck up a casual conversation with his potential accomplice. They strolled to the lounge and headed for a corner booth. A waiter sat two drinks in front of them as they sat down. After introductions and some small chitchat, the conversation turned to money.

McGruder asked in his best English accent, "What kind of business are you in, Alcatraz?"

"I'm in the business of making money. And you?"

"Likewise. Have any connections with people employed at the refineries?"

"Maybe."

"I'll take that as a yes. I could use some help."

"And?"

McGruder stared into Alcatraz's eyes, sipped his drink, and said, "My company needs a few barrels of fuel that's manufactured at the Borco plant."

"And why can't your company just buy some of this, ah, fuel?"

This guy is being noncommittal. He's careful. Cautious. Smart. Ugly. And probably dangerous. I like that, McGruder thought.

"It's manufactured exclusively for the military. Not sold to civilians."

"Really?

"Yep. Only the military uses this type fuel."

"For what?"

McGruder ignored the question and said, "Alcatraz,

perhaps we should discuss this further in a private setting."

"That so? Well, I'll have to give this some thought and get back to you. Check you out. For all I know, you're a kingpin from an intelligence agency or cop trying to entrap me. Where can you be reached?"

Oh, you're really going to check me out all right. Very thoroughly, using my false name, and fake country. Ha. Oh yeah.

McGruder ignored the question and asked, "You play golf?"

"I swat a few balls now and then. Wanna play?"

"I've got a ten o'clock tee time tomorrow here at Sandollar. Care to join me?"

"Sure. Why not. A free round of golf and a chance to pick up some pocket change. Hundred bucks a stroke?"

McGruder stood and said, "Fine. See you at ten tomorrow."

The following day, they finished nine holes without the subject of fuel surfacing. McGruder parked the golf cart under the shade of a large palm. Adding the scores, he said, "Good round so far. Thirty-nine. That's good. Beats my forty-two by one shot."

Alcatraz turned, looked at McGruder, and said, "Your math stinks. Fork over my three hundred bucks."

McGruder decided it was time to dominate Alcatraz. Make it perfectly clear that he was not dealing with a weakling. Scare him into rethinking any inclination he may harbor, such as a rip-off.

McGruder reached in his pocket and retrieved a one hundred dollar bill. He slapped it down into Alcatraz's open hand and barked, "My math's fine, acid face. And, so are my eyes. I saw you move your ball twice. I suspect you moved others while you were out of my sight. I'll give you the benefit of the doubt on the others." McGruder rammed his large elbow into Alcatraz's rib cage, stared at him with narrowed, steely eyes, and added, "Don't try any more funny business. Understood?"

Alcatraz grimaced and nodded affirmative. He stuck the bill in his pocket and said, "You don't miss much do you?"

McGruder ignored the question and said, "I suppose my credentials met your basic requirements or you wouldn't be here."

Alcatraz tossed a golf ball back and forth from one hand to the other without responding. After a long silence, he said, "I know some people that work at the Borco Refinery. They may be available. Depends on how much money is involved, risks, danger, and so forth."

"How do I get in touch with them?"

"Through me."

"How much?"

"Five grand up front. Used U.S. bills. If you hire them, I get a ten percent bonus of what you pay them."

"What's the deal if we don't dance to the same tune?"

Alcatraz responded weakly, "Five grand's mine."

"Too complicated, too expensive, and too much risk taking for me. I'll pay you a grand now and three grand later provided your people meet my requirements and if they accept the contract."

Alcatraz grabbed a towel and wiped sweat from his pock marked face.

He picked up a golf ball and resumed tossing it back and forth. Finally he said, "Two thousand now and three more if you accept them and they agree to do the job."

He'll take any final offer I make. McGruder thought for a moment and said, "Take my offer or leave it."

Alcatraz nodded his head and said, "I'll take it."

They skipped the back nine and proceeded to the Sandollar lobby.

Alcatraz waited in the bar while McGruder retrieved the money from his safe.

When McGruder returned, they headed toward the men's room. It was empty except for an attendant. McGruder glanced around for hidden cameras. None were visible. He motioned for Alcatraz to join him in a stall for the disabled. McGruder locked the door after Alcatraz entered but kept a cautious eye on him. Any unintentional or unusual move from Alcatraz and his head would be slammed into the commode bowl.

McGruder pulled a bundle of one hundred dollar bills out of his pocket. Alcatraz reached for them. McGruder didn't let go and injected, "Let's see your info, scarface."

Alcatraz grinned sheepishly, pulled a folded piece of paper from his pocket, and handed it to McGruder. "Robello owns a taxi," he said. "Desperate for more money. His relatives work at Borco. You can reach Robello at his cab number or at his apartment. I'll tell him to expect a call from you. He's dependable. I've used him before. If they accept, they'll do a good job. Don't forget, if you make a deal with Robello, you owe me another four grand."

McGruder leaned forward near Alcatraz's face. "How much?" he said, thumping on his chest with his large index finger.

Alcatraz quickly said, "Oh I forget. It's three thousand if Robello and you agree to a contract."

McGruder leaned further into Alcatraz's face and said, "This information better be on the up-and-up. If not, I'll find you and spoil your entire day. Got it?"

Alcatraz nodded meekly. "You have my word."

McGruder put the paper and money in his pocket, opened the stall door, and said, "I want to meet your Robello here, and now. If I accept him, I'll pay you a thousand bucks. By the way, your breath smells like a sewer."

McGruder grilled Robello and Alcatraz as they strolled along the beach for almost twenty minutes. When he had finished, he knew an enormous amount about Robello. McGruder had been formally trained and was an expert interrogator, asking the same question at varying time intervals in a completely different format. He could filter out untruthful answers in short order. He decided Robello might be suitable for the task at hand. Not too dumb and not overly smart. Manipulative. And his relatives with inside information about the refinery were a big plus. McGruder peeled off ten bills from a roll and paid Alcatraz as Robello watched intently, wondering what was in store for him.

The next morning, Robello picked up McGruder at the Sandollar as planned. He stopped the Volvo under the portico. By the time he got out to open the door, McGruder had already crawled into the back seat clutching his attaché case and said, in his English accent, "Let's roll'em, mate."

"Good morning, Mr. Goodwin."

"I'd like to see your refineries."

"Which one?"

"Borco. Where your relatives work."

"Pelican Point?"

McGruder nodded.

"Yes, sir, mon, Pelican Point Borco it is."

Robello studied him in his rear view mirror, wondering why his relatives and the refinery were of such great interest to this stranger.

McGruder asked Robello, "How much per KM?"

"Depends."

The hot, prickly wig and beard was beginning to agitate McGruder. "On what?" he snapped, forgetting to use his fake accent.

"It varies on how far you be traveling," Robello replied, gesturing with both hands to emphasize the point. "The further you go, the less I charge per kilometer. Petrol is very expensive here on our beautiful islands."

"I'd appreciate it if you'd pay attention to what you're doing and keep at least one hand on that wheel while you're motoring," McGruder said forcefully. "I didn't come over here to get killed by a reckless motor car driver. I could do that at home in England."

McGruder couldn't reveal that traveling on the left hand side of the highway was very nerve-racking to him. Especially if someone else was driving.

"How much for your taxi all day?" McGruder asked.

Robello's eyes brightened, and a large smile displayed a set of almost perfect white teeth. "Two hundred fifty American."

"That's the same as stealing from tourists. Why American money? British sterling is still known around the world."

"It's easier to exchange than British pounds."

Wiping perspiration from his forehead with his index finger and smearing it on his jeans, McGruder said, "Two hundred, but only if you turn that air conditioner on."

"Air conditioners use more petrol. Two hundred and a quarter, and it's a deal."

"Turn the air on. You're hired," McGruder mumbled, as if he really cared about the fare.

"Thanks, mon, appreciate your business. That will be half up front and the balance this evening." As the windows went up and the air conditioner came on, McGruder reached in his pocket and retrieved some cash. He handed the fare plus a nice tip to Robello.

He had tracked the serial numbers obtained from fuel barrels at MCAS Beaufort to the Borco Refinery. One of his golfing buddies, retired Master Sergeant Bowker, and now Mr. GS-14 Bowker, civilian manager of the base computer system, allowed McGruder to use the base's computers to ostensibly research jet fuel acquisition procedures to be used in his M.B.A. thesis. McGruder discovered some startling data along the way. The Pentagon had not selected the lowest bidder for naval jet fuel in 2004 and again in 2007. Instead, the contracts were let on a quarterly basis, which put the total cost under the umbrella of a no-bid regulation. The resulting cost of fuel was generally 20% higher than if sealed bidding had been used. This same company, under a no-bid contract, had charged $5.00 to launder a military shirt and $20.00 per soldier per meal, regardless of whether the meal was consumed or not. And $5.00 per gallon for gasoline was the standard. This type of thievery had gone on for years in Iraq and Iran. When he discovered the unorthodox and illegal acquisitions, McGruder gritted his teeth, clinched his fists in disgust, and cursed the military/industrial complex for their continued practice of exchanging the blood of the U.S. military for money. Revelations such as this magnified his determination to get even. To set the record straight.

"How many relatives of yours work at the refinery and what are their jobs?" It was a test. He already knew the answers.

"One brother and two cousins. One cousin be a woman. Makes more money than either of the other two. It really sticks in their craw. Women don't suppose to be better'n men here in the islands. But I guess we're slowly getting used to it. Seeing all those crazy shows on American television be causing lots of problems for us."

McGruder nodded his head in agreement when Robello glanced at him in the rearview mirror. "Yeah, I could understand that," he said. "The U.S. is going to the dogs, and fast. Too bad we didn't get serious and kick those ruffian's butts during the revolution. America would be British and a better place for all of us."

"Yeah mon, I couldn't agree more," Robello quipped, hoping to sweeten the next tip. "Them Americans think we're just here to serve. Come over here, throw some money 'round, and expect us to kneel down. It's tough, but most of us don't have any choice, you know. Gotta eat and have a place to sleep."

McGruder interrupted. "Speaking of money, could you, your brother, and your cousins use some extra cash?"

"Course, mon, who can't? What's on y'r mind?"

"Let's motor by Borco and then maybe we can have some lunch. Know any good spots?"

"Know 'em all," Robello said, nodding his head. "Depends on what you want and how much you willing to pay. You buying?"

Approaching the Borco entrance, McGruder instructed Robello to park on the north side of the Grand Bahamas Motorway at a fast food restaurant.

"This is no real island food," moaned Robello.

Ignoring Robello's comment, McGruder asked, "Tell me what you know about the operation at Borco."

"Operates day and night. Lit up at night like a big city. Never shuts down. If the wind's blowing in the wrong direction, it stinks up the island a lot. Don't know how you can work all night, but the pay be good."

Robello pointed toward a tanker anchored offshore.

"Big ships, tankers they called, dock a couple miles offshore and pipe oil through a line to the refinery. I guess the water be too shallow for them monsters to come in close. The oil goes through all them pipes and lines and comes out as different kinds of oil and fuel. Whatever they want it to be, that's what it is."

McGruder reached into his attaché case and pulled out a set of high-powered binoculars, courtesy of the Marine Corps.

He pressed the electric switch, lowered the window halfway down, and then pointed the binoculars toward the bay area. He scanned for several minutes.

"Do they make gasoline and jet fuel?"

"Sure do. Not that it helps us. They puts most of it on ships and transport it to other places, probably to the States."

McGruder raised the window and stored the binoculars in his case.

"What type of work are your relatives involved in at the refinery?"

"Truck driver, janitor, and Tabatha is a…what you call it…a QA technician. She checks to make sure everything is up to par."

I believe I've found my man, thought McGruder.

"Seen enough. Take us to a good restaurant. Lunch's on me."

"Yes, sir. Mon, you are going to love where we're going."

They were ushered to a sun-drenched patio with a shiny marble floor. Palm trees swayed in the gentle breeze, and the tables were adorned with fresh cut flowers, fine linen, and expensive silverware. Birds of several species chirped, sang, and generally enjoyed themselves in their paradise. McGruder carried his attaché case. A magnificent view of the busy bay lay before them. After a fine lunch and two large drinks at the Neutered Lobster, Robello was in a talkative mood.

"I only been here at Port Lucaya Marketplace and Marina to deliver and pick people up. Mon, it's a beautiful place. Often wondered how all these rich people gets so rich." Pointing at a yacht preparing to depart, he continued. "I bet one of them thangs costs millions. And this food is great, mon. And all these women in bikinis. This is the way to live. Where did you say you live, Mr. Goodwin?"

"Birmingham."

"But I thought you're from England?"

McGruder thought for a moment, leaned back in his chair laughing heartily. “Okay Robello, that’s Birmingham, England.”

Robello grinned and said, “Oh, I knowed that, just checking ya out.”

McGruder already knew Robello’s full name. It was prominently displayed on his taxi license, which was attached to the back of the front seat of his taxi. It matched the information given by Alcatraz. He had passed the first test. At least he hadn’t lied about his name, unlike McGruder.

McGruder decided it was time to talk business before Robello became too intoxicated. “Better ease up on those drinks,” he suggested. “I might decide to tour the island this afternoon.” When Robello turned his head to look at the scenery, McGruder poured their drinks into a flowerpot. Robello turned toward McGruder and carefully studied the virtual stranger sitting across the table from him with a large, hairy, ape-like body. McGruder returned the stare, then they clicked their empty glasses together.

Robello laughed and said, “Yeah, these things sho go down easy.”

McGruder began. “You related to Alcatraz?”

Robello’s perpetual grin disappeared. His face turned serious. “Know him. He calls me when he needs some work done. Just like he did with you. Business only.”

“You get along okay with your brother and cousins that work at the refinery?”

Robello slowly pondered the question as he gazed at the busy marina. *This guy be for real or maybe an undercover cop? I’m half-drunk, and I'd better be careful what I say. I could lose my taxi license. That crooked Alcatraz will do anything for money.*

"Oh mon, we have great times together. Very good family, we have."

Glancing around to make sure no one was in earshot, McGruder inched his chair closer to Robello and said, in a hushed tone, "Robello, my real estate investment organization needs some important work done. You and your relatives just might fit our bill. My company will pay all of you handsomely, all U.S. cash, untraceable, and nothing larger than a hundred. I would like you to be in charge. Can I trust you to handle a big operation?"

"What kind of operation?"

"Two projects. First, we want a section of a small island partly cleared of sand and small bushes, and secondly we need a few barrels of JP-8 jet fuel from the Borco refinery delivered to this location after it's cleared. I will pay for a boat to transport you and your group to and from the island. You would have the option of camping on the island or commuting each day during the clearing project. I'll visit this location soon and decide on how much work is involved in the clean-up operation. I must move quickly to beat our competitors. Are you ready to deal?"

Robello looked around incredulously, raised his voice, and said, "What deal? I make no deal! I have no idea who you really are. Arnold from Birmingham don't give me much to go on. I don't even know if that be correct. And I don't know nothing 'bout no, what you call it, jay eight? If you in drugs, forget me."

McGruder held an index finger to his lips, signaling for Robello to lower his voice.

Robello's eyes grew larger as he moved his chair farther from the table. "I don't want no part in dealing with drugs. Here in the islands, they puts you in prison and forgets you," Robello muttered, feeling the effects of the alcohol.

Patting Robello gently on his arm and looking directly into his eyes, McGruder said, "Jay pea eight jet fuel. Tabatha will know what it is. If you want to make some easy money, you must trust me just as I trust you. Now, the important part: money. Since you would be in charge, I will tentatively offer you 50,000 dollars for your services."

Robello's heart rate increased dramatically until he could hear it thumping in his chest. He tried desperately to act natural, to hide his excitement about the possibility of obtaining a large sum of cash. But McGruder clearly read Robello's facial and body language and thought, *He's mine.*

"The others would be paid half this much. Mind you, this offer is not in concrete. After I visit the site, I may decide to increase the offer, or I may reduce it. But in either case, we're talking about a large sum of U.S. cash."

"That's what I want, mon. Don't want no English pounds. Islanders don't care for it. Usually won't take it." Robello was in a bargaining mood and continued. "That's only 25,000 dollars apiece for my relatives."

McGruder raised his hand, stopping Robello, and emphasized, "Discuss this with the others. Remember, I'm tentatively offering you 50,000 dollars in cash. No taxes to pay. How many years would it take you to save that amount,

Robello?" Before he could answer, McGruder added, "I think I know the answer. Not in your lifetime. You'll never move from that flat without some real money. I might talk my associates into sweetening the pot slightly, but I wouldn't consider asking for a substantial increase. I don't think you should push the issue too much and break the bank. We'd be forced to look someplace else for help. I'm sure there are thousands of capable islanders that would jump at this opportunity."

Robello squirmed in his chair.

"And for a lot less. Think about how lucky you are to have this golden opportunity. You've got a short time to decide. Robello, don't procrastinate."

"Oh, don't worry 'bout that. I'm a one-woman man. No sir, no monkey-business for me."

McGruder shook his head, a disgusted look on his face, then leaned back in his chair and laughed so hard he shook.

The following morning, while McGruder was searching for tractors on the hotel's computer, a loud knock on the door interrupted his train of thought. McGruder moved the safety bar on the door and cracked it just enough to see Robello nervously glancing around. McGruder retrieved and donned his wig, opened the door, and watched as Robello scanned the wide hallway in both directions to see if anyone noticed him before quickly entering the room. McGruder hung the "do not disturb" sign on the crystal doorknob and closed the door.

"Cup of java?"

"Yeah, please."

"Help yourself and have some of the pastry if you like. It's very good."

"Yeah thanks, I will," replied Robello, as he scanned the ornate room with heavy draperies, elegant woodwork, and expensive art displayed in an exquisite fashion.

"Have a seat, Robello, and tell me what's on your mind this morning."

"Is it safe to talk in here? I mean, could it be bugged?"

"It's as safe as can reasonably be expected. If you are concerned about a bobby or any other government agency monitoring me, forget it. No one knows my whereabouts except you and some members of our company. Trust me; you have nothing to worry about."

"If you say so, but I hear it said that when somebody say to trust them you better run the other way." Robello bent the truth again and said, "I got to tell you, I never done nothing like this before. I'm definitely scared mainly 'cause I don't know what this is about. I could use some extra cash to help me get my family out of that crowded apartment, but I don't want to be up in jail."

"Robello, you've come to the right place. We run a clean, legitimate, and safe operation. I've got a lot of experience in this business, and I know what I'm doing. I'm a real estate barrister."

"What's that, mon?"

"Attorney—lawyer. Robello what have you done since yesterday?"

"You mean other than drive my cab, eat 'n sleep?"

McGruder sighed, looked away, and said, "Yeah of course."

"Talked to my brother and my cousins last night. They're as skittish as I am, but we want to know more about your offer."

McGruder stood, tightening the belt on the terrycloth robe, courtesy of the hotel. He moved to the black leather couch and sat near Robello. Lowering his voice, he said,

"I've already told you what we need, but I'll review it again. I want your group to clear a small area on an island. Clean an area of small shrubs and some sand. Once that's complete, I want six barrels of JP-8 petrol, jet fuel, delivered to that same location. This fuel cannot be contaminated and must remain in the original refinery barrels. The details of how you secure the fuel and make the delivery will be primarily left up to you. But the delivery must be done during the hours of darkness. I don't need to know all the small details of how your group carries out this operation. I will visit this location soon and determine the amount of labor required. Then I'll make an official offer based upon the amount of risk and labor involved. That is, if you're really interested."

Robello's forehead wrinkled, and his eyes opened wide as he pondered the possibility that big money was in the offing.

"Questions, Robello?"

"Yeah! Lots. Actually, my head's spinning…Are we buying or…stealing this here fuel?"

"If I could buy it, we wouldn't be having this discussion."

Robello nodded, sipped his coffee, and lowered his head in thought. "That's what we were afraid you'd say."

After a long pause he asked, "Cousin Tabatha says jay bee eight is fuel for military planes. That true?"

"It's jay pea eight, and she's correct. And I won't disclose to you why I need it."

"You in the military?"

"Do I look like a military type?"

"No…just trying to reason all this out."

Robello stared out the window as the bright orange sun peeped over the horizon. *What if this dude is part of a sting operation?* he thought. *I could be in big trouble. But I didn't agree to nothing. I've never been in no trouble with the police except for speeding and double parking…'cause I never got caught. A sting operation on me wouldn't make no sense. But why would this dude be spending so much money on clearing an island and some stupid jet fuel? Don't add up…*

McGruder glanced at his Rolex, stood, and walked toward the door, signaling to Robello that the meeting was over. To turn the screws slightly tighter, McGruder ended the meeting by saying, "I don't want to miss my tee time. Robello, I hope to see you soon with some good news. Otherwise, I'll be forced to look elsewhere."

The next morning, a loud series of raps on the door finally aroused McGruder. He rubbed his eyes and half-way focused on his Rolex, which indicated 7 AM. He turned over and covered his head with a sheet. The raps became louder and persistent. He slowly pulled himself out of bed. He had played blackjack in the casino until almost 3 AM, and his lack of sleep, secondary smoke, and alcohol consumption was taking its toll. His head throbbed when he sat upright.

After plopping on his smelly wig, he stumbled toward the door and cracked it, expecting room service, although he didn't think he had ordered anything. It was Robello.

McGruder removed the security bar and opened the door, squinting with one eye as the bright sunlight poured in from a large, oval shaped window across the hall. He opened the door, motioned for Robello to enter, and mumbled, "You're mighty early, I think."

"Yeah, wanted to talk to you. Unless you want to hire me today, I've got to hit the streets. Got two kids and a wife to feed, rent to pay, you know."

"Understood. Just a second while I throw some water on my face and go to the loo." When he rambled back, McGruder studied Robello carefully. He plopped down in an overstuffed leather chair wearing only his underwear and wig. Thick black hair covered his entire body, some of which would make a razorback hog envious. "Well, Robello, do we have a deal or not?"

Robello nodded. "We accept the offer, but my brother and cousins want an extra 2,000 dollars each when we completes the delivery. That will be 27,000 dollars each. They want more, but I was able to change their mind. I don't believe they will budge from this here offer. And they need another 20,000 dollars for payment to a, whats you call it, a computer operator and a security guard."

McGruder leaned forward, snorted, and shot back, "You say you accept my offer. But you're not. You're asking for more money than I offered, plus you have added two extra people. I can't let this operation get out of control. Too many people can spoil the pot."

"Yeah, but it's very expensive just to survive here in these blessed islands. You got to remember Tabatha is a high paid woman compared to what most folks make. We've got to weigh the possibility of being caught."

Robello kept his eyes on McGruder, trying to feel him out.

McGruder got up, poured two cups of day-old coffee, and popped them into the microwave. He offered the cup to

Robello, all the while staring down at him. Robello's hand quivered slightly as he reached for the cup, which didn't go unnoticed by McGruder. He was prepared to pay considerably more, but Robello would never know this. Finally McGruder spoke, hoping to build-up Robello's battered ego.

"Robello, you strike me as a man of courage that stands behind his word. I'll pay the new amount but not a penny more. Got that?"

"Yes, sir, I have."

"That seals the deal."

McGruder sipped his coffee, puckered his mouth as if he'd swallowed a swig of vinegar, coughed, and said, "How about some breakfast while we finalize our operation, Robello?"

"Sounds great. I haven't eat nothin' this morning. Too early, and my stomach is churning. Didn't sleep well last night at all. My wife thinks I be coming down with something. But this operation and the prospect of having fifty thousand dollars of my own keeps running through my mind."

"Yeah, you look like you've been dragged through a hedgerow backward."

Robello let McGruder's words soak in, then he slapped his legs, leaned back, and laughed. "You British folks can say some funny things."

After ordering breakfast, McGruder decided he had heard enough of Robello's motor-mouth lamentations and interrupted him in mid-sentence.

"I will mail two phones to you next week. Keep these phones in a safe place and don't use them but once."

"One time? That's strange. What will I do with 'em after I use 'em?" he inquired.

McGruder exhaled loudly and said, "After you remove the sand and undergrowth, take several pictures from different angles. Send them to the pre-programmed number in the phone. Toss that phone into the ocean on your way back to the marina. After I receive the pictures, I'll fly back over from Birmingham and pay you the first installment. That's provided you have completed the work as I specified." McGruder walked across the room to a desk. He made some calculations on a sheet of hotel stationary.

"I'll pay you 75,500 dollars. That's 40,500 dollars for your three relatives, 25,000 dollars for you, and 10,000 dollars to be divided between the guard and the computer operator."

A sharp rap on the door interrupted McGruder. After he verified that it was room service, he opened the door and the waiter rolled a large, stainless steel cart into the room containing just about anything a palate could imagine.

While scarfing down his breakfast, Robello said, "Mon, this is getting awfully complicated. I thought you said it would be simple."

McGruder nodded. "You'll see. We'll go over these procedures until you know 'em by heart. The exact time to clear the area will be left up to you, considering such things as weather, and if your relatives can all get off work at the same time and so on. But I want it done within two weeks if possible."

Robello returned to the breakfast cart and reloaded his plate.

McGruder's eyes followed him. "Robello, this will take some expert coordinating among all these people, and I know you're the right man to do it. And do it right the first time. I'll leave 38,000 dollars with you to purchase a small tractor, and another 1,000 dollars for wheelbarrows, shovels, gloves, food, and so forth. Purchase a Caterpillar skid steer tractor with a bucket attachment at the Machinery and Energy Limited. Do you know where this company is located?"

"Yes, sir, I do."

"Fine.

"Robello, this is a tough little tractor that should navigate the marshy conditions surrounding the island. Practice operating it before you take it to the island. It's tricky to use, but it's very efficient once you learn its nuisances. I suggest you make training a part of the deal when you purchase it. The second phase, delivery of the fuel, must be done on a more precise date. I will provide this date when I return with your money. That should be in approximately three weeks. Hopefully you can transport the barrels from the boat to the platform using the tractor. If not, you will have to roll 'em to the platform. Place the barrels near the edge of the platform, clean them of any debris, and take photos, as you did before.

"Robello, you seemed to enjoy the Neutered Lobster, didn't you?"

"Yes sir, that was some fine stuff. Won't have to twist my arm for another run at that place. No sir."

"I agree. So from now on, we'll refer to the delivery site as 'Lobster,' okay?"

Robello grinned and said, "Yeah, that'll be easy to remember."

McGruder nodded. "I thought so. Take several photographs of the barrels, then cover them with freshly cut foliage. Send the photographs to the pre-programmed number, then destroy the phone, as you did before. After I receive the photos, I'll contact you and advise when to meet me at Lobster. If you have completed the operation as agreed to, I'll pay you in full. Another 75,500 dollars. Again, all money will be in U.S. untraceable hundreds. This would complete our first contract."

Robello continued, unsuccessfully, to link some logic to what McGruder was saying. *What if this money is counterfeit? Guess we'll find out when I buy that tractor. Up to that point, we ain't committed no crime. Contracting to clean up some sand and brush on a small deserted island we call 'Lobster.' That ain't no crime in my book.*

"How do I know you'll return with our money? If you don't, the others might think I've lied to them. It might not be pretty, especially if one of them involved threatened to go to the police."

"You've made a good point, Robello. But think about the situation right now and see who's got their neck on the chopping block. I wouldn't cut you short for four good reasons. Number one, as you stated, someone not fully paid might anonymously tell the police what they know just for revenge. Number two, if this operation is successful, my organization would probably contract with you for other projects. Three, I'm going to leave 39,000 dollars with you for a tractor. And last, after you spend a few days cleaning up one small area, my organization will fork over 75,500 dollars with nothing to show for it other than a picture for collateral. Isn't that trust?"

Robello nodded his head in agreement. "Yeah, yeah, mon, it is. It sure is."

"You betcha it is. So Robello, please tell me who's putting forth the most trust here?"

"Yeah, I see. Yeah, sure you are. I admit you are. I want to go over this plan until I have it all straight in my head."

"Robello, you're reading my mind. We're going to be a great team."

Over a cup of coffee, Robello recounted each step several times until he was able to accurately articulate them to McGruder's satisfaction. At this time, McGruder walked over to his safe, plugged in the correct code, opened the door, and removed three rolls of one hundred dollar bills. He removed the rubber bands and slowly counted out 393 bills. He laid them on a coffee table and began pressing them flat with his hand while Robello observed, an astonished look on his face. It was probably the most money he had seen at one time.

"Robello, this is for the tractor, tools, and 300 dollars for your services today. Oh, there's one important item I failed to disclose. I will need a pump to remove the fuel from the barrels. I will ship this pump to your flat if that's satisfactory. This will be done sometime after I receive the first set of photos. Please do not unseal the shipping container. If foreign objects such as sand or grit should get inside the pump, it wouldn't be usable. The shipping box is not large, but it's quite heavy. Deliver the pump with the fuel. Is this agreeable?"

"I see no problem here," replied Robello, his eyes glued to the money like radar locked on a missile. McGruder continued smoothing the wrinkled bills.

"Good. Now, speaking of trust, Robello, my organization would be very upset if you should decide to keep this money and not carry out the contract. Do you understand?"

"Yeah, honestly, you have my word," Robello said, as he continued to stare at the stack of bills, anxious to get them in his hands.

Finally, McGruder slid the money slowly across the slick mahogany table to Robello. He snatched it up, held it under his nose, sniffed, grinned, and crammed it in his pocket.

"Robello, I want you to start thinking, analyzing, and planning for this operation. You're in charge. No doubt there's going to be some unexpected challenges. So act like you're in charge and be in charge. So what will you and your helpers do when you arrive at the island?"

"Clean up some brush and sand. Actually, my mind is not clear on this. How much sand to move? And where?"

"I thought so. Robello this is another example of when you should have been asking some critical questions. You will be required to analyze, make critical decisions, and so forth. Otherwise, this whole project could fall apart.

Robello, I'll be leaving here in a day or two and our organization is depending on you to get the job done, and on time.

"Who did you say would take us back and forth to the island?" Robello inquired.

"I didn't, Robello. But that's a good question. That's what I want you to do. Think. Any recommendations?"

"Yes, sir. I know a very reliable captain at the Blue Ocean Marina. Captain Saint George. Worked with him before. Hauled some stuff for me. Never any problems. Keeps his mouth shut."

McGruder nodded his head and said, "Might be what I need. I'd like to see the boat. Maybe talk to the captain."

"It's the Windjammer Company. Got several large boats. Big outfit."

"Excellent. Pick me up at ten, motor me to and from Windjammer, and then take the rest of the day off and relax with your family," McGruder suggested. "You look bushed. Have some fun with your kids. Go to a movie and eat out if you like. You've earned it. Tomorrow we might visit Lobster if your captain at Windjammer fits the bill."

I'd give anything if I could be with my kids, McGruder thought, as Robello nodded and grinned. *And I wish those Iranian kids were still alive…*

"Great idea, Mr. Goodwin. See you in a couple hours."

Robello proceeded west on the Queens Highway for three miles, exited onto Mango Street, and stopped at the marina twelve minutes later. McGruder hopped out of the cab and said, “Let’s take a look at Windjammer’s boats.” They walked around the large marina on a wooden walkway observing various types of rental boats. The jingling sounds from the rigging of countless sailboats clustered around the marina reminded McGruder of happier days he had spent on his small sailboat. A pair of graceful pelicans glided by silently and gently settled onto a wooden post. McGruder wasn’t overly impressed with Windjammer’s boats until he saw the *Andros Angelica.* It was clean and had the appearance of being well maintained. A radar antenna, several radio antennas, and a crane large enough to lift a heavy load complimented the vessel. The *Andros Angelica* just might meet the minimum prerequisites of McGruder’s plan.

He climbed aboard and verified the boat had in fact all the capabilities advertised by Windjammer. The navigational aids and radios were more than satisfactory, and the maximum load stamped on the crane was well above McGruder's needs. A sign, with an arrow pointing toward the office, said the boat was rented by the Windjammer Company, LLC. Robello said, "That's Captain Saint George's boat. You like it?"

"Looks promising. Let's talk to Saint George."

They proceeded to the Windjammer office. Captain Saint George was leaning against the office counter scanning a computer for weather reports and notices to mariners. His white uniform was overdue for the laundry. His protruding belly raged a war with the buttons on his shirt. He carefully eyed McGruder from head to toe as he stroked his pencil line mustache. Puffing on his crooked pipe, he slowly exhaled the smoke through his nostrils.

Robello introduced the two. Saint George extended his hand and said, "I'm Captain Saint George, Captain of the *Andros Angelica.* She's a fine vessel, and I'm glad you chose Windjammer."

McGruder shook his hand and said, "I'm Arnold Goodwin, and I'd like to charter your boat for tomorrow if the price is right."

Captain Saint George pointed to an overhead sign listing various prices and said, "Those are our standard prices, Mr. Goodwin." He keyed in some information on a keyboard and said, "We're booked solid every day for the rest of the month except today.

McGruder studied the price list as if he really cared about the cost and said, "Let's go for a ride."

Captain Saint George grinned and said, "Welcome to the finest boat in Freeport. Judging from your accent, I'd say you're from England. Get lots of you folks over to avoid your dreadful winters. He sucked on his crooked pipe, slowly exhaled the smoke through his nostrils, and said, "What kind of fishing are you interested in, Mr. Goodwin?"

"Actually, fishing is not my primary reason for contacting you," McGruder replied. "But, I might want to do some sport fishing out and back. How much weight can your crane lift?"

Captain Saint George blinked twice. He was thinking fish. McGruder was thinking tractor. Captain Saint George chuckled and said, "It's strong enough to handle anything you'll catch."

McGruder ignored the Captain's comment and handed him a piece of hotel stationary with a set of hand-written lat/long. "This is where I wish to go today."

Captain Saint George placed his pipe on the counter and removed a mariner's navigational chart from his black leather bag. He unfolded the chart and skillfully ran his fingers up and down the chart until he located the lat/long, then drew a circle around the tiny speck of land, which was barely discernable on the chart. Captain Saint George moved sideways, giving McGruder and Robello a better view of the map.

"The water's very shallow in that area and may be impassable," he said, pointing at the map. "Depends on the tide, winds, and so forth at the time we arrive. I can't afford to jeopardize my boat. If necessary, we may be able to use our inflatable raft to go ashore. Would that be satisfactory with you, Mr. Goodwin?"

McGruder continued to scan the detailed map and replied, "No problem with the raft."

McGruder had spent several hours rehearsing his story until it started sounding real even to him. "My company is in the real estate business. We're interested in developing a series of these small islands. Dredge the sand and soil, connect the islands to make one large, man-made island rising several feet above sea level. It would be a project similar to the one in the Persian Gulf. My job is to evaluate these islands and determine if such a project is feasible from an investment standpoint. Obviously, this information is strictly confidential. If word were to leak out, the price of this property would skyrocket. If such a project should emerge, we would look favorably upon your company for further business. That is, of course, if we could depend upon Windjammer to provide adequate services and retain highly confidential information such as what I have just divulged to you."

Captain Saint George inserted his pipe into the corner of his mouth, glanced slyly at Robello, and intoned, "Of course, sir. You can be assured that all of our personnel here at Windjammer are of the highest level of integrity and will treat this information as you wish. Much of our business is with well-known clients who are in the entertainment business. In fact, one of our mottos is…'confidentiality greatly helps our survivability.' It's part of our creed." He folded the chart and placed it in his navigational bag.

McGruder pulled a roll of one hundred dollar bills from

his pocket and paid the rental. Captain Saint George glared at the large roll with raised eyebrows, glanced over at Robello, and winked.

Arriving at the island some two hours later, he circled it at a safe distance. Rounding the western side of the island, he spotted an area of blue-water that was deep enough to safely anchor near the shore. It was the handiwork of Seabees who built a platform on the island in 1942.

McGruder's great-grandfather was a daring Seabee during World War II. He told McGruder many fascinating war stories when McGruder was a young boy, and McGruder hung onto every word. One of his stories was about a secret project his unit constructed on a tiny island in the Bahamas. Their assignment was to construct a heavy-duty, steel reinforced concrete platform on a tiny speck of land. It supported a large radio antenna used by the Navy to communicate with their submarines, ships, and aircraft.

McGruder researched the project at the Naval Historical Center. There he found declassified photographs of the construction site taken while the platform was being built. Among those was a photograph of his great-grandfather in a group picture. He also discovered the platform's precise location. Recent satellite photographs indicated the platform was overgrown, but a definite outline of the platform was visible—that is, if you knew where to look. And McGruder knew.

Captain Saint George instructed Ramos, his deck hand, and Robello to assist McGruder. Constantly swatting insects, the three slowly worked their way through the thick brush until they came upon an elevated area. Reaching the top, which was approximately four feet higher than the surrounding terrain, McGruder could easily ascertain the outline of the platform. The brush struggling for survival on the concrete platform was stunted compared to the brush and small trees outside the platform. The differences perfectly outlined the platform boundaries.

He walked to a point near the center and told Ramos and Robello to dig a hole in the sand. They both dug the loose sand with their bare hands and soon found concrete about eight inches below the surface. A large grin spread over McGruder's face. He knelt down and rubbed his hand along the exposed concrete. He instructed Robello to accompany him while he measured the distance around the platform by stepping-off three feet at a time. This served two purposes: to verify if the actual size of the platform would be suitable for his project and to determine the number of man hours needed to clear it.

McGruder looked at Robello and said, "Robello, here's what I want you and your associates to do." McGruder pointed at the outline of the platform. "Clean all the sand and debris from the platform and sweep it perfectly clean. I estimate it will take you three days. You may have some difficulty driving the tractor from where it's off-loaded. If it bogs down, lift the wheels out of the muck using the bucket. In other words, the tractor can free itself. Don't leave the tractor here on the island overnight unless you camp with it. Captain Saint George will leave it on the deck of his boat if you decide to transport it back and forth. Windjammer will provide necessary security at night. After the project is completed, the tractor's yours."

Robello grinned from ear to ear and said, "Yes, sir, Mr. Goodwin. I like the way you operate. We'll clean this place up just as you wants. It'll be spick and span."

The three hurried back to the boat. McGruder explained to Captain Saint George, "There's a concrete platform on the island. It must be cleared of sand and brush before I can make an assessment of the island's value. I estimate three full days will be required to complete the project. I'll need to have this work done in the near future. Would you be interested in providing the transportation for Robello and his relatives, who will perform the work?"

"Yes, sir. Indeed we would. It would, of course, be at the regular non-fishing rate. That's unless heavy, bulky items are transported, in which case that would be extra."

"I don't know what your classification of heavy equipment is. There is a substantial amount of material to be moved. A small tractor capable of maneuvering through the soft, marshy surface will be needed. Is your crane capable of lifting a tractor—such as a Caterpillar skid steer?"

"As I recall, that's a relatively small tractor. I'm sure I transported one from Nassau for a customer. No problem."

"It weighs approximately 6,000 pounds."

"As I said, no problem. I can lift substantially more than that."

McGruder already knew the crane's lifting capacity. He was simply testing the captain.

"Perfect," McGruder said. "Probably use two

wheelbarrows and some shovels. I don't know the exact date this will be accomplished. Since I can't sign a contract for a specific date, would you agree to a floating contract with a, say, fifteen percent bonus?"

Becoming suspicious, Captain Saint George asked. "Exactly what do you mean by a floating contract, Mr. Goodwin?"

"When Robello calls you to schedule a date, any other conflicting agreements would be voided."

"Hmm, such an agreement wouldn't adhere to our principles of fairness and solid business ethics. Our well known reputation might be tarnished." Captain Saint George nervously stroked his mustache, gazed at the small island for a moment as in deep thought, then said, "Twenty-five percent bonus—I must have at least twenty-five. And half of the total cost up front."

"You drive a hard bargain, Captain. But since I don't have the luxury of time nor an inclination to seek out other companies, you're hired. Done deal."

They shook hands. "Let's head for Freeport. I'll sign our contract and make partial payment today."

Thursday, March 17, 2015
Caribbean Sea
1430 Hours

The *USS George H. W. Bush* recovered the last of her sleek F-35s. The Navy's F-35Cs, affectionately known as Rattlesnakes by the first squadron to acquire them, was later shortened to Snake. The Marine Corps version, the F-35B, is different in that it is capable of a short take-off and vertical landing—STOVL. Both models are extremely maneuverable, stealthy, and capable of supersonic speed. The Marine Corps version, codenamed Stove, obtained its odd name in a rather humorous manner. During development of the STOVL, an engineer wrote an e-mail erroneously referring to the STOVL as STOVE. Spell-check didn't have a problem with the word, the engineer didn't notice his typing error, and the e-mail was transmitted. The error was immediately noted in the military/industrial complex. He took a lot of good-humored ribbing from his friends, but as it turned out the name caught on, and the engineer unwittingly dubbed the Marine's F-35B, the Stove.

At 1510 hours, with her aircraft safely on board, *Bush* turned left out of the wind toward the assigned operating area near the Puerto Rican Trench. The Snakes, pride of the Navy, and the Marine Corps' lone Stove, assigned to the development and testing program, would be thoroughly inspected, refueled, and readied by the deck crews for the next launch.

Final testing of the top-secret SAID was to begin at 1930 hours. In slightly less than five years, the promising SAID program was ready for its final exam, known as an Operational Readiness Exercise—ORE. If this extremely difficult test was successful, Congress would appropriate necessary funds to begin production. If not, …

SAID is a remarkably sophisticated instrument of war. Its brain is the recipient of sonar, radar, laser, and another highly classified electronic device. However, what sets SAID apart from anything yet developed is its top-secret ability to merge all the incoming data and paint a picture of an object, such as a submarine, in its brain. If the dimensions of the object, such as the hull of a submarine, are stored, SAID has the ability to analyze and identify the object, known officially as Automatic Target Recognition and Classification. This information is relayed by satellite to a Combat Direction Center (CDC), aircraft, and to other command operations centers anywhere in the world. Search patterns are programmed prior to launch. Controllers in an E-2 Hawkeye are responsible for the SAID operation once it is launched. The Hawkeye team monitors the movement of the SAID, and has the capability to modify the search pattern in real time, initiating manual navigation and detonation.

If appropriately coded instructions were transmitted, SAID could, theoretically, destroy the object with conventional or nuclear warheads. In effect, SAID is an intelligent, stealthy killer. If a SAID is not detonated while on a mission, it is recovered and used again

The revolutionary sub hunter and killer is compact enough that one can be tucked into the modified internal weapons bay of an F-35. Transporting a SAID by air instead of a surface vessel to the general location of a search area saves valuable time and substantially increases the operational on-station time of the SAID.

Instructions had been issued that an all hands briefing would be at 1600 hours in the wardroom. Exactly at the prescribed time, Commander Scott J. Wallace, the respected, redheaded, and chiseled-faced Commander of Air Group (CAG) 15, called the room to attention as Admirals Clarence Gibbons and Scott Hayes entered. Gibbons, in charge of the SAID program from its start, and Hayes, the commander of CVN-77, the *USS George H. W. Bush*, stopped in front of the sailors and marines and gave a sharp salute.

"At ease, everyone," Gibbons began. "First, I wish to thank Admiral Hayes and his staff for their excellent support during the past two weeks. And it goes without saying that Commander Wallace and his Air Wing have their act together. Every launch was on time and without incident or failure. Now, let's review what we have thus far accomplished. Then I will review tonight's all important ORE."

Gibbons pointed his red laser at a screen, and it came alive with data from the exercises. "During the past two weeks, we have launched twenty-eight SAIDs and recovered twenty-eight SAIDs. Some of them were re-cycled and used three times. Out of the twenty-eight reconnaissance missions, the SAID located and successfully identified our Remote Controlled Submarine (RCS) twenty-one times, a remarkable record for this stage of development. Five of the seven failures were caused by high-g impact with the ocean during launch at excessive height and speed. This problem has been corrected through revised launch procedures that are published in your ops manuals. The other two failures are being studied at our Naval Technical Laboratory in Virginia. Fortunately, all four of the ultra-deep tests conducted today were successful. The RCS was detected, correctly identified, and SAID was in a position to, we believe, destroy same."

The admiral stopped short of mentioning that the obsolete US Navy submarine in question had been modified to the exact dimensions of a Cockroach. Nor did he touch on the method of searching, locating, and identifying objects used by the SAID because the majority of personnel in the briefing room were not cleared top secret. And no one in the room except the admiral knew the source of the detailed dimensions of the Cockroach.

"The ORE will consist of three launches beginning at

2330 Zulu. Two Snakes and one Marine Stove will each carry a SAID."

A low boo resounded from the audience. Major Vance R. McGruder rose and took a bow. Admiral Gibbons paused, cleared his voice, and continued, his way of letting the audience know that they were wasting his valuable time and horseplay was not fitting to the occasion.

"Lieutenant-Commander Hause will have the honors of the first launch of SAID. Lieutenant Driscol will launch after control is confirmed by the Hawkeye team, and Major McGruder will launch after confirmation that both SAIDs are under control. In case you're wondering, the ORE evaluators restricted the number of SAIDs to three. That's probably realistic. All three of these men were chosen for this momentous occasion due to their outstanding flying skills and safety record during this work-up."

At this time, everyone in the room rose and gave a roaring ovation, including the admiral.

Admiral Gibbons finally held his hand up, a signal to quiet down and let him finish. "Ladies and gentlemen, I can't overemphasize the importance of a successful mission tonight. The security of our nation might very well depend upon the outcome of your endeavors. Good luck, good hunting, and God speed."

Commander Wallace called the room to attention, and the admirals and their entourage vanished as quickly as they had appeared. He began his briefing as everyone else sat down.

"I'll make this sweet and to the point, as we will need to strap-in and light the fires in less than two hours. The

Admiral mentioned the names of the lucky pilots selected for the final phase of the ORE. I was on the board during the selection process, and it was a difficult decision because of the great job all of you have done.

"Now for tonight's ops…the CDC headed by Admiral Gibbons and his staff will be in overall charge. Contact CATCC shortly after launch and monitor the CDC on your second radio. Two Seahawks will be airborne for rescue or other emergencies. Two Vikings will loiter in the area at angels ten and fourteen. A Hawkeye will remain on station Quail at angels one six to authorize the actual launch and of course to control same. Additionally they will advise of any intruding aircraft or surface contacts. I suspect at least one Russian Bear will launch out of Cuba to observe our operation. Normally they remain well clear and don't interfere with our tests. Nevertheless, let's stay on our toes and identify all intruders. *Bush's* search radar will assist in this endeavor. SAID launches will not be authorized if any unknown air, surface, or sub-surface target intrudes within fifty miles of the launch location.

"Lieutenant Commander Hause will take the catapult first and proceed directly to station Whale. We expect he will be given authority to launch upon arrival. Lieutenant Driscol will be second and proceed directly to station Shark. Major McGruder will be last and proceed directly to station Shrimp. All three aircraft will maintain angels six.

"All SAID launches will follow the revised standard profile—two hundred feet mean sea level, into the wind, and not greater than 150 knots indicated airspeed. Major

McGruder will use a discretionary speed between 120 knots and thirty knots. Use the current winds obtained on board your aircraft and the carrier winds as a back-up.

"You will be given a sealed envelope containing the classified IFF codes, maps, and common operational frequency just prior to boarding your aircraft. Double-check your IFF to make sure the correct codes are selected just as diligently as you would in a combat zone. Although the common operational frequency is encrypted, make only necessary transmissions. We don't want the bad guys hearing a lot of radio chatter even though it will mean nothing more to them than gibberish."

"I expect Admiral Gibbons will push SAID to its designed limits, or possibly beyond. We knew the location of the RCS five hours ago, but it's probably been under full steam since then, and it'll be up to you as a team to locate and make the kill. The RCS will likely be at least 7000 meters or deeper. The RCS team will try to foil us by using all known evasive tactics and probably some they've recently invented.

"Let's all keep safety in mind as we go about our business. Double-check everything. If you're not sure of what you observe or hear, check it out. Challenge anything that doesn't feel, look, smell, or sound right. Remember, this is the real deal. We must destroy that RCS. Good luck and good hunting."

Thursday, March 17, 2015
1745 Hours
Aboard the USS George H. W. Bush
Caribbean Sea

Immediately after the briefing, all hands proceeded to their designated work stations to prepare for the upcoming launch. Major McGruder detoured to his compartment and locked the door behind him. He pushed a button on his cell phone and speed-dialed an international number. The phone rang four times, clicked, and then a female voice with a thick accent answered in a hushed tone.

"Hello, may I ask who's calling?"

"Could I speak to Robello, please?"

"Who's calling?"

"A business friend. It's very important."

The woman did not respond.

McGruder almost cursed but decided she might hang up if he did.

"Ma'am, he would want to speak to me."

After a long delay she said, "Oh okay, but make it quick."

McGruder could hear rustling sounds and footsteps in the background.

Finally, an agitated Robello answered the phone.

"Yeah, this is Robello."

"I received the Lobster picture. You've done well. Meet me at Lobster tomorrow after dark. If everything is in order, we'll pump the fuel, and you'll be paid in full. Questions?"

"Oh, Mr. Goodwin. Didn't expect a call from you so soon. But thanks, mon, for the compliment. Tomorrow after dark. That's not much time."

"Robello, make it happen if you want the green stuff I'm holding in my hands at this moment."

"Yeah, sure. We'll be there. Tomorrow after dark."

"Good."

"You say you'll meet us at…Lobster?

"That's affirmative… ah correct."

"You got your own boat?"

"Negative Robello."

"But I thought you would use Windjammer's boat. Remember you told me to think these things out, to ask questions. So, how you going to meet us without a boat, Mr. Goodwin?"

"Maybe I'll walk on water. Just be there, Robello."

"Yes, sir. You can count on us."

McGruder clicked the phone off and tossed it on his bunk. It slid under the pillow and out of sight. He didn't have the time or inclination to listen while Robello whined at this late hour. Robello thirsted for more money, and McGruder knew it. He would show.

He pulled his hidden attaché case from the closet and laid it on his bunk. After entering a series of numbers in the lock, he opened it. It was nearly full of neatly stacked one hundred dollar bills wrapped by a bank sorting machine. The money had originally been set aside for the remaining debt to Robello and his associates. But McGruder had pondered over the verbal contract and come to the conclusion they had already been adequately paid.

Robello is crooked as a dog's hind leg, and Captain Saint George is far from being a saint.

He scribbled a note on a piece of stationary stating the money was to be distributed in accordance with his current will dated December 12, 2014, then placed it on top of the money.

He unzipped a pocket on his flight suit and stuffed it with Power Bars. After hesitating for a moment, seemingly in deep thought, he filled a pocket on his flight suit with bundles of bills.

McGruder verified that his M9 Beretta was loaded, clicked the safety switch to on, then strapped it on. He picked up the family photograph from his desk, stared at it wistfully for a short while before replacing it. Next he glanced in a mirror to reassure himself. His tailored marine flight suit fit perfectly. He smiled maliciously, snapped a smart salute, and headed for flight operations.

After more briefings, he signed enough flight authorization documents to create a small book, donned all the necessary flight gear then hurried up to the flight deck. He completed a thorough preflight of his aircraft, closely scrutinized the GAU-22/A Gatling Gun for proper installation and verified the drum was fully loaded with ammo. Then he cross-checked the installation of the SAID. He gave thumbs-up to his crew chief, Sergeant Turk, scrambled up the steps of the F-35B, and slid into the cockpit with the agility of a much younger man.

He plugged the cord into the communications outlet, pushed the main power switch, and flipped on the intercom, which allowed him to communicate with Turk by voice. A screaming F135 jet engine set on max power prior to launch vibrated the huge carrier. Turk buckled McGruder's shoulder harness, keyed his mike, and wished him a safe flight.

"Thanks, Sarge. By the way, I want a catapult launch tonight."

"Can't show those airdales how we do a STOVL if we catapult, sir."

"Yep, I know, but I want to conserve fuel."

"Yes, sir, Major. Catapult it'll be."

Sergeant Turk saluted and climbed down the ladder totally unaware of McGruder's real mission. McGruder's demeanor was unchanged. He was an excellent actor and impersonator.

McGruder closed the canopy and started the detailed

checklist. He could locate all the physical switches and buttons in the cockpit and operate the PCD with his eyes closed, using only memory and touch. But in a complicated machine like the Stove, pride must be set aside and the checklist used. The PCD confirmed that a gatling gun and SAID were on board and properly installed. He was number three in line for launch behind an E2C Hawkeye and an F-35C flown by Lieutenant Driscol. He was always amazed after every launch that each aircraft was maneuvered in place at the exact time and in the correct sequence. To the untrained observer, the flight deck reeked of bedlam. Night operations cast a mystical, almost surreal atmosphere. But, he reckoned it was nothing more than a product of many years' experience and training that produced a safe and finely tuned choreography of men and machine.

The F-35's PCD glass cockpit is a marvel in itself, with many pieces of information combined into one display that requires less pilot scanning and more time to look outside the cockpit. McGruder enjoyed flying the Stove on non-combat missions, except for one item. He preferred a large "stick" mounted in the floor of the aircraft rather than the small side-stick and throttle controls mounted on the side of the Stove's cockpit.

By 2000 hours, McGruder's Stove was attached to the catapult shuttle. He powered up the F-136 engine to burner. It screamed like a caged tiger. All instruments read normal, so McGruder gave a snappy salute to the catapult officer and pressed his helmet backward against the restrainer. Instantly men, lights, equipment, and the flight deck became a blur. He was airborne. Without conscious thought, he raised the gear and flaps, reduced power to minimum climb, and turned left toward Shrimp.

"Rawhide, Varmint 2, with you climbing to angels six direct Shrimp."

"Varmint 2, Rawhide, radar contact."

Whew. Got off that flat top with a gatling gun and a full load of ammo. Fortunate. If the CO had not been wrapped up in the SAID ORE, I probably could not have pulled it off…Their inventory boys and bean counters will go nuts over a missing cannon.

Twelve minutes later, McGruder entered an oval shaped holding pattern at station Shrimp.

"Varmit 2 at Shrimp, entering holding."

"Varmit 2, Rawhide, concur."

Senior Chief Fred Donelson expelled air from his lungs and gave a sigh of relief. Several data blocks, called *bogies* by the military since Word War II, reflected in his glasses as he intently stared at his radar display in the dimly lit CATCC. Carbide 8, flown by Lieutenant Commander Hause, had just seconds ago successfully launched an operational SAID. He remained in a holding pattern at station Whale. Ramrod 4, piloted by Lieutenant Driscol, was in a holding pattern at Shark, his position confirmed by Donelson's long-range search radar. Varmit 2, piloted by Major McGruder, was entering his holding pattern at station Shrimp.

The pilot of Greyhawk 1 maintained a speed for maximum endurance utilizing the Hawkeye's round, aerodynamic radar dome for lift and greater efficiency. The Hawkeye has an advantage over the ship's radar in that it can search further over the horizon due to its height. This radar data is then merged by computer software and displayed in a mosaic fashion on the radar displays of the Hawkeye, CATCC, and the CDC. The Hawkeye's had been modified recently with a display used to monitor and control SAIDs after launch.

Two Vikings and two Seahawks meandered around the confines of a fifty-mile moving circle centered at the carrier's current position. Several other unknown and fast moving targets on his display, all well clear of the operating area, were probably airliners and box haulers controlled by the FAAs CERAP located in San Juan, Puerto Rico. The radio chatter finally ebbed and was now subdued.

It was time for Donelson to refresh his non-spillable cup with some good Navy Joe. He pushed the intercom button and advised Petty Officer First Class Morrison that he was stepping away from his position for a moment. Morrison, using an exact duplicate radar display as Donelson's, had been monitoring Donelson and didn't need a detailed briefing. He was Donelson's next in command, knowledgeable and capable enough to handle the operational position by himself.

McGruder unzipped a pocket on his flight suit and removed a navigational chart. The previous day he had printed a series of numbers along the top edge of the chart that represent latitude and longitude. These numbers were identical to those given to Captain Saint George—the latitude and longitude for Lobster.

McGruder set his inertial navigation/global positioning

system on standby. He held the chart under a map light in order to see the numbers and quickly entered them into the PCD INS/GPS, then verified their accuracy. Next, he set both radar altimeters to two hundred feet. The power to the SAID in the belly of his F-35B was switched to off. He turned the INS/GPS to NAV. The Stove made a steep left turn to a heading of 310 and started descent to 200 feet above the ocean. McGruder reached behind his seat and switched the IFF master power to the off position and pulled the circuit breaker for added assurance. Next he turned all navigation lights off and dimmed the cockpit lights. The radio remained on.

A minute or so later, just as Senior Chief Donelson was pouring his coffee, Morrison abruptly stood up and yelled, "Senior Chief, come here and see what this is."

Donelson was startled by Morrison's unusual behavior. He was normally calm and unflappable, even under the most strenuous conditions. Now, he had a strange, distraught look on his face. He forced words out of his mouth with great difficulty. Donelson, startled, set down his cup and darted toward Morrison. As Donelson neared Morrison's radar display, Morrison pointed at Varmit 2's computerized data block.

Donelson glanced at the data block, and immediately recognized that something was missing. It was Varmit 2's IFF. Without saying a word, he hurried to his display, plugged his headset into the radio jack, keyed his mike, and transmitted: "Varmit 2, Rawhide Control, how do you read, over?" While Donelson was transmitting on the radio, he moved his slew ball on his radar display over the last known position of Varmit 2 and pressed the enter button. This action placed an X on the radar display at the last known position of Varmit 2, including the latitude, longitude, military, and Zulu time. He adjusted his radar to ensure that primary targets, radar reflections from solid objects such as an aircraft, were being displayed on his screen and called Varmit 2 a second time. "Varmit 2, Rawhide, radar contact lost, repeat, radar contact lost—reset your IFF, over."

Dead silence.

An unusual, devilish smile slowly crept over McGruder's face. He ignored the calls from Rawhide.

"Greyhawk 1, Rawhide, radio check."

"Loud and clear, Rawhide. We've lost radar contact with Varmit 2 also. Want us to call 'em?"

"Greyhawk 1, Rawhide, affirmative. Also try guard frequency."

"Varmit 2, Greyhawk 1, radio check."

Again, nothing but silence.

McGruder mused, *They're not tracking me on their radar. Ha, stealth's really working.*

McGruder turned the cockpit lights up enough to read the INS/GPS. It read:

>AIRSPEED 310 KTS

>GROUNDSPEED 312 KTS

>HEADING 317

>TRACK 310

>DISTANCE 803 NM

>ETE 02+33

>ETA 0245

>FUEL 02+48

>FUEL EXHAUST 0302

The fuel warning light flickered occasionally. McGruder would soon climb to a higher altitude for improved fuel consumption. But for now, he hugged the ocean surface at 200 feet until he was out of range and clear of the Hawkeye's search radar. He had nursed his fuel since engine start. Even so, his fuel reserve was too close for comfort. Although fuel consumption would improve after he climbed to a higher altitude, he would need to land as soon as he reached Lobster.

McGruder listened closely to the communications of the other ORE participants and kept his eye on their position on his PCD. Ramrod 4 was holding at shark, angels six. McGruder's route would pass about twelve miles west of Ramrod 4's holding pattern. The other participants would not be a factor because of their distance from his flight path.

Ramrod 4 can't see me visually. Can't see me on his radar even if he was looking for me. Shouldn't be able to see me on his HMDS.

The last weak radio transmission McGruder heard was when Rawhide asked Bargain 4 if he saw any debris or other signs of impact.

They've bought the bait—believe I crashed.

When McGruder estimated he was out of radar coverage, he started a very slow cruise climb, milking every molecule of fuel to angels 330. Reaching 330 he leveled off and selected auto pilot on the PCD. He removed a one-inch square data card from a pocket and inserted it into the PCD. The screen blinked and displayed ten different options. He selected REVISE/UPDATE ORDINANCE. As he scrolled through the procedures, he deleted the current data stored in the SAID computer and inserted his data—data containing all the details he had gathered about Norris Dam.

Meanwhile, a frantic search was underway to find him. While en route, McGruder observed several southbound airliners on his PCD taking excited vacationers to the islands and northbound airliners returning them home, sun burnt, tired, broke, but presumably happy. He remained well clear of their visual range. Although his navigational lights were not on, it was possible some sharp-eyed pilot might see his aircraft glistening in the bright moonlight and question the FAA controller. McGruder didn't want to leave any, or at least, minimum evidence of his flight to Lobster.

Donelson's years of training for such an event kicked into gear. He pressed his intercom button to the CDC Officer in Charge, Commander Scott Wallace, and transmitted: "Probable crash, Varmit 2."

Donelson knew, as did most personnel on board, that Commander Wallace and Major McGruder had been close friends for many years and that the commander was instrumental in the assignment of Major McGruder to the SAID program. In their younger years, they could often be found standing at attention before their commanding officer for infractions, such as hot-dogging in their F-14 Tomcats or starting a brawl in a dingy bar in the wrong end of town. Another story, probably embellished somewhat over the years, followed Scott and Vance wherever they ventured.

During their sophomore year at the University of Tennessee, they were on a double date with their future spouses. Scott wanted to impress Jacqueline, a very attractive and popular sophomore who just happened to be the tennis champion at UT. He proceeded toward a trendy restaurant near Oak Ridge. En route, a computer chip in his BMW broke. Cell phone coverage was marginal and balked each time road service was dialed.

Scott walked to a farmer's house, explained his dilemma, and asked to use the farmer's phone. The farmer, suspicious of strangers, ordered Scott off his property. His first impression with Jacqueline was a dud.

Days later, Scott convened a group of dormitory pals for the sole purpose of "re-paying farmer X for his kind and gracious assistance to a stranded motorist." Halloween was nearing, and someone suggested a prank on farmer X might be in the offing. A suggestion was made to disassemble a piece of farmer X's machinery, put the parts on his barn roof, and reassemble them. The measure was agreed to.

The following day, Scott and three of the committee members surveyed the farm and noted that the farmer owned an old horse drawn wagon. And the barn roof was painted with large letters urging passing motorists to "SEE ROCK CITY," sparking the group's interest even further. Another meeting was held to decide how they could safely disassemble, raise the heavy parts onto the barn roof during darkness, then reassemble them. Two engineering students were brought into the fray, and a method was quickly devised that worked flawlessly.

The morning after Halloween, amused motorists created a traffic jam staring at the wagon parked on the barn's roof. The new advertisement read: SEE ROCK CITY FREE TAXI SERVICE CALL 462 9962. The phone number of course belonged to the uncooperative farmer.

However, they were always ready and eager to get back in the air, a place they loved. Some referred to them as unsafe risk takers, hotshots, not worthy to be a part of their elite group. However, the naysayers grew quiet after they distinguished themselves at NAS Fallon's Top Gun School and in air combat over Iran. But the war in Iran downed the fast-rising star, Major McGruder.

In 2011, five Iranian girls were accidentally killed as they walked home from school in an upper middle class section of the once beautiful city of Esfahan. They had stopped for a short time to socialize at one of the few remaining bridges in the city, the popular Khajo that spans the Zayandeh River. Afterwards, they began their casual but fateful stroll home. A handful of U.S. Marines on what was supposed to be a routine patrol, in an area of the city that had been relatively quiet, encountered a larger group of determined insurgents near the bridge. A tough firefight ensued, leaving one marine dead and two seriously injured. Outnumbered and low on ammunition, they called in air support. Major McGruder, a volunteer after the scheduled pilot became ill, had just finished air-refueling his F-18 and reentered an assigned anchor, or holding pattern, over Hamadan.

His arsenal included the desired ordinance, a 2,000-pound smart bomb. An AWACS controller entered the requirements for this mission into his computer. It immediately selected Hunter 2, flown by Major McGruder, as the closest aircraft to Esfahan, carrying the necessary armament and plenty of fuel. He was issued a radar vector by the AWACS controller toward Esfahan and instructed to increase speed to Buster, maximum speed without using afterburner.

A short time later, as he approached Esfahan, the lat/long of the insurgents was transmitted to McGruder over a weak and garbled radio. Under fire and traumatized, the young marine transposed two of the numbers when he gave them to McGruder.

He carefully copied the lat/long on his knee-pad data sheet, and confirmed the numbers with the desperate marines now under heavy small arms fire and an occasional RPG. The error went unchallenged. The major dropped the laser-guided smart bomb on the erroneous location. He had complied with standing orders that, time permitting, all lat/long would be read back for verification.

After returning to Tabriz Air Force Base, the video from McGruder's aircraft was reviewed at the debriefing, a standard practice. When the video was played a second time, everyone in the debriefing room, including Major McGruder, yelled in unison, "goodbye," as the bomb exploded with a bright flash. Yelling "goodbye" by flight crews had become a tradition after a successful mission.

The following day, Qatar's Al-Jazeera Television splashed the horrible scene around the world by satellite. A reporter looked directly into the camera and deliberately asked the audience how any civilized nation could commit such an atrocity. Then they flashed on the screen a grisly close-up of charred textbooks, a piece of a shoe, and smoldering chunks of metal that had once been vehicles. Collapsed buildings with red splotches of blood were scattered around a gaping crater. McGruder had glanced at the revolting scene on TV only once, but once was too much. At the time, he didn't realize the carnage had been caused by the bomb he'd dropped. A day later, he was shocked when he was called before a safety committee investigating the tragedy. His bomb had exploded close enough to the insurgents to force a retreat, but it had also killed five teenage girls.

The Marine Corps exonerated the major from all charges, but he couldn't shake the horrible scene from his mind. It haunted him constantly. Against advice from his attorney and psychiatrist, he visited the site where he'd dropped the fateful bomb. Afterwards he started to drink heavily, was involved in two serious altercations at work with a superior officer, and was finally disciplined and grounded.

After many agonizing months of pleading with McGruder to change his lifestyle without success, his wife filed for divorce and left with their two daughters. Months later, he crawled out of his hellhole, voluntarily entered a rehab program, and finally regained his flying skills.

Losing his best friend would be difficult for Commander Wallace. He'd encouraged Major McGruder to join him in the SAID program and was instrumental in his selection. Assignment to the SAID program would be career enhancing for the major, who had acquired all the necessary qualifications and time-in-grade for promotion to Lieutenant Colonel.

Scott immediately replied, "Have you lost radar and radio contact with Varmit 2?"

"Affirmative sir—no radio, both primary radar and IFF lost," Donelson replied.

"All IFF modes lost?"

Donelson replied, "Affirmative, sir. I'm afraid so."

Commander Wallace's preference would have been flying his beloved Snake, but Admiral Gibbons had assigned him to the CDC during the ORE. This was not what he was trained for and loved to do, but he would give 110 percent to whatever he was charged to accomplish.

"Get those choppers headed in the direction of the last radar plot of Varmit 2. Find out how long they can remain on station, and let me know if any other Seahawks are available."

"Sir, we have two additional Seahawks fueled and ready to fly. Both airborne Seahawks have the lat/long coordinates and are proceeding to that point at this time. Standby for the other," Donelson said.

A SAID controller in Greyhawk 1 transmitted over his radio in an excited voice: "SAID Alpha has located and identified the RCS."

A rather subdued cheer resounded throughout the CATCC, then the controllers returned to the task at hand.

"Senior Chief, did any of our aircraft report seeing anything unusual, such as an explosion or fire?" Scott inquired.

"Negative sir, nothing."

"Senior Chief, direct Bargain 4 and Greyhawk 1 to station Shrimp to help search for Varmint 2. And Chief, make sure they're assigned individual angels. We don't need a mid-air collision tonight."

"Aye, aye, sir," Donelson responded. "And sir, the Seahawks estimate they have enough fuel to remain on station for forty-five minutes."

"Roger that, Chief. Arrange for the two standby Seahawks to relieve them. And Senior Chief Donelson, I'm now monitoring the radar and radios and it won't be necessary for you to advise me concerning routine items."

Donelson nodded. "Thanks Commander."

At this time, a controller in Greyhawk 1 transmitted: "RCS destroyed, listing forty degrees port."

This was such great news that all controllers stood up and gave a loud whooping yell. Then immediately they returned to the more sobering thought—they may have lost one of their family and the first F-35 at sea.

Fifteen minutes passed before Bargain 4 arrived at station Shrimp. Donelson waited until the Snake turned and descended to five hundred feet above the ocean before he transmitted:

"Bargain 4, Rawhide, see any debris or other signs of impact?"

"Negative Rawhide, got our lights on and the area is well lit, but nothing to report. Have you calculated a drift angle?"

"Affirmative Bargain 4—it's two-seven-zero at 8 knots. Any debris should be located very near your location. Our computer calculates the current drift position to be one mile west of—" Donelson almost referred to the location as a crash site but realizing his mistake, cut it short and continued with "—ah one mile west of Varmit 2's last known position."

About ten minutes after the two Seahawks and the Hawkeye arrived at Shrimp without sighting any debris, Commander Wallace decided the time had come to brief Admirals Gibbons and Hayes.

McGruder began a slow descent direct to Lobster. Lightening flashed almost continuously at 3 o'clock. The radar displayed on his PCD confirmed a heavy line of weather approaching from the east. He would make the approach under combat conditions without any assistance from the ground and with the Vertical Approach Lights off.

Good. No surface vessels showing on radar or HMDS.

No lights. Weather too bad for small craft…

He pictured in his mind what the landing area should look like from his survey and Robello's photographs. The sand and concrete slab had retained more of the sun's heat then the surrounding vegetation At five miles distance the thermal imager depicted a faint heat signature of the landing area in his HMDS. This image coincided with his INS/GPS presentation and would greatly aid McGruder in his approach and let down. The INS/GPS depicted the surface winds as strong and dangerously gusty. Two miles to go, he switched the INS/GPS to a four-mile range and slowed to one hundred knots. Ground speed, sixty-two knots.

Gonna be a tricky landing… strong, gusty wind… no vertical lights.

Final checklist. Gear down…radar altimeters on, set ten feet…fuel balanced… fifty knots…lift fan and roll nozzles on…pitch and yaw nozzles on… engine nozzle vertical…ten knots, INS/GPS one half mile range…vertical…zero knots…sink rate fifty…drifting left… correcting…severe drift…GO AROUND!

Without a second of hesitation, McGruder added burner power, selected FORWARD, gear up and began climbing. During the shallow climb, transition was made to forward speed. He made a left turn at 300 feet, reduced power, and returned for another approach.

This time I'm landing…May be bumpy, but I'm setting you down, baby…not gonna use all my fuel and crash.

The port gear struck the concrete platform first, the nose gear a split second later, followed by the starboard gear, which slammed down hard. Very hard. McGruder's head and limbs whipped around the cockpit like a rag doll. Anything not secured in the cockpit was flung back and forth. Naval aircraft are stressed for hard landings, but not this hard. The 34,000-pound Stove would have stressed the old platform, even with a soft landing. A hard landing was too much. A rapid descent into darkness and a sharp wind gust at the worst possible second was the culprit.

As the starboard gear struck the concrete, the tire exploded and the rim punched through the concrete, making an eerie scraping sound that McGruder heard over the screaming jet engine. The rim became entangled in rebar, stopping the Stove just inches before the exhaust nozzle made contact with concrete. The gatling gun wasn't as fortunate. McGruder was aware, even in the darkness, that the jet was not sitting level. Its nose was pointed upward and to one side. The cockpit instruments confirmed his perception. Totally frustrated, he removed his face mask and helmet.

I can't believe it! I've collapsed the gear. Possibly destroyed the nozzle. I'll never get outta here. I've never put a scratch on an aircraft. Now this. He slammed his helmet into the canopy screaming obscenities. *What rotten luck!*

McGruder opened the canopy slightly to allow fresh air in, then meticulously followed the checklist and shut the Stove down. He would sleep in the cockpit until dawn to avoid insects and snakes. At least that was the plan.

At the first hint of dawn, he awoke from his restless dozing. During the night, hundreds of biting insects found the small opening in the canopy and sucked their first human blood. His back and legs were stiff and his neck was sore from the near crash landing. The Stove's seat was comfortable for a few hours, but it wasn't intended to be used as a substitute bed.

He carefully surveyed the outside environment. An occasional squawk from a seagull and chirping insects were all but drowned out by the howling winds. Six barrels of JP-8 were aligned along the north perimeter of the platform. He turned the master power switch on, opened the canopy, and removed the survival kit from beneath the seat cushion. After splashing insect repellent over his hands and face, he cut off a piece of the mosquito net and tied it around his head. After removing his survival vest, he tossed the emergency escape ladder over the side. Not until he climbed down from the cockpit did he realize how close to the edge of the platform his starboard landing gear had touched down. But McGruder's spirits were lifted when he examined the gear and found it intact, with no apparent damage.

Gear survived, but it's jammed in the rebar… like the jaws of a bear trap.

The rim was entangled between several pieces of heavy-duty rebar strong enough to support three large diesel engines and a metal radio tower when first constructed. *Tire's destroyed, but that's insignificant. With a full load of fuel, I doubt if I'll be able to defy gravity with a vertical takeoff and at the same time break loose from that rebar.* He comprehended the danger in such an attempt and ruled that possibility out of the equation. McGruder would have to invent a way to release the wheel from the shark-like grip of the rebar.

He continued the inspection and was stunned to see the extremely small clearance between the platform and the exhaust nozzle. Damage to a gear or blown tire wouldn't necessarily ground him, but a damaged nozzle definitely would. The rebar had snagged both sides of the upper section of the rim, stopped further descent, and prevented catastrophic damage to the nozzle. He crawled underneath the injured Stove for a closer look at the wheel. Then he noticed the cannon pod. It was touching the concrete and the outer skin was bent. Only time would tell if it was operational.

Wonder how long the rebar will support that load, especially in this gusty wind? If the gatling gun pod had not been mounted, most likely the nozzle would have been damaged. McGruder pondered. *If the pod collapses, the gear will probably fall further through the concrete and damage the exhaust nozzle.*

With this thought in mind, he scrambled up the emergency escape ladder and slid into the cockpit. After the main power switch was turned on, he selected NOZZLE FORWARD on the PCD. When the exhaust nozzle locked into the horizontal position, he gave a deep sigh of relief.

Unfortunately, at least for McGruder, he hadn't factored in the weather in his grandiose plan. Caribbean weather can be quirky and difficult to predict. His schedule was driven by the ORE, not weather. But weather was the non-factored item that jumped up and bit him where it hurt the most.

Another annoying matter that concerned him was the possibility that a prying satellite might be searching for him. He suspected that the latest satellites could see through clouds and darkness, so he collected some of the brush cut by Robello and placed it on the wings for camouflage. Almost immediately a strong gust removed the limbs and cart-wheeled them across the platform. Disgusted, he looked up, shook his fist at the dark rolling clouds, crawled under the Stove, and rested his head against the nose wheel. He removed a power bar from his pocket, raised the mosquito net, and ate slowly. His brain kicked into high gear.

I've got to look at this situation in a positive manner. Rely on my training and skills. I've overcome many hurdles to get this far. I must not collapse at this juncture in time. Most likely, in a few hours this weather will subside, Robello and his gang will show and help me re-fuel. Perhaps we can find something on the boat and pry the gear loose. Then I'll be on my way to fulfill the Pact.

He drifted off to sleep while the ever-increasing wind temporarily kept the bugs at bay and soothed his aching body, unaware that Robello had not delivered the fuel pump as promised.

Friday, March 18, 2015
Conference Room 0600 Hours
Aboard the USS George H. W. Bush
Caribbean Sea

While McGruder was inspecting his Stove for damage and fuming over the weather and his bad luck, Commander Wallace entered the conference room. Commander Robinson, XO and Operations Officer, called the room to attention. The board members, mentally and physically drained, rose slowly in unison and stood at attention. The possibility of losing one of their own cast a spell of gloom.

As he closed the door, Commander Wallace gave the command to be at ease.

He sat his briefcase beside his chair and took his position at the head of the table. Even in his flight suit, the redheaded, six-foot, thirty-five-year-old Wallace gave off a certain aura that demanded attention. His piercing eyes could melt men in their tracks if a dressing down was necessary, or arouse confidence and enthusiasm in subordinates with only a smile and a nod. At any rate, he would probably be promoted from commander to captain soon after he met the time in-grade requirements. Success as the commanding officer of an Air Wing usually assured a promotion.

Although he hadn't retired until well after 0200 hours, he appeared fresh and ready to head the preliminarily investigation into the causal factors of the first loss of an expensive F-35B, its pilot, and a top-secret weapon.

Lieutenant Moss's seat was near the refreshments, so she volunteered her services and inquired, "Juice, sir?"

"Coffee with cream and sugar. And one of those sweet rolls, please."

This surprised those who personally knew the disciplined Commander. He was health conscious and usually ate only nourishing foods. In order to fly an F-35 near the edge of the designed operational envelope, or in his case, slightly outside of it at times, physical conditioning was paramount. And Scott was determined to stay even with or ahead of the young airdales assigned to his air wing. But, he was physically and mentally drained, just like the other members of the board, despite his crisp look.

"Good morning, everyone. I apologize for the quick turnaround," he began. "Commander Robinson, are all the players present?"

"They are, sir."

Scott nodded, glanced around the table, acknowledged

each member, and began. "This investigation will be recorded by voice and by steno.

"March 18, 2015, 0600 hours, at sea, aboard the *USS George H. W. Bush.* My name and rank is Commander Scott James Wallace, commander of Carrier Air Wing Fifteen. I have convened this preliminary investigation, commonly known as an Aircraft Mishap Board, to assemble facts as to the causal factors surrounding a missing Marine F-35B STOVL aircraft presumed lost at sea during carrier operations on March 17, 2015 at approximately 2017 hours. This is a class A flight mishap. The missing aircraft was piloted by—" Scott paused and took a sip of coffee, stalling while he regained his composure, then continued with, "—piloted by Major Vance R. McGruder, assigned IFF mode 1, code 4314 and call sign of Varmit 2. According to the CATCC logs, entered by Senior Chief Fredrick S. Donelson, and the CDC logs entered by myself, radar and radio contact was lost with Varmit 2 at 2017 hours, at latitude 190503, longitude, 681007. All radio and radar data have been captured, reviewed, and secured for one hour before until one hour after contact was lost with Varmit 2. Major McGruder gave no indication of a problem at any time or in any manner that we know of as of this moment. His flight appeared normal from launch until he disappeared from our radar.

"At this time, each department will add any factual information they have. Keep in mind that nothing should be withheld, even if in your opinion it is insignificant. Sometimes small things are the key to solving the cause of an accident. Don't get tunnel vision, jump to conclusions or focus on just one cause. A mishap is the culmination of a number of apparently unrelated events that creates an environment for a mishap to occur. Do not give your opinion at this time unless asked. Stick to known facts and do not speculate. The deliberative analysis, conclusions and recommendations of this Aircraft Mishap Board are privileged information. It cannot be used except to improve naval flying safety. Unauthorized disclosure of any information in our Safety Investigation Report is a criminal offense. Therefore, you should not feel reluctant to withhold any pertinent information. We'll start with our aircraft maintenance and engineering and safety officer, Lieutenant Moss."

A very nervous Moss turned toward the recorder, laid her arms on the table, and interlocked her fingers. Her knuckles turned white. It was her first interaction with such an investigative board. And being first to respond made her even more apprehensive.

"My name is Lieutenant Margaret T. Moss…I serve as the aircraft maintenance and engineering as well is the safety officer aboard this ship." She paused, her face reddened, and the document from which she read shook like a leaf in a storm.

Scott switched the recorder off and motioned for the stenographer to stop. He glanced at the petrified lieutenant, smiled, and said, "Try to relax, Lieutenant Moss. Just take a deep breath of air and exhale. You'll do just fine."

She glanced around the room and said in a somewhat normal tone, "Thank you, sir. I'm sorry." Scott nodded and punched the recorder button. With her composure almost under control, she exhaled and continued. "I have two hard copies of all the maintenance and modification history concerning the subject aircraft number M-C 1839 since its delivery to the Marine Corps twelve months ago. I wish to enter one set of this data into the investigative records. The missing aircraft has not been involved in any incidents and has less than the average amount of pilot gripes. According to the records, all required maintenance was done in accordance with regulations and at the appropriate time. Before last evening's flight, as you suggested at our brief, I had two separate crews perform a detailed preflight on all aircraft involved in the ORE. As you know, specially trained technicians perform maintenance on the F-35B Stove. I instructed the teams to double check the engine nozzle, control ducts, and the lift fan. No discrepancies were noted by either team. Our fuel and oil analysis met specifications. Mike charlie 1839 has a very clean record, with no known emergencies or incidents. Major McGruder has logged 420 hours in the F-35B. No previous incidents or mishaps have been entered in his flight records. His physical is current until June of this year." With a sigh of relief, she added, "That concludes my report, Commander."

"Thank you, Lieutenant Moss. The maintenance records are accepted as part of our investigative data.

"Next is our air wing XO and Operations Officer, Commander Robinson."

"My name and rank is Commander Craig M. Robinson, Executive and Operations Officer for Carrier Air Wing 15. On the evening of March 17, 2015 I was on duty assigned as the Air Boss. Launches and recoveries were conducted in an orderly, safe and timely manner. I did not observe any incidents nor were any reported on the flight deck or within the immediate vicinity of the boat. The only thing I noted that might be of interest was the manner in which Varmit 2, Major McGruder, reduced power from burner shortly after the catapult sequence began. Even though it was dark, I followed his aircraft visually for a short while because his climb rate appeared to be unusually shallow. Just as I started to verify if Varmit 2 was having any difficulties, he called Rawhide in a routine manner, without any apparent problem. Consequently, I didn't quiz him concerning his flight profile. I believe the radar tapes will confirm my observations. That concludes my AMB report."

"Thanks Commander Robinson. Why do you suppose Major McGruder operated his aircraft in what seems to be a non-standard manner?"

"I'm not certified in the B model but I have run his launch sequence through my mind several times. The only logical explanation I could draw was that the major was conserving fuel."

"Conserving fuel? On such a short flight?"

"That's my conclusion, Commander."

Scott paused, looked up at the ceiling in thought, then said, "Thanks Craig. Next is CVN-77s Catapult Officer Lieutenant Mark A. Goldberg."

"Yes sir, my name is Mark A. Goldberg, Lieutenant, United States Navy. I was catapult officer in charge during March 17, 2015, 2100 UTC until March 18, 2015, 0500 UTC. The pilot of Varmit 2 requested a catapult launch rather than a STOVL. The launch was routine, with no unusual delays or noticeable problems."

"Lieutenant Goldberg, did Major McGruder normally prefer a catapult launch over a STOVL departure?"

Goldberg shook his head. "No sir. Just the opposite. He seemed to enjoy demonstrating how quickly he could lift off the deck in the STOVL mode."

"Would you consider it unusual that he requested a catapult launch last night?"

"Well, I wouldn't go so far as to say it was unusual, but perhaps somewhat surprising to me."

"Do you keep records of launches?"

"Yes sir, we do. We log all launches regardless of their kind. A record is kept for one year of anything that leaves the deck, including copters."

"I want a copy of all launches and recoveries of Major McGruder during this deployment and note the type of launch."

"Will do, sir."

Next is Lieutenant Commander Hause, pilot of Carbide 8.

"Good morning. My name and rank is Lieutenant Commander Eugene W. Hause. I am assigned to Air Wing 15 as an F-35 Charlie pilot. Yesterday evening I flew the first tactical aircraft to launch as part of the ORE. I proceeded directly to my assigned orbit pattern at whale, angels six in accord with the ops order. Six minutes after arriving at whale I was given authority to launch my SAID. I descended to the appropriate altitude and successfully launched the SAID. I climbed to angels six and remained at whale until the RCS was destroyed. I returned to the ship and made a routine recovery. The entire flight was without problems and in accord with the ORE operational plan. I did not observe anything abnormal."

"Thanks Lieutenant Commander Hause. Next is Lieutenant Driscol, also of Air Wing 15."

"My name and rank is Lieutenant Randolph A. Driscol, F-35 Charlie pilot assigned to Air Wing 15, currently aboard the carrier *Bush*. I was the second tactical flight to launch yesterday evening as part of the SAID ORE. After launch I proceeded direct to shark and held at angels six. After I launched my SAID I climbed back up to angels six, remaining in the assigned area at shark. I remained on station until we had a kill on the RCS. My entire flight was without incident, routine in every respect except for one item. During my climb shortly after launching the SAID, I observed the signature of an F-35 in my HMDS. I was in a climbing right turn and only saw it briefly. At about the same time I was distracted by a radio call followed by a false overheat light and didn't pursue the image any further. Normally I probably would have brushed this off as an anomaly and put it out of my mind. But after this Stove incident I thought it might be of interest. That's all I have, sir."

"Lieutenant Driscol, do you recall the approximate direction of flight and estimated angels of this thermal image?"

"Well sir, it was definitely below me. My orbit pattern was northwest and southeast heading 140 and 320. I was about half way through a right turn from 140 to 320. I estimate I was passing through heading 240 when I observed the image. It was moving from my left to right, tracking north or northwest."

"Are you sure it wasn't Lieutenant Commander Hause you saw?"

"Yes sir. I'm positive. According to my PCD Commander Hause was holding at whale, almost forty fifty miles from my holding area. This image was fairly close, maybe ten miles or less."

"Thank you very much Lieutenant Driscol. This is very interesting. Lieutenant, I want you to do some investigating. Check with the manufacturer of the HMDS and determine if there has been any case of false targets reported, reflections from other aircraft similar to false IFF targets and so forth. Keep me apprised."

"Yes sir. Will do."

"We will now hear from Marine Corps Staff Sergeant Turk, Major McGruder's crew chief."

"Thank you, Commander. My name and rank is Staff Sergeant Bobby G. Turk. I serve as Major McGruder's crew chief, or aircraft captain, on the F-35B STOVL aircraft. I supervise eight enlisted maintenance personnel. I served as Major McGruder's crew chief yesterday evening. By this I mean that I personally supervised the preparation of the F-35B for its mission. This included a very thorough inspection of the aircraft and monitoring the ordinance team as they armed the aircraft. I was pleased with the manner in which all of these functions were carried out. All hands knew how important this mission was and demonstrated extra diligence in every move they made. I met Major

McGruder at the aircraft and assisted him in a routine manner. That concludes my report."

"Thank you, Sergeant Turk. Sergeant, you were the last person to personally talk to Major McGruder last evening. Did you notice anything unusual or different about the Major? His composure? Attitude?"

"No sir, not his composure or attitude. He was his normal self. A guy—excuse me, an officer that we all admire and enjoy working for. However, I have thought about his last launch many times. Three things have struck me as being different, ah well, maybe somewhat different. Of course if he had not crashed, or whatever happened, I'm sure that I would not have given these things a second thought."

"Please continue, and take your time, Sergeant."

"Yes, sir. He didn't want a STOVL launch, which he normally does as you probably already know. Said he wanted to conserve fuel."

Scott interrupted the sergeant. "Major McGruder said he wanted to conserve fuel? Are you sure?"

"Yes, sir. I remember it well. You know, it's not as if he was going to fly a great distance from the boat and possibly have a legitimate concern about fuel. The other thing out of the norm was the M9 pistol he wore. Normally marine pilots don't like to wear a weapon while flying except when over enemy territory where they might be needed in case their aircraft goes down. The third thing, the one that puzzled me the most, was his verbal order to mount a GAU-22/A Gatling Gun loaded with ammo."

Scott abruptly stopped taking notes. "Did you comply?"

"Yes, sir, I did. I supervised the mounting of the cannon and the SAID. Major McGruder said the CO had verbally authorized the cannon because he was too busy with the SAID test to cut the orders. It seemed reasonable at the time even though I knew we were bending the rules."

"Sergeant Turk, did the major give any indication as to why he wanted the cannon?"

"No, sir, he did not. And, of course a sergeant doesn't question a superior officer even when inadequate time is allowed for a project. My team worked continuously through the afternoon and early evening without a break or to eat."

"Thank you, Sergeant Turk. Your information may help us solve this mystery."

Now came the part Scott would have preferred to skip. "Next is our medical officer, Lieutenant Commander Richardson."

"My name and rank is Lieutenant Commander Gwendolyn A. Richardson, Flight Surgeon for CVN-77. I have reviewed all on-board medical records of Major Vance R. McGruder. He had a sterling medical record throughout his Marine Corps career until late 2011. At that time, Major McGruder was grounded from all flying duties and ordered into alcohol and psychiatric treatment for post-traumatic stress disorder. During this time, he was given an article fifteen for assaulting a superior officer. Unless he satisfactorily completed all of those programs, he would have been forced to resign from the Marine Corps. He did successfully complete the treatments and returned to flying status. Upon his return to flying status, he was ordered to wear corrective lens for near vision when piloting an aircraft. A request from the Major to have corrective laser surgery on his eyes was denied. He had no serious illnesses during his career except those just mentioned. He was given a routine HEENT exam four months ago. Everything was normal except his near visual acuity. His medical record is otherwise un-remarkable. During the past week there has not been an increase in sick bay patients aboard this aircraft carrier, and no complaints of food or water contamination or poisoning. All personnel involved have been given the required post mishap physical exams and the Aeromedical Analysis will be completed sometime this morning."

"Why was the request for surgery denied?"

"Laser surgery can adversely affect night vision and in rare cases cause other serious complications."

"Has anyone examined his eyes since the request for surgery, and would this type of laser surgery be obvious in a routine examination?" Scott asked.

"He has had semi-annual eye examinations. I suppose laser surgery could be overlooked. Actually, I don't feel qualified to answer that question. I have not examined Major McGruder's eyes. That concludes my testimony."

"Thank you, Commander Richardson, for that in-depth report. Your Aeromedical Analysis will become a significant part of the Safety Investigation Report. Next we'll hear from our meteorologist, Lieutenant Commander Whitaker."

Commander Whitaker turned towards the recorder and cleared his voice. "My name and rank is Lieutenant Commander Curtis E. Whitaker. I serve as the meteorologist for CVN-77 and for aircraft squadrons or air wings when deployed to this carrier. Last evening's weather was typical Caribbean weather for this time of year. The sky had scattered clouds at 5,000 feet, visibility 30 miles. The winds at 6,000 feet were from 090 at 12 knots and on the ship from 080 at 6 knots. No turbulence was forecast or reported. The sea was relatively calm, with two-foot swells. All in all, the weather was ideal for air operations. A low trough is approaching the Bahamas from the east. It's an unusual storm for this time of year and has winds of a category one hurricane. This weather pattern did not impact our operation. That about wraps it up, sir."

Scott nodded. "And now let's hear from Senior Chief Donelson of CATCC."

"Thank you, sir. My name and rank is Senior Chief Fredrick S. Donelson. I am the senior enlisted person assigned to the CATCC. Ensign Holmes is the CATCC officer, but he's currently on emergency leave. During the loss of Varmit 2, I was on duty in the CATCC and reported directly to the CATCC officer, Commander Wallace. After all aircraft were on station and two SAIDs were successfully launched, I stepped away from my station momentarily for coffee, leaving Petty Officer Morrison in charge. A moment or so later, he excitedly requested my presence, and I proceeded directly to his station. I immediately noted that Varmit 2's data block was not normal in that the aircraft target or primary radar target, as well as the IFF transponder, were missing. It's not unusual to lose the primary or IFF for various reasons. But when both of these returns are lost as well as communications, this is a good indication that an aircraft is down. This is especially true when the radar and communications are functioning normally with other aircraft, as they were last evening. With this in mind, I immediately returned to my radar position and called Varmit 2 on all my radio frequencies, including guard, with no response. I then requested Hawkeye 2 to call Varmit 2, which was also negative. At this time, I notified Commander Wallace of the situation. Commander Wallace ordered available aircraft and the stand-by helicopters, the Seahawks, to proceed to the last known position of Varmit 2.

"After an extensive search, no debris or petroleum liquids were found on the surface. After I was relieved from my position, I contacted the legal office and requested a witness. Lieutenant Smith accompanied me while I retrieved and reviewed all the radar data and communications tapes. Nothing unusual was found on the communications tape. The radar data shortly after the disappearance of Varmit 2 is somewhat puzzling. Again, I definitely don't want to speculate on this matter. Shall I continue, Commander?"

"By all means. I haven't heard any speculation so far, and I consider you our legal expert in long range shipboard radar."

"Yes, sir, thank you. Several small pieces of raw radar data are displayed that, I believe, is an aircraft flight path originating near the last known position of Varmit 2."

Everyone in the room turned their head and gazed at Donelson with a stunned or puzzled expression on their face. No one spoke. Commander Wallace looked around the table and finally nodded his head for the young Chief to continue. Donelson, apparently awakening to the potential bombshell he had just dispensed, paused for a moment, and then continued.

"Uh, these radar hits, if you will, leave a signature consistent with the F-35 airframe. However, they are unevenly spaced, but seem to form a track in a northwesterly direction of approximately 310 degrees. I want to emphasize that occasionally other small bits of radar data also exist in all quadrants. This clutter is caused by normal electronic interference and occasional returns from waves or swells on the ocean surface. But, the swells were only two feet high yesterday evening, and I would not expect any significant radar reflection from them. The ship's powerful radar transmits energy bursts in all directions as the antenna rotates. A small amount of this radar energy is reflected from an object, and returned to the ship's radar antenna where it is digitally processed and displayed as a blip or primary target on our radar display. The F-35 is not a totally stealthy aircraft. It does have many stealthy characteristics, making it difficult but not impossible to reflect some radar energy back to our radar antenna. The pieces of data displayed are consistent with the F-35 skin or primary target. The cannon pod mentioned by Sergeant Turk would also reflect a small amount of radar energy. Some of this information is, of course, classified. That's all I have, sir."

"Thank you for that thorough review of what transpired last night. Senior Chief, I want all board members to review this information. All members are reminded that disclosing classified information to any individual not properly cleared is a very serious offense. We will reconvene at 0800 hours to review this information on our large MBS screen and then wrap up our preliminary investigation as to the disappearance of Varmit 2."

Some of the board members were not versed in radar presentations. Consequently, the board could not agree that enough data existed to positively conclude that the returns were from an aircraft. On the other hand, they were unable to totally disregard the possibility that the scant returns were indeed those of an aircraft. They recommended further expert analysis of the data.

Scott resumed the investigation, "Senior Chief Donelson, I understand the shipboard radar and the Hawkeye airborne radar data is interchanged and displayed in mosaic fashion on the E-2, CDC, and in the CATCC. Is this correct?"

"That's correct, sir."

"Have you reviewed the radar data from the Hawkeye?"

"No sir, I have not."

"Why not?"

"Because I assumed it would be a duplicate of ours."

"That's probably true, Senior Chief, but just in case we're

wrong let's also review the Hawkeye data and compare the two."

"Yes sir, will do."

"Senior Chief, have you explored the possibility that another military or civilian governmental agency could have useful radar data?"

"No sir, but at one time the FAA CERAP at San Juan used the Navy's long range radar located on the eastern tip of Puerto Rico. This was possible through a joint use letter of agreement between the Navy and FAA. Roosevelt Roads Naval Station no longer exists, but it's highly likely the FAA still uses the same radar."

"If the FAA is still using this radar, does it depict raw or what the FAA calls 'primary' radar?"

"It did when the Navy used it, and it's highly likely that it still does. Also at one time the Puerto Rican Air Guard used a long range radar for their drills, but I believe it was decommissioned several years ago."

"Chief, check out the Puerto Rican Air Guard and verify whether they still exist. If so, see if they have some information we could use in our investigation."

Donelson quickly grabbed a pen and jotted down Scott's orders.

Scott glanced around the room at all board members and commented, "During my career, I was with an air wing temporarily deployed to Roosevelt Roads. We needed some airspace for a special mission outside our warning and restricted areas. The FAA's Naval Liaison Officer and I worked with a gentleman from the CERAP named Dan Allen who was both knowledgeable and congenial. Let's see if we can obtain some more information from the FAA. Is the DSN still down for maintenance?"

"Yes sir, down until midnight Zulu," replied Donelson.

Commander Wallace scanned his laptop for old phone numbers, then dialed Allen's number in San Juan using his cell phone.

A cheerful voice with a distinct Puerto Rican accent answered. Scott switched his phone to speaker and placed it on the table.

"Good morning, San Juan CERAP, may I help you?"

"Good morning to you. My name is Commander Scott Wallace. Mr. Allen please."

"We have two Allens, sir. Do you know which one you wish?"

"I'm sorry. Yes, Dan Allen, please."

"One moment, sir."

On the second ring, the phone clicked.

"Dan Allen, San Juan CERAP."

"Dan, this is Scott Wallace. How are you?"

After a slight pause, Allen said, "Scott Wallace from air wing seven, the F-14 hotshot?"

"I'm afraid so. It's been a while."

"Yeah, you were a young Lieutenant last time we met. Do you have an air wing yet?"

"Yep, I do. And several young hotshot pilots that remind me of my earlier years in the Navy. I try to keep them on the straight and narrow, but it's a full time job and tends to accelerate the graying process. How about you?"

"Still in the same job as when you were at Rosy Roads. After my contract in Puerto Rico expired, I took a similar job at the Center in Hilliard, Florida. Although my wife and I tried, we finally admitted that we longed for the mountains and beautiful scenery here in Puerto Rico. I bid on my old job and returned three years ago. Plan to retire here. It's very expensive compared to the States, but we think it's worth it. What can I do for you, Commander?"

"Dan, since we're not on a secure phone, I must be careful what I say. What I'm about to divulge to you must remain confidential. I'm on the aircraft carrier *George Bush* headed for Mayport. Last evening we apparently lost a Marine F-35 north of Puerto Rico. Our radar data is very limited. Is there a possibility your radar could have painted this aircraft?"

"Sorry to hear bad news. Whether we saw this aircraft on our radar depends on a lot of factors, which you probably already know. Our long-range radar is located in the El Yunque Rain Forest on the eastern and highest portion of the island. Our maximum range is two hundred miles. It would help if the aircraft had a transponder. If the aircraft was within two hundred miles of our radar antenna, we might be able to help."

"Do you have the exact location of your antenna?"

"Yes we do. It'll take a moment to locate that information in my computer."

Clicking sounds from Dan's keyboard emitted from Scott's phone.

A moment or so later Dan said, "Ready to copy?"

Commander Wallace and Senior Chief Donelson

grabbed a pencil. Scott replied, "Yes we are."

"Okay, the lat/long is 181702 north, 654807 west."

"Got it, Dan. Stand by while we do some plotting."

Seconds later, "Dan, the location from your radar site is 330 degrees at 90 nautical miles, angels 6."

"That's in an ideal location. What was the transponder squawk and time of the lost contact?"

"Mode three was on 4000, and the date and time was March 17, launch time 2000 hours."

"Fine, Commander. I'll get my people right on this. How can I reach you?"

"Our DSN is down for maintenance. I'm on my personal cell phone now." Scott gave Dan his cell number. "Please don't let this information out of your office. We haven't notified the pilot's next of kin."

"Wilco. Nice to hear from you but saddened to hear about your loss. Get back with you ASAP."

After disconnecting the call, Scott remarked, "About two months of red bureaucratic tape was just cut." The board chuckled and nodded in unison.

"I have one more question before we disband. I've been brainstorming, and I wonder if there is any way we can determine the speed of Varmit 2 shortly before his disappearance. His forward and vertical speed."

No one responded.

"Okay. Let's ponder this. If Varmit 2 was at a very slow hovering speed, could his aircraft enter the water and sink without shedding parts or spilling fluids?"

No one responded, but several sidebars sprang up as a murmur filled the room.

"Lieutenant Moss, get in touch with our F-35 rep at Lockheed Martin and ACETEF. Find out if any slow speed crash tests were conducted, and if so, what the results were."

Commander Wallace dismissed the board until he heard from Allen in San Juan.

At 0900 hours, Scott's cell phone rang. He glanced at the incoming number and said, "Dan, Commander Wallace. Didn't expect your call so soon. Hope this doesn't mean you were unable to locate our aircraft."

"Well Scott, the data was readily available and no big deal for my specialist to retrieve and print it in a hard copy format, which I have in front of me. As I said earlier, the aircraft was in an ideal location for detection. Our radar first received the aircraft's transponder about thirty miles from the location you gave me. It was at flight level six, tracked 113 degrees at 300 knots ground speed. At 0012 UTC it entered a racetrack pattern at flight level six and remained in this pattern until 0017 UTC, when our radar lost contact with the transponder. We did paint what appears to be a primary target at that location seconds after the transponder failed. We also painted what could be—and I'm being cautious here—a weak radar target tracking northwest bound. Our radar did not paint any other unknown aircraft—that is, aircraft not under our control—in that area before contact was lost."

Scott doodled on a sheet of paper, shaking his head in disbelief at what he was hearing.

Allen continued. "I believe you could therefore rule out a mid-air collision. As I said, the primary targets are rather small and unevenly spaced. Our specialists could not rule out the possibility of this being nothing more than ocean clutter or interference."

Scott swallowed hard, his mind racing, trying to sort out what he'd just heard.

How could a primary radar target exist from an aircraft that was not supposed to be there? And why didn't the board think of a mid-air collision as a possible reason for the disappearance?

"You still there, Scott?"

"Yeah sure, just a little confused. Actually, I'm really confused."

"Scott, if you'll give me your ship address we'll zap a copy to you."

"Okay, just a moment."

When Scott asked Senior Chief Donelson for the address, he replied, "Sir, our satellite receivers are down for routine maintenance until midnight Zulu. That's the reason the DSN is down"

Scott glanced at his watch and said, "Sorry Dan, we're down for maintenance. I could fly down and pick it up."

"Now?"

"Dan, I really need this data."

"Absolutely Scott. Just give me the details."

I anticipate it'll take me an hour from now to coordinate this with the admiral, kick the tires, and light the fire. Probably be forty minutes flying time. Let's guesstimate an ETA of 1120 hours or 1520 UTC. I'll park at the Air Guard and refuel. Could you meet me there?"

"Love to. Maybe we can have a cup of real Puerto Rican coffee and chat about old times. Do you want our folks in the CERAP to assist you? It's beautiful VFR weather here today, but I'll be happy to file a flight plan for you and have it ready when you call."

"That's just great, Dan. You're one of a kind. My call sign will be Rifle 1, an F-35 Charlie slant whiskey at 510 knots. Request flight level 470 from approximately 200 miles north of San Juan direct to San Juan airport. The rest will be on file at the boat."

"Got it. See you at the guard operations. Fly safely."

At 1503 hours, Rifle 1's tail hook grabbed CVN-77's second arresting wire as everyone expected. The second wire was Scott's favorite, and he seldom missed. *Bolter* was not in his vocabulary. As far as he was concerned, the other two arresting cables could be disconnected. And he expected nothing less from his more experienced pilots. He handed the roll of paper with the crucial radar data to Turk, climbed down from his F-35, and preceded directly to the conference room where the board members were waiting.

Without taking his seat, he removed his helmet and other flight gear, then spread the FAA document on the table. The data was printed by a computer on a sheet of paper approximately two feet by two feet. Aircraft without transponders, or IFF in Navy jargon, were represented on the print-out as a small x. Scott inquired if anyone had a suggestion on how to merge the two computerized documents with software that was worlds apart. Senior

Chief Donelson suggested doing it the old-fashioned way, by simply plotting the Navy data onto the FAA chart.

"Is it technically possible to obtain the exact lat/long of the radar data in question, Senior Chief?"

"Yes sir, we have that capability. We simply slew a trackball over the piece of radar data, push the entry button, and the lat/long of that location is displayed on the radar display. Won't take very long to obtain this data."

"Outstanding. Let's merge that data ASAP, Chief."

"Right away, Commander."

Forty minutes later, Senior Chief Donelson entered the conference room.

"Sir, I have the lat/long of all the pieces of radar data considered relevant."

Scott and all the board members quietly observed while the lat/long was called out. The first position coincided with the FAA's radar data, and as more positions were plotted, a definite track emerged—a definite radar track. Interference or clutter was displayed randomly, not in a neat, straight line.

"What do you make of this, Chief?"

"To be honest, sir, I'm stumped. And a bit bewildered. This is definitely an aircraft track."

"What's the speed and altitude?"

The groundspeed is 312 knots. We were unable to obtain an altitude readout on our height finding radar, which indicates the bogey is either very high or very low."

Scott looked down at the floor, rubbing his chin while in deep thought.

312 knots. The recommended speed for maximum fuel

conservation at low altitude. What have we got here? And where does Lieutenant Driscol's HMDS sighting fit in?

Scott issued two quick orders. "Chief Donelson, plot Lieutenant Driscol's shark orbit fix on the FAA chart. Then determine the time the radar track would be abeam of shark." Lieutenant Driscol was out of the room searching for answers to Scott's earlier questions concerning reflections or false targets in the HMDS. Scott looked at Lieutenant Commander Hause and said, "Get Lieutenant Driscol in here on the double."

A scurry of activity took place in the room as Scott's orders were carried out. By the time Driscol arrived, Donelson had the shark fix plotted. Scott glanced at Donelson and Hause, nodded his approval. He pointed at the chart and said, "Lieutenant Driscol, we have plotted shark on this chart. I want you to plot your orbit on the chart then review what you said in your statement concerning the HMDS. Lieutenant Driscol moved the chart for a closer look. He picked up a plotter and carefully drew his orbit pattern with the southernmost part over shark. He turned to look at Scott and said, "Sir, there are no known reports of false targets or reflections with the HMDS. As I stated in my interview, I was in a right climbing turn to angels six." He demonstrated the actual flight pattern with his hand. "Just seconds before leveling off at six, turning through a southwest heading, I briefly saw an F-35 in my HMDS. I estimate the time to be 0030 Zulu."

"Chief, what was the time our mysterious aircraft passed abeam shark?"

"Exactly at 0029 Zulu, sir."

"I think that we can only draw one conclusion. We now know with certainty that the FAA radar as well as ours painted a real aircraft. And Lieutenant Driscol saw a real F-35 on his HMDS that matches the radar data. There was only three F-35s airborne at that time. Two of them are accounted for. Therefore, this board can conclude that the mysterious aircraft is in fact the F-35 Stove flown by Major McGruder." Finally, he nodded his head and declared, "I deeply appreciate the professional help and technical expertise contributed from each of you. This board is in recess until further advised."

When Scott briefed both Admirals on the board's findings, they were perplexed and dismayed. Admiral Hayes slowly shook his head and said, "What logic could materialize from an F-35 thought to have crashed only to appear on our radar like a ghost and fly off into the unknown?" Regardless of Scott's presentation, the admirals agreed that the next of kin must be advised as quickly as possible and instructed Scott to inventory Major McGruder's personal effects. His next of kin and the news media would be informed that his aircraft had been missing since the previous evening and was presumed lost at sea for unknown reasons, and that search and rescue operations were continuing around the clock.

When Commander Wallace opened the door to McGruder's compartment, he was stunned. Normally it was kept in immaculate condition. But now the closet door was open and uniforms hung haphazardly. Dirty underclothes were scattered on the floor. Commander Scott backed out of the doorway and said to Lieutenant Smith, who was assisting him, "This place is a mess. Just to be on the safe side, let's put on our mask, latex disposable gloves and shoe covers. They cautiously entered the compartment. An open attaché case stuffed with money and a note was on McGruder's bunk. A laptop computer sat on his desk.

Scott instructed Lieutenant Smith to photograph the room from four different angles without disturbing anything. Scott shook his head in bewilderment when he read the note and counted the money. The laptop computer intrigued Scott. He had played chess and blackjack with McGruder at least two times since they'd sailed from Mayport. While not necessarily unusual, he thought it somewhat odd that he hadn't noticed McGruder's computer during his visits. Perhaps he'd elected to keep it in a safe place to prevent it from falling onto the floor in case of rough seas.

"Lieutenant Smith, do you have any doubt as to the ownership of the uniforms, books, shoes, and so forth?"

"No sir, it's pretty obvious since Major McGruder was the only Marine Corps officer on board. Why do you ask?"

"I agree with you, Lieutenant. The reason I asked is I'm puzzled as to the disposition of this laptop. It doesn't have any identification on the outside. Therefore, we're not really sure who it belongs to, are we?"

"No sir. Not unless we look inside."

"Exactly. I don't believe we would violate any privacy or legal laws by turning this computer on in order for us to determine its rightful owner. As our JAG officer, I want your opinion and I'll abide by whatever you decide."

Lieutenant Smith stared at the computer, rubbed his chin in thought for a moment or so, then said, "I recall a similar case in which the appellate court upheld the breaking and entering under similar circumstances. My opinion is that it is legal to enter the computer."

"Okay, Lieutenant Smith, you're my witness."

Scott pressed the on/off switch. When the log-on page appeared, it was labeled V. McGruder.

"Okay, so we know who this belongs to. Got any ideas for a password?"

Lieutenant Smith shook his head and said, "None whatsoever."

After many unsuccessful tries using familiar passwords such as family names and birth dates, Scott entered the word "Stove" and the desktop appeared. It didn't contain any unusual icons. He clicked on "my documents." A list of normal or expected files popped up except for one labeled, "The Pact." Scott opened "The Pact" file, and two folders appeared. When he clicked on the first folder, a digital picture of a lake taken from an aircraft popped up. The picture was dated April 11, 2014.

As he scanned through numerous photographs of the mysterious lake, some taken with the aircraft in a steep bank, a dam appeared. It was apparent the aircraft had been at a very low altitude and was flying directly toward the dam when the photograph was taken. The next photograph was snapped as the aircraft started a steep climb to fly over the top of the dam. Next to last was a shot taken as the aircraft was level with the top of the dam. It contained a blurred image of the upper portion of a white SUV. The last picture showed the aircraft nosed over on the other side of the dam.

Wonder what nut risked their life to take these? Scott thought.

"Recognize that lake or dam, Lieutenant?"

"Negative sir. But it was nearly full of water when those pictures were taken. The foliage is light green, and the trees are not fully leaved. Considering the date, foliage, and hilly terrain, I'd say the latitude is probably along the middle of the U.S., near the Ozark or Appalachian Mountains."

"Good observation, Lieutenant. Let's continue and see if we can make an identification." The next set of images were an architect's rendering of the construction of Norris Dam.

Scott clicked on the other folder. It contained a photograph of a creased and weathered handwritten document. It began:

THE PACT

Throughout the course of history, man has struggled with nature and man himself for survival. Oppression, treachery, and slavery imposed by pompous tyrants devour the spirit and livelihood of just men who are perceived by these degenerates as being vile and from a lower order. In due time, such intolerable conditions forces the just to resort to whatever measures are necessary to rectify and rebalance the power between the people and their government. Such is our dilemma today. Our forefathers gallantly volunteered their services to establish and protect our great nation, beginning with the ultimate sacrifices at the battle of Kings Mountain during the Revolution. Our third president perceived that this country might in time produce men with an unquenchable thirst for power. He foresaw the necessity to refresh our liberty when necessary with the blood of patriots and tyrants. His vision has manifested itself through the TVA. They have trampled on the Constitution by illegally taking private property for purposes other than the public good and without just compensation. I alone cannot overcome such a giant, but I will not be forced from my birthright by these renegades. I will succumb here in my beloved land and be buried in what will, in time, become my watery grave.

Therefore, it is incumbent upon my issue through this solemn pact to succor, and assure that justice will eventually be achieved, that our land will be restored, and allow God's sun to once again cast its caressing rays upon my earthly abode.

William McGruder January 3, 1936

Ronald McGruder January 9, 1936

Craig R. McGruder May 1, 1957

Aaron W. McGruder March 15, 1977

Vance R. McGruder February 11, 2014

When Scott saw McGruder's signature and thumbprint on the document, his body began to convulse. He barely made it to the head before heaving up his last meal. When he returned, he sat his shaking body down on McGruder's bunk. A cell phone slid from beneath the pillow.

Friday, March 18, 2015
1700 Hours
Aboard the USS George H. W. Bush
Somewhere in the Caribbean Sea

Scott returned to his quarters, showered, and dressed in his formal Dinner Dress Blue and White uniform. A burning sensation gnawed deep in his stomach. Several words used in the Pact haunted him. At times, he felt himself defending the original cause, even feeling sorry for the family so long associated with his own.

That Pact has survived through four generations. Has anyone attempted to implement it before now? Apparently not, but who knows for sure. Regardless of what may have happened in the past, he's obviously adamant about carrying out its commands. Its goal is very explicit. Destroy the dam and uncover the land, restoring it to its original grandeur. Wonder where the original document is stored? Or even if it still exists. Probably locked away in his bank safe deposit box. It's amazing. McGruder has apparently been faking, just biding his time since he regained flying status. He's one crafty individual. A chameleon. All that camaraderie was faked. Why wasn't I cognizant of what was going on inside the head of my closest friend?

He probably realized that he wouldn't be able to pass the Pact resolutions on to his daughters. Or maybe he didn't want to. Most likely he surmised that he was the last person in his family that had a real chance to carry out the commands of the Pact—the last member with the motive, means, and volition to do such a nefarious act.

Three VIPs—Senator Vernon Davis, Chairman of the powerful Armed Services Committee; William Bradley, Under Secretary Of The Navy; and Ted Armstrong, Director of Operational Testing and Evaluation—were en route to the ship for dinner and a formal briefing on the SAID program. Scott was expected to attend dinner with the Admirals and the VIPs, and would probably give a briefing on the outcome of the ORE. The briefing might be worthwhile, but he didn't relish the idea of entertaining civilians who usually drank too much at dinner and became obnoxious. Then came the loosened tongues invariably bragging about their great achievements. But rubbing elbows with VIPs was unfortunately a necessary step if you had aspirations to be promoted to a rank above captain. And Scott did.

But the VIPs were not utmost on his mind at the moment. He picked up the phone and dialed Admiral Gibbons' suite.

"Admiral Gibbons."

Speaking in a rather strained voice, Scott said, "Good evening, Admiral. This is Commander Wallace. I would like to discuss a matter that I consider of extreme importance."

"Commander, have you forgotten the VIPs?"

"No sir. I'm dressed and prepared for the brief. However, I would not have disturbed you unless I believed this to be an urgent situation that demands the attention of a higher authority."

"Commander, you know I hold you in high esteem. Your voice sounds strange, different. Are you feeling okay?"

When Scott didn't answer, the admiral said, "All right, Commander, come up to my quarters and we can talk while I dress."

"Sir, could we meet in the conference room? I would appreciate it so that I can use the MBS. Communications has built a formal briefing and downloaded it into the MBS."

After a long pause, Gibbons exhaled his breath and said, "I'll meet you there shortly, as soon as I can put my uniform on. This had better be important."

The phone clicked and went dead in Scott's ear.

Admiral, Scott thought, *this might be the most important briefing you've ever had.*

Twenty minutes later, Scott turned toward the admiral and stood at attention as he entered the conference room in his impressive formal uniform, adorned with several rows of miniature medals of various shape, sizes, and colors.

"At ease, Scott. Is this going to be a one-on-one?"

"I would prefer that it be for now, sir."

Admiral Gibbons nodded as he sat down. "Then go ahead. I'm anxious to see what's so important that it interrupted me at this inopportune time."

Scott pushed the view button on the MBS panel and immediately the large plasma HD screen came alive as the lights in the conference room automatically dimmed.

He directed a laser pointer at the screen. "Sir, this is the radar data you were shown earlier today. Now I will superimpose radar data obtained from the FAA's radar in Puerto Rico. It fills in the blank areas for the most part."

Scott pressed the control screen. The additional FAA radar data depicted an unmistakable radar track of an aircraft.

"Our best analysis of this data confirms this track is indeed that of Major McGruder's F-35. What I'm about to show you, sir, will, I believe, shock you as much as it did me."

Admiral Gibbons slowly tapped the conference table with his right index finger and nodded, his thoughts more focused on the VIPs than on what Scott was saying.

"Among Major McGruder's personal effects was a laptop computer. These images were found in his computer."

Scott displayed the first picture.

"Admiral, this is one of a series of photographs taken from what appears to be a light civilian aircraft. Note the date, April eleventh of last year."

Each picture was flashed on the screen until a dam appeared, the flyover, and then the last photograph of the series, a breathtaking view of the Clinch River south of the dam.

"We believe these photographs are of Norris Dam in

Eastern Tennessee. The next photographs led me to reach this conclusion. However, we are in touch with Homeland Security to verify the identity of the bridge. I was careful not to divulge the reason I requested this information."

Admiral Gibbons nodded his head in approval.

Scott continued his brief with several other photographs of the construction of Norris Dam. Of particular interest to Scott was an architect's rendering called Plan-Elevation and Sections. These drawings were in great detail. The dam was constructed with two large metal tubes almost 21 feet in diameter, called *penstocks*. Their purpose was to deliver water from the reservoir through the dam. The force of this water surging through the penstocks turns large turbines, which creates electricity. In one photograph, both penstocks were circled in red and a handwritten note said: "soft spot."

Scott held up a plastic bag containing a cell phone.

"This cell phone was taken from Major McGruder's room. It has several stored numbers. Most appear to be routine numbers for friends, relatives, restaurants, and so forth. But there are two numbers that intrigued me. I called the first one and a cab company named Robello's answered. When I dialed the second number, a woman answered. It was Robello Martinez's residence. Both of these phone numbers are in the Bahamas. Could be nothing but a friend or relative, but I have a hunch they have something to do with this problem. Major McGruder called the second number last night shortly after our briefing. Just moments prior to the ORE launch. I have known Major McGruder practically all my life, and he never mentioned anyone he knew in the Bahamas."

Scott held up a large plastic bag containing McGruder's money. "This bag contains money found in McGruder's attaché case. He signed and dated a document yesterday that includes this money in his will.

The next image was a plain sheet of white paper with the following statements written by hand:

Society in every state is a blessing, but Government, even in its best state, is but a necessary evil; in its worst state an intolerable one: for when we suffer, or are exposed to the same miseries BY A GOVERNMENT, which we might expect in a country WITHOUT GOVERNMENT, our calamity is heightened by reflecting that we furnish the means by which we suffer. —Thomas Paine

The tree of liberty must be refreshed from time to time with the blood of patriots and tyrants. —Thomas Jefferson

"Admiral, I'm not a handwriting expert, but I'm positive these were copied by McGruder."

Scott pressed another button on the MBS and the top third of The Pact appeared. This was intentional, as Scott didn't want the admiral to see the signatures and start asking questions before he finished the brief.

"Admiral, this document was written by Major McGruder's great-great-great-grandfather in 1936. Apparently this is a contractual obligation handed down from generation to generation to reclaim their homeland, which was covered by water when the Norris Dam was built."

Scott slowly scrolled the picture, making sure the admiral was able to read the entire document. Major McGruder's signature finally came into view. Scott paused to observe the admiral's reaction. Gibbons was obviously without words as his brain strained to sort out a large volume of data that seemed irrational, illogical, and unreal. His hands trembled as he rubbed his chin. His wrinkled forehead was raised, accentuating his bushy eyebrows and premature crow's feet. The room was quiet except for the slight hum of the nuclear heated steam boilers and hundreds of other electric motors that powered the many different parts of the gigantic carrier.

"That concludes my briefing, Admiral."

After a long pause, Admiral Gibbons shifted in his leather chair and stared at Scott with eyes that seemed to beg for assurance.

"Commander, what's the relevance of the fingerprints?"

"No one on board is an expert in this area, but the flight surgeon believes these are all thumbprints stamped with blood. Notice how the colors change from red to dark red or almost black in some of the older imprints."

Admiral Gibbons stared straight ahead and said, "Commander, this is very troubling. Thank you for your courage and foresight in insisting that this matter be brought to my immediate attention. I apologize if I seemed overbearing. Who else knows about this?"

"Lieutenant Smith, our legal officer, who assisted in the retrieval of Major McGruder's personal effects, the communications technician that developed this briefing, and the flight surgeon. I took the liberty and gave a direct order to all three that disclosure to anyone else was prohibited."

"Excellent thinking, Commander. What conclusion have you drawn from this data?"

"Admiral, I can only draw one conclusion. That the Major never really recovered from his traumatizing experience in Iran, has been faking, despises what he perceives as a lying, degenerate government that destroyed his life as well as the lives of his ancestors, and now he intends to fulfill the commandants of The Pact."

"What traumatizing experience are you referring to?"

"Sorry Admiral, I thought you knew. You may recall the beating we took from world opinion after we bombed the wrong target and killed several Iranian girls, I believe in two thousand and eleven."

Admiral Gibbons looked up toward the ceiling momentarily, cracked his knuckles, and asked, "Was that the Esfahan incident?"

"Yes sir, it was. Major McGruder was the pilot that dropped the bomb. The Marine Corps cleared him from any wrongdoing or mistakes, but soon afterwards he spiraled into deep depression, heavy drinking, and finally a nasty divorce."

Scott frowned. "Admiral, I feel somewhat responsible. I have known Major McGruder since our college days. Our family ties go back to the start of the Revolution. After he recovered and attained flying status, he became one of the Marines' top aviators. Partly because of his flying skills I recommended his selection for this project, and I admit, Admiral, in reflection, that knowing him personally factored into my selection."

"That's perfectly understandable. Let's not get hung up on these matters and concentrate on what could become one of the greatest homegrown terrorist acts ever carried out in this country. If he's planning on destroying that dam, it could make Oklahoma City, 9/11, Katrina, and the New Madrid quake look like child's play. I assume the reason the laptop remained in his room is because he would be unable to place it in the cockpit of his aircraft without being noticed. Of course he could have just tossed it overboard or deleted the compromising data. But that doesn't explain the cell phone and cash. It's as if he wanted to leave a trail—to let us know his intentions. In any case, he probably could care less about evidence left behind."

"I agree with your assumptions, Admiral. "

"What's your recommendation as to how we should proceed, Commander?"

"Well sir, what's troubling me is where Major McGruder and his Stove are at this very moment. He could be en route to the dam as we speak. Or he could be sitting on some military base in Florida after faking an emergency, having the Stove refueled in preparation for an attack on Norris Dam. Or he could have run out of fuel and crashed. The possibilities are nearly endless."

"Commander, I'm sure I know the answer to this, but I need a confirmation. As I recall, Major McGruder was carrying an armed SAID."

"That's correct, Admiral. He flew the third aircraft that was to launch a SAID."

"And, I assume it was not launched."

"We assume that to be the case; however, we do not have any hard evidence as to the location or disposition of that SAID."

"Any other ordnance? Missiles?"

"No missiles. But he did have a gatling gun mounted with a full load of ammunition."

"You're speaking of the GAU-12/U?"

"No sir. They installed the GAU-22/A Gatling Gun. It only has four barrels, is lighter, but is deadlier than the GAU-12/U. It's carried externally, which increases drag and thereby reduces the range. Major McGruder ordered his crew chief to mount the cannon and a full load of ammo the day he disappeared. He could cause us some trouble with this gun but compared to the SAID, it's nothing more than a pea shooter."

"I see. Do you think there's a possibility he would sell or give the Stove and SAID to the bad guys for profit or spite?"

"Sir, I'm sure just about anything's possible. Of course, he could have defected to Cuba or Venezuela. But my hunch is McGruder is bent on destroying Norris Dam with his SAID. He would accomplish two things at once. One, he would fulfill his signed obligation to uphold the commands of The Pact, and two, he would even the score with a government that he apparently sees as being out of control."

"Commander, this may be too immense for us to handle. Obviously, time is critical. We must think clearly and move quickly. As a starter, what do you think we should do?"

"I suggest we immediately send a routine overdue aircraft inquiry or MINOT to all military bases east of the Mississippi. If we should get lucky and locate the aircraft, we could have it seized and detain McGruder until this matter is settled."

"Good idea, but make sure the inquiry looks routine, nothing unusual. Let's keep this to ourselves for now."

"Yes sir. I'll have Cherry Point transmit the MINOT and advise me by phone of the results. This would be normal procedure for a ship at sea."

"Good. Commander, what's the range of the F-35?"

"The Marine version has a combat radius of slightly over 600 nautical miles. Of course the actual radius depends on many variables, such as cruising altitude, upper winds, speed, and armaments attached to the outside of the aircraft such as the gatling gun. All of these factors have an effect on the range, some positive and some negative. I know for certain and without making any calculations that McGruder could not fly from our location last night to Norris Dam without refueling. To our knowledge, he didn't air-refuel, so in order to attack that dam, he would have to land someplace and take on fuel. Admiral, I suggest we pause now and allow me to have the MINOT prepared and assign some of my pilots to calculate the maximum distance McGruder could fly under ideal conditions. Maybe we can start our own search after we get this information."

A slight thump and shudder of the carrier confirmed what the overhead TV monitor displayed. The COD aircraft delivering the VIPs had arrived.

Admiral Gibbons stood up, took a deep breath, and patted Scott on his arm. "I'll entertain those three for a while and then try to hand them off to someone else. Get in touch with me as soon as you have additional information. In any event, I'll rejoin you as soon as possible."

As the admiral turned to leave, Scott added, "And sir, on second thought I suggest we transmit an alert message to all military bases ordering them to exercise diligent control over all jet fuel until this problem is resolved."

"Good idea, Commander." The admiral thought for a moment and replied, "But an all service order would require the signature of the Chairman of the Joint Chiefs of Staff, unless that authority has been delegated. We'll consider that option later. In the meantime, let's treat McGruder's room as a crime scene and secure the items you've shown me."

Friday, March 18, 2015
1900 Hours
Aboard The USS George H. W. Bush
Caribbean Sea

The MINOTs returned with negative results. Calculations on the maximum range of a Stove aircraft under ideal conditions were complete. Forecast and actual upper winds for various altitudes were factored in for flight in several directions emanating outward from the last known position of McGruder' Stove. Scott decided the time was ripe for further discussion and investigation. In his judgment, the VIPs could cool their heels for a few moments if necessary. In any case, entertaining civilians was not high on his agenda. He called Admiral Gibbons's private shipboard number.

Admiral Gibbons's aide-de-camp answered the phone in a tone similar to an electronically generated voice.

"Admiral Gibbons's office, Lieutenant Farnsworth speaking, may I help you?"

"Yes, this is Commander Wallace; Admiral Gibbons please."

"Sir, the Admiral is having cocktails with Admiral Hayes and some visiting dignitaries. Sorry, he mustn't be disturbed."

"Lieutenant, this is a matter of national security. I suggest you get the Admiral on this phone now unless you want to spend the rest of your Navy commitment swabbing decks."

"National security? Just a moment, sir."

Lieutenant Farnsworth cautiously approached Admiral Gibbons, who was chatting with the VIPs.

"Excuse me, Admiral Gibbons. Sir, I'm very sorry to disturb you, but Commander Wallace demands to talk to you. Says it's a matter of national security or I wouldn't have interrupted you."

Admiral Gibbons swore under his breath but quickly realized he hadn't told Farnsworth to expect an important phone call from Commander Wallace. Admiral Gibbons grabbed the phone and walked a few steps out of hearing from the others.

"Yes, Commander."

"Sir, the MINOTs were all negative. I can give you the details concerning the range of the Stove or brief you in the conference room."

"I'm on my way to the conference room. We've got to formulate a plan of action, and quick."

Admiral Gibbons returned the phone to the lieutenant, turned toward his guests, and announced, "Gentlemen, if you'll excuse me I have a matter that I must look into."

Senator Davis, capable of detecting the most intricately woven military snafu, sensed that something unusual was afoot—and it was apparently being kept from him by Admiral Gibbons.

"Admiral, uh, Gibbons, your aide mentioned, I believe I heard, 'national urgency'; no, 'national security.'"

"'National security' is what I heard," mumbled Under Secretary Bradley as Admiral Hayes nodded, a look of consternation on his face.

Admiral Gibbons looked at Admiral Hayes for assistance but realized he had not been briefed on all the details of the missing Stove.

"Admiral, is there a problem with the SAID program that we should know about?"

"No sir. The SAID ORE went beautifully. But we have an unrelated problem with a SAID. A big problem. At some point in time you would have, of course, been informed of what we currently know. Gentlemen, if you'll accompany me to the conference room, Commander Wallace will brief you on this entire matter."

When they entered the conference room, Admiral Gibbons remained standing and introduced the VIPs to Scott. Then he looked around the room, smiled, and said, "Gentlemen, I'm happy to report that the ORE was a total success. The SAID performed magnificently, as advertised, and destroyed the RCS, at a very deep depth where the

Cockroaches are known to operate. Unless you have questions I'll turn the brief over to Commander Wallace, who has some startling revelations."

Gibbons' statement about startling revelations plus his ultra-short brief got the VIPs' attention. They all stared at the admiral, a surprised look on their faces. No one spoke.

Scott stood up and began a detailed briefing. He'd only expected Admiral Gibbons, not the entire retinue. Not that it really mattered. Scott was well adapted to rapidly changing scenarios. As an air wing commander, impromptu briefings, some on the carrier's live TV, were common.

At the end of the briefing, Scott mentioned the negative results of the MINOT search and continued with a detailed analysis of the Stove's optimum combat radius.

Tension in the room increased until it was thick enough to be cut with a knife.

"Gentlemen, this analysis is based on the best-case scenario, or we could view it in this case as the worst-case scenario."

Senator Davis, who had been, or at least appeared to be, taking notes, twiddled with his pen, staring in disbelief at nothing in particular. Under Secretary Bradley unconsciously stroked the smooth edge of his empty, lead crystal glass engraved with an artist's conception of the *Bush*.

Scott continued. "Major McGruder is an expert in Stove performance. The Stove's range is slightly less than our Snakes'. The Stove's fuel tanks are smaller than the tanks on our Snakes. This extra space is used to house the STOVL computer, fan, and other components. The upper winds were favorable to extend Major McGruder's flight. That's assuming he continued on a course to the northwest."

Scott displayed a detailed satellite map centered on the location of McGruder's disappearance. A computerized, somewhat oval shaped circle graphically depicted the estimated maximum range McGruder could have flown before fuel exhaustion.

"As you can see, it is very probable that Major McGruder's range could extend as far as the Florida panhandle, the Bahamas, the Leeward and Windward Islands, Venezuela, northern Columbia, and Cuba. He could have flown to any of these locations—could have defected to some of these countries. There's a possibility that he rendezvoused with a civilian supertanker and they're halfway around the world with an F-35 and a SAID aboard. No doubt he would be treated royally and live in luxury hereafter if he should deliver an advanced aircraft and a top secret weapon that was, and hopefully still is, unknown outside the United States. However, all indications are that Major McGruder is determined to consummate The Pact." He paused, to let his last statement sink in, then continued.

"Homeland Security experts have developed videos using data from computer models for all domestic dams. These models depict the theoretical results of a terrorist attack. They're based on explosives inside the dam cavity that would crack or perhaps breach a dam. Their models use an average amount of water in the reservoirs. Unfortunately, the Norris reservoir is full of water due to the excessive winter and early spring rains. And, I believe the SAID would destroy a large section of the dam or obliterate it if struck in or near the penstocks."

Scott started the Homeland Security video. It began with panoramic views of the dam and surrounding terrain near the dam. Then a very realistic computer animated description of the unfolding events began. The solemn commentator opened with a vivid description of the detonation of a bomb within the dam. A thunderous roar was followed by two huge vertical cracks in the dam. Water gushed out of the cracks, spewing outward for approximately 100 yards. Within moments, the entire middle portion of the dam collapsed.

"As the water roars out of the reservoir, it obeys the law of centrifugal force, churns southward instead of winding to the southeast, as the Clinch River does. Three of the University of Tennessee's seismographic stations come alive, registering between a continuous 4.1 and 5.6 on their Richter scale. The massive force will carve a new canyon out of the hills located slightly over a mile south of the dam. Charging southward at an enormous speed, it crosses the Clinch in a short time, disrupting its flow. Minutes later, it reaches Interstate 75. A swatch of the road almost a quarter of a mile wide will vanish in the blink of an eye. All the unfortunate motorists on, or close to, this portion of the interstate would never know what hit them. The worst-case scenario would be at a time shortly after dark during peak traffic. Estimated casualties, two hundred ten lives lost."

Some of the men shifted in their chairs, stared at each other, or slowly shook their heads in disbelief.

The video continued. "The wall of water will be sixty to

eighty feet high in the valleys between ridges and knolls. It will cascade southward, generally paralleling the Clinch River. When the water reaches the foothills of the Lone Mountain, it will deflect the mass and turn it slightly southwestward along Highway 61. This pent-up kinetic force crosses the Clinch again and enters the outskirts of Clinton, home to slightly over nine thousand people. Along the way, it will accumulate tons of wood, trees, and any material with buoyancy. Submerged and tumbling along the surface are large boulders, vehicles, farm machinery, animals, and human remains. People hear the roar and feel the ground shaking before the deluge arrives but there is no time to escape. Instead of turning left with the river, the preponderance of this giant savage continues straight ahead between two knolls located on either side of Clinton, striking the little town head-on. In an instant, an estimated six thousand inhabitants will perish and ninety-five percent of the town's infrastructure and buildings will be destroyed." The video switched to a bird's eye view of a gigantic wall of water careening through the small city.

"After the water subsides, little evidence will remain to indicate that a thriving city once stood at that location. It will appear as if a giant hand scooped down Main Street, leaving nothing but exposed soil, rocks, and a few recognizable man-made objects such as automobiles and farm machinery. It is possible the location of the Clinch will be permanently changed. If so, it would continue flowing through what was once the town of Clinton. The Pine Ridge will deflect the man-made tsunami, and turn it slightly to the right. The churning and screaming water crosses its father, the Clinch again. Without warning, this brainless, uncaring, and merciless mass thunders into Oak Ridge, killing thousands of innocent inhabitants. The water will inundate the National Nuclear Security Administration's Y Twelve facilities, unearthing and unleashing hundreds of casks containing the world's most dangerous and feared substance known to man, enriched uranium and lithium six. Within hours, the reservoir will be fully drained and return to its original state, except for the desert-like appearance on either side of the river where lush foliage once stood.

"As the water subsides downstream, new lakes will be formed in low lying areas, completely changing the appearance of the landscape. The loss of life and property could exceed any catastrophe that has ever struck our nation." The video ended with a dire warning. "Nuclear radiation would sicken and kill untold thousands in future years and lay waste a large portion of our country indefinitely."

Senator Davis, now ashen-faced, sensed the gravity of the situation. He slowly stood up and moved to the head of the table.

"Gentlemen, without a doubt this is one of the most difficult problems to hit us since the Cockroaches appeared. What's so troubling is we don't have the luxury of time to fully explore, to investigate, or to bring others aboard. If we don't take immediate action and that dam is destroyed, every one of us in this room is doomed, and well we should be. On the other hand, if we recommend a national emergency be declared, and nothing happens, we could be the laughing stock of this country. So gentlemen, what will we do? Sit on our hands and dillydally while a national calamity unfolds? While thousands drown—men, women, and children? And if Y Twelve in Oak Ridge is destroyed, as Homeland Security predicts, it could be the worst ecological disaster since Chernobyl."

"Therefore, I believe we must all, here in this room, put

our personal lives and ambitions aside. We are all representatives and servants of the people of the United States. If we don't take action, we could be guilty of an enormous crime, and rightly so." Senator Davis turned toward Scott and said, "Commander Wallace, what recommendation do you have?"

"Senator, I believe we must use every means available to locate and destroy this aircraft, if necessary. As you have seen, it's difficult to detect and track the F-35 but not impossible. Since we don't know the whereabouts of Major McGruder or when, or even if, he intends to strike, I recommend we immediately dispense fighters to the Knoxville Air National Guard Facility. Sufficient fighters should be activated to maintain a continuous CAP over the dam, and should be properly armed to destroy the F-35. Two E-3 Sentry aircraft should be ordered airborne immediately with direct communications, command, and control authority over the fighters. Our job of detecting and tracking this aircraft would be immensely simpler if all airborne aircraft were identified and under FAA control."

Under Secretary Bradley made a T with his hands signaling for a time out.

Scott stopped his briefing and acknowledged Bradley.

"Commander, are you suggesting we ground all aircraft, except some military flights, as we did shortly after the 9/11 tragedy?"

"No sir, not entirely like 9/11. Similar, but not to that extent. The procedure I propose will have less impact on our economy, less disruption in the civilian aviation industry.

We could sanitize the appropriate airspace, force all aircraft to be equipped with a functioning radio, IFF, or transponder and under FAA control. I propose an area east of the Mississippi River and south of the thirty-eighth parallel. The thirty-eighth parallel would be on a line approximately from Evansville, Indiana direct to a point forty miles south of Washington, D.C and continuing along the thirty-eighth parallel to a point twelve nautical miles offshore."

"Could such a measure be implemented on short notice?" Senator Davis inquired.

"Yes, Senator, there is a plan in place. It's called SCAT, short for security control of air traffic. Appropriate military authority, probably the Joint Chiefs of Staff or possibly the SecDef, would implement this procedure through the Secretary of Transportation or the FAA Administrator. Once the FAA is ordered to implement SCAT, they will issue a NOTAM for all aircraft to land as soon as practical and file either an IFR or DVFR flight plan. After word has spread through the news media and the FAA, any aircraft operating in the area described without FAA authorization would be treated as a suspect and intercepted by our fighter aircraft. Our job of identifying McGruder's Stove would certainly be easier.

"Short-range mobile radars should be established at the dam site and on top of several ridges upstream from the dam. As to whether evacuations should be ordered is not in my area of expertise; nevertheless, I believe we should address this subject. Some diplomatic effort should be expended by the appropriate agency to determine whether

Major McGruder intends to or has already handed over the F-35 along with the SAID to a foreign government, such as Cuba, Venezuela, Columbia, or perhaps Argentina. The Pentagon should consider issuing an immediate order to all service commanders to ensure all military jet fuel depots are appropriately guarded and tighten controls on fuel delivered to aircraft.

"The full resources and expertise of all federal agencies that can assist us—such as the NIA, FBI, Homeland Security, the FAA, and possibly the CIA—should be brought aboard ASAP. In addition to the SCAT zone, I highly recommend necessary protection for Washington, D.C. That's all I have, sir."

Senator Davis forced a slight smile and said, "Thank you, Commander Wallace. Admiral Gibbons, you have demonstrated your knowledge, expertise, and can-do attitude in many tough situations in the past. Do you have any ideas or suggestions in addition to Commander Wallace's?"

"Commander Wallace has laid out a very thorough and realistic plan of action. One area not considered, which could become troublesome at some point in time, is the news media. Perhaps if they are brought aboard initially we could use them to our advantage, particularly if an evacuation is implemented. And last, but of utmost importance, is what level and what department in our government we initially contact.

"I assume that you and Under Secretary Bradley will make those decisions. If I may, sir, I believe this should be forwarded directly to the SecDef. I'm not talking about the secretary's assistant or anyone else but the secretary himself. Otherwise, valuable time may be lost. This started out as a military problem and it seems reasonable for the secretary to implement what action he deems necessary. In the interest of time, I recommend that our thoughts and conclusions be included in that notification. After the Secretary is briefed, I intend to notify the Naval Chain of Command above me to avoid confusion and possible embarrassment."

"Of course we must keep everyone informed that have a bona fide need to know. That's an excellent point, Admiral Gibbons. Admiral Hayes?"

"This is a potential disaster that could easily surpass those that have recently ravaged our country through fires, floods, the mid-south earthquake, and several devastating hurricanes. We must exert every effort, use whatever resources are available, to stop this madman. I agree with Admiral Gibbons and Commander Wallace. You should personally contact the Secretary immediately by secure phone and apprise him of this serious situation. Perhaps we could help you convey the seriousness of this situation if the conversation were conducted over the MBS. In order to save time and accuracy, I recommend Commander Wallace brief SecDef."

"Gentlemen, I agree wholeheartedly with everything all of you have said. I'll speak to Secretary Donaldson initially, lay out the overall problem quickly, and then ask Commander Wallace to complete the brief. Gentlemen, would you contact the secretary for me please?"

Admiral Hayes replied, "Of course, Senator."

Scott glanced at the admirals for assistance. Admiral Hayes' aide-de-camp was on the ball and was entering the codes to open a black case attached to his arm with a strap as Admiral Hayes spoke. The aid opened the case and handed Admiral Hayes a key on a large, gold-colored ring along with a card about the size of a U.S. savings bond. Admiral Hayes carefully studied the authentication data for a moment, signed and dated the card, and handed it and the key to Scott.

Scott inserted and turned the key. A brass cover moved upward, exposing a red button labeled, PENTAGON EMERGENCY USE ONLY. A screen flashed the words, "ENTER AUTHENTICATION CODES NOW." While Scott was entering the numbers and letters for authentication, Admiral Hayes added, "The MBS communications system is scrambled for security at the highest level. Commander Wallace will use the split-screen so that we can simultaneously observe ourselves as well as the other party."

Scott completed the entries, pressed the emergency communications button, and a very hesitant, yet military sounding voice answered on the second ring.

"Pentagon, OSD…Colonel Sterling speaking."

"Colonel Sterling, my name is Senator Vernon Davis. I'm aboard the *USS George Bush*, somewhere in the Caribbean."

"Senator Davis. How may I help you, sir?"

"This is a matter of utmost importance affecting our

national security. I must speak to Secretary Donaldson immediately."

"Senator, the SecDef is at a reception at the White House with POTUS. I'm not able to—"

Senator Davis interrupted Colonel Sterling.

"Colonel, apparently you don't understand the meaning of a national security breach. We're in a crisis mode, and you're creating a speed bump—no, a roadblock. Now get moving and contact the Secretary now."

"Yes sir, stand by please. I'll do my best."

On the first ring, an official-sounding female voice answered. "SecDef, may I assist you?"

"Colonel Downing, this is Alex at OSD. I have a Senator Davis—I believe his first name is Vernon—calling on the emergency MBS phone. He says it's about a national security matter. He's very persistent and demands to speak to SecDef. Patricia, this is very awkward for me. I've never seen that phone ring, much less answered it. I guess they didn't cover everything in our OSD training after all. What's your take on this?"

"Well, Alex, he's probably for real. Only a few top people have access to that mode of communication. Stand by, and I'll see what I can do."

Unknown to both of the OSD Colonels, their conversation was overheard by everyone in the conference room. Almost five minutes passed as Senator Davis paced back and forth, becoming more and more agitated. Then a strong and dignified voice broke the silence.

"Vernon, old boy, still steaming about the beating you took at our last golf outing?"

A large grin appeared on Senator Davis's face.

"Good evening, Fred. We'll settle the golf score sometime soon. The news media might put this in their believe-it-or-not column, but I'm on a constructive junket in reference to the SAID program."

A loud chuckle emitted from Secretary Donaldson. "Did you say junket or boondoggle?" More laughter.

"Fred, I'm sorry to disturb your evening with the president and his charming wife, but a very unusual and troublesome matter has ensnared us. I could brief you now, but I highly recommend you proceed to your office immediately. I can give you a broad overview of the situation while you're en route, if you like, which would save time. After you arrive in your office, we can video conference using the MBS. I'm on the Carrier *George Bush*. I have with me Under Secretary Bradley; Ted Armstrong, Director OT and E; Admiral Gibbons, who is in charge of the SAID project; Admiral Hayes, Commanding Officer of the *George Bush*; and Commander Wallace, C-A-G of Air Wing 15. Commander Wallace is most knowledgeable of the facts of this critical matter and can provide an in-depth briefing for you."

"Honestly, Vernon, I'm relieved that I have an excuse to escape from that boring party. I only attend to appease my wife and naturally you attend if the boss invites you—which he usually does. I've faked a smile so much tonight for the photographers and guests that my face may have a permanent crease on it. It'll be a pleasure to get this monkey suit off and breathe some fresh air. Those Cuban cigars are disgusting and make me nauseated. But, you can't beat the food. I'll say good night to POTUS and resume this conversation in my limousine."

"Fred, time is of the essence."

Friday, March 18, 2015
2030 hours
Aboard the USS George H. W. Bush
Atlantic Ocean

A moment of silence ensued after Scott completed his briefing to Secretary Donaldson using the two-way, split-screen MBS.

After a short pause while he gathered his thoughts, the SecDef spoke.

"Gentlemen, thank you for bringing this matter to my attention. General Morgan, Chairman of the JCS, rode over with me from the party. The other members will join him in the Tank shortly where they will plan and direct this enormous effort. General Morgan is currently implementing all of your recommendations pertaining to the military authority. I will brief the National Security Council immediately and request the full assistance of the newest organization on the block, the National Counterterrorism Center. How effective they will be in switching their mode of operation to a homegrown act of terrorism by our own military remains to be seen. But we need all the help we can muster in this gigantic effort.

"Mr. Myers, Assistant Secretary of Defense for Public Affairs, will inform the media at the appropriate time. I will personally authorize all news releases. I request that all others who are cognizant of this situation please refer media requests to Mr. Myer's office. Undoubtedly, this will be a media circus before it's over. I'm sure they already suspect something big is in the works.

"General Morgan has requested Commander Wallace's presence in the Pentagon to assist and advise the JCS. Please release Commander Wallace and instruct him to report to General Morgan as soon as weather conditions permit his passage. Most likely we'll all be on duty through tonight and probably tomorrow. Please assist the JCS in any way you think appropriate. I'm leaving now to inform POTUS of our situation. Vernon, again I appreciate your quick response to this potential tragedy. And the same is true for the other gentlemen and officers there with you. Good luck, and may God bless our country."

An operator at the Pentagon disconnected the MBS. The VIPs thanked Scott for his resourcefulness and dedication to duty, shook his hand, and departed the room with Admiral Gibbons.

Admiral Hayes glanced across the table at Scott.

"Commander, are you in a launch mode?"

"Affirmative, sir. The sea condition and wind are considerably worse than routine flight operations would allow. However, we would not hesitate to launch if we were in a combat situation, and this crisis certainly qualifies for that elevation of risk."

"You have my permission to launch, Commander. I know you will be cautious but I just want to emphasize it one more time, be careful. Our country desperately needs your assistance."

Scott explained his tentative plans. "I will brief the launch crew, maintenance, and everyone else involved on the flight deck as quickly as possible. I'll proceed directly to Pax River. Initially I'll operate under ICAO rules for state aircraft using due regard rules. When I'm within radio range, I'll contact the FAA in New York for an IFR clearance. Wouldn't want to spoil the NORAD boys mid-shift by sneaking through their radar. And now if you'll excuse me, Admiral, I've got a tough job ahead of me."

An hour later, Scott sat strapped in his F-35. A painting of a long-rifle, barely visible in the downpour, decorated each side of the fuselage and underneath the painting was written, CDR SCOTT WALLACE, RIFLE 1. If you looked closely, you could see the word "Lucy" written on the stock. The real Lucy of Kings Mountain fame hung over the rock fireplace in the home of Scott's parents.

As he scanned the checklist, the launch crew valiantly struggled to stand upright against the wind howling across the pitching deck of the 98,000-ton behemoth. Scott inserted the lat/long of KNHK, the international identifier for Patuxent River Naval Air Station, in the INS/GPS. Instantly the PCD depicted a magnetic track of 354 degrees for a direct flight. The checklist completed, he increased power to the launch position, crosschecked the instruments once more, and saluted.

Leaving 3,000 feet, he turned left to a heading of 003 degrees to correct for the strong winds blowing from the east and checked in with Rawhide.

Even though airliners would not likely be flying in severe weather, Scott nevertheless kept a close eye on his PCD radar display just in case. He relied on Rawhide for additional information on weather and traffic. However, it was Scott's sole responsibility to remain clear of any other conflicting aircraft until he obtained an instrument clearance from the FAA.

Two hundred and eighty miles west of Scott's launch position on a tiny speck of land, a very agitated Major McGruder cursed his luck, the weather, and seemingly every species of insect known to man. He sat in his closed cockpit, sweltering, to escape the swarming bugs, gusting wind, and drenching rain, which was steadily increasing in depth. Several hours earlier, he had removed his weapon and flight suit in order to deflect some of the stifling heat and humidity. But in doing so, he'd provided the insects with more opportunity for a fresh meal. If McGruder's plan had been on schedule, he would have been delivering his SAID on Norris Dam, perhaps at that very moment. But since it was not, his emergency food and insect repellent were almost depleted. The only thing in abundance was water, severe weather—and McGruder's increasing anger. Doubts sprouted in his brain and quickly metastasized. He wiped perspiration from his burning eyes with the back of his hand and pulled his flight suit on.

Maybe Robello's smarter than I thought. If he'd delivered the fuel pump, I would've had a chance. Probably forgot it. Or he may be holding that pump as insurance on the remainder of the money. That's probably it. That sneaky bastard…In any case, I can't leave this hellish hole until I have that pump and break the gear loose. Maybe when this weather subsides he'll show with the pump, we'll transfer the fuel from the barrels, they'll have some more money, and everybody'll be happy. But what if he never shows?

Two hours later, McGruder suddenly woke from a restless cat nap when a small mangrove limb crashed into the canopy with a loud thump. The wind was howling. Leaves, sand, and anything not sufficiently attached to the ground swirled by. *If enough of that junk blows into the engine intakes it may destroy the turbine blades when, and if, I start'er up.*

He scrambled out of the cockpit. His hands slipped on the wet emergency rope and he awkwardly dropped to the concrete platform, twisted his left ankle, and fell backward into the water. He winced, massaging his ankle for a moment, then stood up and hobbled over to the fuel barrels in water now halfway to his knees. If he could move a barrel in front of each intake, perhaps it would provide some protection.

He pushed a barrel over and rolled it to a position in front of the Stove. Although he strained with all his might, his ankle throbbing with excruciating pain, the barrel still lay on its side. After several more attempts, he decided the barrels were not tall enough and wouldn't help much even if they were sitting upright. He kicked the barrel with his good foot and slowly pulled his drenched body back into the cockpit, cursing his misfortune and the elements.

Scott changed the radio frequency on his standby radio and called the New York Center.

"New York Oceanic Control, Rifle 1."

After a short pause, a controller with a distinctive Brooklyn accent responded.

"Calling New Yok Centa, say again."

"This is Rifle 1, request to file IFR with you."

"Okay, Rifle 1, you just might be the TOI NORAD is interested in. You squawking four thousand on your mode three?"

"That's affirmative, New York. And just what is a toy—something NORAD plays with?"

The controller laughed with his mike keyed then said, "I believe, to the fly boys, it means track-of-interest. Rifle 1, squawk 4217 and go ahead with your flight plan."

Better look at the traffic situation. Who knows what those edgy fly boys might try, thought Scott.

He pressed Program Select on the PCD screen and touched a square labeled ACID.

There she is. Now I've got a complete picture of all traffic. At least that's what we're told. Bet some high-flying, ultra secret CIA nerd is trailing me right now. Not a good feeling…

"Roger, New York," Scott transmitted, "4217 on the squawk, F-35 charlie slant whiskey, true air speed, 511, currently at angels, er flight level 450." Position is 2515 north, 7257 west; request flight level 510 direct Patuxent River, ETA, 0450, three hours ten minutes fuel."

A short time later the controller transmitted, "Roger, Rifle 1. You're cleared to Patuxent River as filed. Climb and maintain flight level 510 Report reaching. Should pick you up on radar in about thirty minutes."

"Rifle 1, wilco. Leaving flight level 450 for flight level 510."

One hour later, New York Center switched Rifle 1 to a new frequency for the Washington Center. The radio chatter with Washington Center eventually dwindled to an occasional call from a box hauler or foreign air carrier. Under these circumstances, it would be too easy for Scott to doze off. To break the monotony and keep his mind active, he switched the radio he was using to communicate with Washington Center to speaker and slightly reduced the volume. He tuned the other radio to his favorite radio station, WPYA, Bob FM in Norfolk and switched it to his helmet speaker. The coastline moved slowly across his PCD screen. The weather had slowly improved, and now the cities were clearly visible. He peered out the port side of the cockpit. Norfolk shone like a twinkling jewel.

Home. That's Virginia Beach almost dead ahead. Nice place. Fine beach and restaurants. We've spent some great times there, Jacqueline and I.

But Norfolk was where he longed to be. A good night of rest in his own bed would do wonders. His thoughts drifted to his family.

Friday night. Jacqueline and the kids probably watched a movie and ate popcorn or had some friends over. Some of my favorite times have been with them just doing simple family things like that. Kids can sleep in tomorrow. Bet Craig is trying to beat one of those crazy games. Pushes those wacky knobs and buttons much too fast for me. Great kid. Wish I were there with them. Jacqueline will probably go shopping tomorrow either at Norfolk or Oceana. Or decide to drive over the bay all the way up to Langley. Sincerely believes the fly boys have a better selection of everything. Maybe she's right on. And in the afternoon take the kids for their golf lesson. At the rate they're progressing, they'll soon kick my fanny. I'd like that. Ha…They're growing up much too fast. I'm definitely keeping my promise to them. This year we're gonna spend a week at Disney World. A promise is a promise. This year we're going. Regardless…Gotta remember to call them this afternoon.

The DJ played several of Scott's favorite hits by Chicago. He gazed out the cockpit as Norfolk slid beneath his port wing. The music brought back many fond memories of places and friends. Time seemed to evaporate. At the end of the 30-minute program, Bob FM played Jacqueline's all-time favorite. As it played, he visualized her in their bedroom lying on her left side reading a novel, one of her long, slender legs partly outside the sheets, long black hair draped over her perfectly shaped shoulders, skin smooth as silk, sultry blue eyes…

The radio speaker came alive with a loud and obviously agitated voice, breaking Scott's ruminations. "Rifle 1, Washington center; how do you read, over?"

Scott fumbled with the radio transmitter and turned the volume up. "Ah roger, center, you're loud and clear."

"Rifle 1, descend and maintain flight level 310. And check your receiver please. We've been calling you for some time."

"Ah, Rifle 1 roger, leaving flight level 510 for flight level 310. I'll check the radio." Scott switched the radio receivers back to his helmet and turned off the commercial station.

He chided himself. *Okay airdale, you've had your fun, now back to TCB.*

At 2352 hours, he turned off runway 24 at Patuxent River and switched one radio to ground control frequency. He was instructed to taxi and park in front of operations near a waiting MH-605 helicopter for transportation to the Pentagon.

As he climbed aboard the gleaming Nighthawk with his small bag containing the basic essentials, it became apparent to Scott that some high level coordination had taken place. The crew wore dress uniforms instead of normal flight suits. This kind of service was sometimes accorded a Vice Admiral or above or a high-ranking civilian but definitely not the rank of commander.

As soon as he was buckled in, they departed and headed northwest following the Patuxent River, avoiding noise-sensitive areas. At Bald Eagle, the pilot headed west until reaching the Potomac, turned right, and then followed the river. Passing abeam the Ronald Reagan Airport, the Washington Monument came into view, proudly standing guard over D.C. Twenty minutes after departure, the pilot began an approach to land at the Pentagon. Scott had never visited or been stationed at the Pentagon and didn't really know what to expect.

As he exited the Nighthawk, he was met by a young lieutenant commander and a senior chief. They both held their hats on their heads with their left hand to protect them from the strong downwash off the Nighthawks swirling blades. After some crisp saluting with their right hand, Scott was welcomed to the Pentagon and escorted directly to the Tank, where he met the chairman, General Armand Morgan, and other members of the JCS. He was surprised and relieved to see some of the members dressed in combat fatigues and regular uniforms rather than the stuffy dress uniforms he'd expected even at this late hour. Consequently, he didn't feel out of place in his flight suit.

General Morgan shook Scott's hand and said, "Commander Wallace, welcome to the home of the Joint Chiefs of Staff. Our situation room, or as some prefer, the war room, is located in a bunker beneath the Pentagon. We've assigned you a small office in the war room and a staff to assist you. That's where we'll formulate and execute plans during this crisis to, hopefully, prevent a major blow to our country. I believe you are the key person to help us understand this marine we're dealing with, how he thinks, and his probable actions. You impressed the SecDef and the rest of us with your briefing. Your military knowledge and grasp of important details both militarily and civil go well beyond what's required of a wing commander."

Scott nodded his head, somewhat embarrassed, and said, "Thank you, General. That means a great deal to me."

As he turned to leave for his office General Morgan said, "Commander, if you have any problems or want to discuss any subject or idea in your endeavors, my door is always open."

Scott snapped to attention, saluted the general, and said, "Thank you, sir. I'll keep that in mind."

Scott was escorted to a set of winding stairs leading down to an entrance guarded by two marines in full battle gear. After his army escort passed the rigid security check—which consisted of voice, eye, thumb print, and full facial biometric identification—he entered a series of letters and numbers into a code box. A computer deep in the bowels of the war room digested all the data. Designed to ensure survivability of the war room in event of a nuclear attack, the computer coordinated the movement of the door with all other doors in the underground bunker. The computer software was designed so that only one door was open at any given time. Layers of precedent allowed authorized users, starting with the SecDef, to pre-empt other subordinate users and open a door at will.

After a short wait, the massive steel door slowly creaked opened, revealing an elevator. A Department of Defense seal encrusted with a steely-eyed eagle clutching three arrows guarded the entrance. The elevator briefly stopped after passing five floors, proceeded horizontally for almost two minutes, stopped again, then continued downward to the war room level. As the elevator doors opened, Scott had a strange sensation. His sense of time, direction, and distance had been honed to a sharp edge from his years as a jet jockey. If his judgment was correct, he was standing beneath the Arlington National Cemetery.

No way. They'd never do such a dishonorable act to our dead heroes. Still, the bad guys might also assume we'd never stoop so low as to bury our war room beneath…No, just forget this thought ever entered my mind. Probably overtired and overstressed.

They walked down a long hallway with highly polished floors and walls adorned with dozens of photographs and paintings of famous military heroes, ships, and aircraft. Muffled sounds of people, computers, and communications apparatus seeped through the thick walls.

After Scott's escort presented proper identification to a heavily armed marine guard, he entered a series of numbers into a touch screen. As the door slowly opened, a dimly lit, cavernous, semi-circular room came into view. It was equipped with banks of computer screens located on various levels according to their importance and manned with both civilian and military personnel.

At the highest elevation, large concave liquid crystal maps displayed every major part of the world. Colored symbols represented the location of air, surface, and subsurface contacts. The different shapes of the military symbols distinguished the United States and its allies from all other countries. Computerized status boards designated the alert level of every major command in the U.S. arsenal. Scott was stunned to see the amount of military and civilian activity taking place around the world.

This is unbelievable. There's the George Bush *not too far from where I left her. Wonder if they're tracking all of the Cockroaches? Or any of 'em?*

They proceeded up a set of winding stairs. Its thick carpet and large wooden banister looked as if it had been removed from an antebellum mansion. The stairs led to a glass enclosed area that overlooked the entire room. It was the nerve center of the war room and commonly known as the fox den. Scott was introduced to the officer in charge, Air Force Major General Marvin Montgomery, and his deputy, Army Brigadier General Westmorland, along with three other lower ranking officers.

"Welcome to Alpine, Commander. We've been anxiously awaiting your arrival," Montgomery said. "As you can see, as usual, it's a rather busy night. We track satellites of all nations, military and civilian aircraft, ships, and submarines. Basically anything that moves. All FAA and U.S. military radars, whether terrestrial or celestial, are merged into one mosaic picture by NORAD, which you see here. We enhanced the PCD you have in your aircraft by adding the National Weather Service's weather radar and two other sensors, the scope of which I am not privileged to reveal."

On hearing this, Scott glanced outside the room at the large displays. He was not accustomed to having information withheld from him, but was in no position to question such a high-ranking officer. And besides, this had nothing to do with his primary mission, to catch the dangerous and elusive Major McGruder. But it did whet his appetite, and he wondered what the two sensors might be.

The general continued. "If this country is attacked, this is where the decisions will be made to defend her. This is where the buck stops after POTUS gives us the green light.

"We saw a recorded version of your briefing to the SecDef," he added. "You did an excellent job of explaining a complex problem."

Scott nodded, glancing at both generals, and said, "Thank you, sir."

The general pointed to a large screen of the southeast U.S.

"As you suggested, we have two Sentry AWAC aircraft from Tinker on station at this time. Two Air Force mobile radars are being offloaded at Knoxville as we speak and should come on line early this morning. They will be located near the dam. Their data will be transmitted to the AWACS aircraft, where it will be merged with their radar and transmitted to NORAD in Colorado Springs, and of course to us. A squadron of F-22 Raptors based at Shaw is at Knoxville providing constant CAP. Another squadron of Raptors from Langley will begin TDY at Knoxville early today. The Kentucky Guard and their F-16 Falcons have been put on alert and are scheduled to arrive at Knoxville in two days. These aircraft will be armed and maintain constant radio contact with the AWACS. We also have capability to immediately communicate with all the players. And the shoot-down authorization will be issued from here. Needless to say, we have substantially beefed-up security here at Washington, D.C.

"Effective approximately one hour ago, all aircraft east

of the Mississippi River and south of the thirty-eighth parallel are grounded unless operating on an IFR flight plan with an operational IFF or under defense visual flight rules with an operational IFF. We won't know until day breaks if this plan will work. The weather is good in the upper half of the U.S., and I'm afraid that hundreds of pilots in small civilian aircraft will not be briefed about the emergency NOTAM and depart VFR. Hopefully, as the day progresses, word will spread and the SCAT procedures will be effective and help us sort out who's who." General Montgomery forced a slight smile and added, "I'm sure word will spread even quicker after we scare a couple of civilians and force 'em to land on a road or in a cornfield." Everyone chuckled and nodded in agreement.

Montgomery continued. "General Lynch, Commander of the Air Combat Command, is on duty at his headquarters at Langley for immediate assistance and consultation. It's my understanding that an evacuation order will not be issued, at least not at this time. The Governor and Homeland Security are reluctant to issue a mandatory or even a recommended evacuation order. They fear panic, looting, and general disorder would kill hundreds as they scramble for perceived safety. I hope and pray our efforts are not too little, too late."

And how many thousands will soon wake up and go blissfully about their daily business not realizing the great peril their lives are in? Scott thought, frustrated.

"Commander, I realize you have been very busy the past two days with very little rest, but we desperately need to know everything you can remember about this nut, Major McGruder. Intelligence briefed us, but most of their information was stale data gleaned from his personnel file. Didn't really tell us much."

Scott thought about what the general had called McGruder, frowned, then realized the general was probably right.

"Major McGruder is unfortunately a very intelligent, cunning, and gifted person," Scott began. "He can think and react quickly to changing scenarios. He's demonstrated some of those traits by successfully stealing the most highly classified weapon in our inventory. Of course, the Major is not the same person I once knew. Or thought I knew. McGruder has always been a very determined person in whatever endeavor he undertakes. He's tenacious, like a pit bull. Once he attempts something, he won't turn loose easily until the mission is completed. And he's probably more determined to execute this Pact than he has been with anything else in his life."

"That's unfortunate…for us. From a technical standpoint, what are our chances of detecting that F-35 on radar and destroying it before he has a chance to launch that SAID?"

"I don't know the AWAC's exact capabilities, nor the mobile radar's effectiveness, but I do know it's not impossible to track the F-35 given enough radars, as we demonstrated in the Caribbean. However, that was over the ocean."

General Montgomery stepped over to the coffee

container, turned toward Scott, and said, "Coffee?"

"Yes sir, black please." Scott accepted the heavy cup emblazoned with an Air Force logo although he really didn't care for coffee and only consumed a small amount. "The rugged terrain near Norris Dam will increase the likelihood that the occasional radar return from his aircraft will be absorbed in the clutter. It's very difficult to track any low flying aircraft without an operational IFF. And stealth multiplies this problem. The SAID is carried internally in a modified bomb or missile bay, which increases the stealth qualities of his F-35 Stove. One thing in our favor is the gatling gun, which is mounted on his aircraft. This cannon is in a pod, which is attached to the underside of the F-35. It does reflect a small amount of radar energy. So, it's not a sure thing. What we've done, of course, is better than nothing, but I believe we must somehow outsmart Major McGruder, design a better mousetrap, and quick."

37

Saturday, March 19, 2015
0700 Hours
The Pentagon War Room

After a short catnap, Scott bent over a stainless steel sink and splashed cold water onto his face in an effort to remove the cobwebs and revive himself. Having virtually no rest since the previous Thursday was taking its toll. But he was on a mission, surviving primarily on grit and fear. At times, he felt confident, believing that his body and brain were functioning normally. Then suddenly, without warning, he would succumb to a world of doubt.

But suppose I'm thinking irrationally due to fatigue and stress? This is such a harebrain idea that I wouldn't dare consider it under normal circumstances. I could ruin my reputation. My career. Maybe I should just keep my mouth shut. Play it safe…No, I can't walk away from this hunch. Too many innocent lives are at stake. If they think it's a stupid idea, I'll just tuck my tail between my legs and run.

His temples pounded, caused by his fast-beating heart, as he mused about the possibilities of his brainstorming.

I must present it and let the chips fall where they will. General Morgan said his office door was always open to me. Let's see if he really meant what he said.

Scott's escort contacted the general's secretary and was told to proceed to the Tank. When General Morgan's secretary opened the door, Scott was momentarily taken aback and stopped at the entrance. General Morgan and his full staff were clustered around a large walnut table conducting their daily staff meeting. Charts of various sizes and colors sat on pedestals in the rear of the room. An MBS screen mounted on a wall depicted a satellite photograph of Iran. Pictures hung on the wall behind the general—pictures of the President at the top, followed by the Secretary of Defense, Joint Chiefs of Staff, and some other officers. A large painting of a Boeing B-52 bomber flown by General Morgan earlier in his career hung on an adjacent wall.

General Morgan motioned for Scott to enter and said, "Morning, Commander Wallace. Come on in and have a seat." The general moved his chair slightly and told his aid to bring another chair to the table. As Scott sat down next to General Morgan, perplexed and dismayed that the general had interrupted his staff meeting, the only thing he could think to say was, "Thank you, sir, for seeing me."

Scott looked around the room. He had never been in a room with so many high-ranking officers staring at him. *Now that I'm committed, there's no turning back. Hope they don't laugh me out of this room.*

After initial pleasantries were concluded, General Morgan said, "What's on your mind this morning, Commander?"

Scott began. "Gentlemen, I would like to present a plan to you that might be the Trojan horse we've been searching for."

Everyone in the room focused on Scott.

Present this in the correct order, in a nutshell, in a manner that all can comprehend. Don't screw up.

He put his hand over his mouth, cleared his throat, and continued. "The SAID normally emits data and receives instructions via satellite through a secure data link. This allows us to track and monitor the SAID at all times, whether inside the belly of an F-35 or thousands of feet beneath the ocean. The SAID was built with this capability for various reasons. The most important one was to prevent the SAID from falling into enemy hands. Of course, none of this is possible if the SAID is in the power off mode. McGruder is a SAID expert, and rest assured his SAID will be in the power off mode while he's en route to his target, as it has been since his disappearance. He wouldn't forget such an important item. Unfortunately, the F-35 has an override switch to prevent the SAID from being activated via satellite. The override switch was installed for pilot safety. Actually, it's not a switch at all. It's part of the so-called glass cockpit concept. It's nothing more than a spot on the PCD touch screen that sends commands to the SAID. This switch would normally prevent us from activating and locating the SAID. During development, we didn't envision such a scenario in which we would need to activate the SAID from another source, and therefore a provision was not included in the contract to do so. However, as I recall, the idea was discussed at least two times, then shelved as an unnecessary cost item with the possibility of delaying the project."

An admiral leaned sideways, whispered in the ear of a lieutenant who promptly retrieved a document from his attaché case containing the classified information on the SAID program. Other members of the board began jotting down key points of Scott's presentation.

"Keep in mind at the time we were in a crash program to quickly develop a viable counter to the Cockroach.

"My proposal is definitely way outside the box, but then so is everything else we're dealing with. Like most munitions of this type, the SAID is armed with a self-destruct explosive. However, the SAID must be in either the standby or power on mode before the explosive can be detonated. Here's the part that's in our favor. The SAID standby mode must be activated at least five minutes prior to launch. During this critical time, the SAID performs a series of internal self-tests. If the results of these tests are satisfactory, the SAID searches several satellites and locks in its current position with extreme accuracy. It's then ready for deployment. If we can break into the SAID's on board computer and activate the self-destruct mechanism, it should theoretically explode when the standby switch is turned on. I propose to do this through one of our satellites or perhaps from an aircraft. McGruder will activate the standby switch several miles from the dam site, and the resulting explosion shouldn't damage the dam. That concludes my proposal."

General Morgan asked if his staff had any comments, questions, or suggestions. A navy captain spoke. "This is the only viable suggestion presented thus far that I am aware of. I recommend Commander Wallace be authorized to proceed."

When no other comments were made, General Morgan turned his swivel chair toward Scott and said, "Commander Wallace, just tell us what resources you need to get started."

At this time, several officers around the table nodded their heads in approval.

"Thank you, sir. I worked with the brains at the Phoenix Corporation as the on-site liaison officer during SAID's development. I personally know most of the top experts. I want to gather several of the engineers, both software and hardware types, who developed SAID, and delve into the possibility of going forward with this idea.

"It'll take some strong horsepower to make this happen. And even more so to make it happen quickly. Sir, with all due respect, I request that you or the SecDef personally contact the CEO of the Phoenix Corporation and request their key people be assembled at their research and development center in Annandale. If approved, I'll leave immediately for Annandale. After a short briefing on what my mission is, we'll proceed to our Test and Development Center at Pax River and get to work."

General Morgan again asked his staff if they had any comments or suggestions. They all concurred that the project should start immediately.

"Commander, I'll leave now for my morning brief to SecDef. I concur and authorize you to proceed as suggested.

I'm sure the SecDef will concur also. My plan is for both of us to contact Bill Warden, CEO at Phoenix. Rest assured, we'll make this happen."

Saturday March 19, 2015
1930 Hours
Patuxent River
Test and Development Center

Scott and his assembled group took a well-deserved break for dinner. The group had been brainstorming in the conference room since midmorning. They wrestled with the bleak possibility that such a mechanism, dubbed *Anti-SAID*, could be developed in such a short time span—a time frame that no one could identify or measure. Unfortunately, little progress was made except to review the initial studies made during the development of the SAID. But the evening meal would be used to continue their brainstorming. Nothing but business would be discussed.

As they carried their trays to a table, Scott glanced at the TV and stopped momentarily in his tracks. A nationally recognized TV reporter was describing conditions in and around Oak Ridge, Knoxville and several nearby villages and towns. Scenes of clogged streets, interstate roads with traffic moving at a snail's pace, looting, and several fires burning out of control in Knoxville flashed on the screen. In one scene, a reporter and cameraman watched helplessly as two men rammed the back end of a dump truck into a bank, hooked a chain to an ATM machine, and careened down the street, sparks flying as the metal machine bounced wildly behind the truck. A young couple in a huge SUV was interviewed as they crept south on Interstate 75 toward Chattanooga. When asked why they were fleeing, the young man replied, "You used the word *fleeing*, not me. I'm employed as a technician at the Y-12 plant in Oak Ridge. If an explosion occurs at Oak Ridge, the upper winds would normally carry radiation to the northeast. And we're heading in the opposite direction. We're just getting out of harm's way."

When asked if his company had issued any special instructions to him, he said they had not, and he didn't know if a terrorist threat had actually been made, but he wasn't taking any chances. The reporter asked if he was supposed to be on duty, and he rolled the window up and abruptly ended the interview.

While the deplorable scenes repeated themselves on a screen behind the reporter, he tried to analyze what could have triggered such a stampede, comparing the frenzy to a herd of African Wildebeest on their annual migration. He concluded that several facts were known: The government had restricted civilian air operations east of the Mississippi, made no-fly zones around Oak Ridge and Norris Dam for all civilian aircraft, and tightened air security within a fifty-mile radius of Washington, D.C. Military fighters and tankers landed and took off on a continuing basis at the McGee Tyson airport at all hours of the day and night. They could be seen circling overhead at moderate altitudes, air refueling with the Knoxville Air National Guard. Military trucks that bristled with antennas were positioned around the dam. Highway 441, which passed over the dam, was closed except for official traffic. All boats had been removed from the marina situated near the dam.

Rumors spread like wildfire that terrorists planned to blow up the Norris Dam and the nuclear plant at Oak Ridge. And a curious news media didn't overlook the military activity in and around Washington, D.C., especially aircraft.

Anxious parents began pulling their children out of school. A run was made on canned goods and bottled water. Most outdoor camping equipment was snapped up in just a few hours. The local news media didn't help the anxious and suspicious public. The media hounded the military and local police authorities for information they either didn't have or were unable to divulge to the public.

As ridiculous as those fleeing people appear, they may well be saving their lives, Scott mused. *We must find a solution to this dilemma, and fast.*

Sunday, March 27, 2015
0100 Hours
High Endurance Coast Guard Cutter Hatteras
Straits of Florida

Excitement rose among the *Hatteras's* crewmembers as they neared the suspect target, tracked intermittently since it left a Columbian port. U.S. agents in Columbia were unable to attach a transponder to its hull before it departed, substantially increasing the difficulty of tracking the small vessel by satellite. Once the boat of interest, suspected of delivering drugs and illegal aliens, entered an area of weather, tracking by satellite ceased. At this point, a computer model used previous headings and speed to project where the boat should be at any given time. This projection was nothing more than an educated guess. But, this educated guess was forwarded to the Cutter *Hatteras.*

She was searching in the vicinity of this projection when she hit pay dirt. At least it appeared so to the Coast Guard.

The target displayed on the *Hatteras's* radar matched the projected position of the suspect vessel. Heading and speed were also compatible. The heavy-duty spotlights of the *Hatteras* made visual contact easy. The crew was somewhat surprised because the running lights were on and its name, *Andros Angelica*, and her registration data were clearly displayed. Professional drug smugglers operate without lights and identification.

As the sleek *Hatteras* neared the target, radio communication was attempted without results. At this time, the suspect increased speed but was obviously having trouble keeping the boat under control due to the rough water. To be legal, boarding must take place in international waters. At its current speed, the suspect would be out of international waters in a short time.

The *Hatteras* captain, Commander John Wilser, ordered the inflatable boat readied, and its crew prepared for immediate boarding of the *Andros Angelica*.

Wolfman, Coast Guard operations at Charleston, S.C., approved an official drug interdiction and boarding of the intercepted boat. Commander Wilser ordered two rounds fired over the bow of the suspect. The *Andros Angelica* slightly changed course but didn't change speed. Two more rounds were fired without any effect. Then all lights on the *Andros Angelica* went out. Commander Wilser ordered the rudder and propellers destroyed.

The tracers and shells struck the boat at water level.

Chunks of wood, metal, and plastic exploded in all directions, followed by heavy black smoke billowing from the gaping hole. The vessel slowly came to a stop, rolling and pitching at the mercy of the large swells. The *Hatteras* drew near and an order was given by loudspeaker for everyone to gather on deck with their hands in the air. Almost immediately, six people appeared on the pitching deck, struggling to remain upright on the unsteady and slippery surface with their hands pointing upwards.

Within minutes, the Coast Guard boarding party was onboard the *Andros Angelica.* Shortly afterwards, the boarding party leader advised, "Preliminary search is complete. Negative weapons, illegals, or drugs. The captain's name on the license posted in the cabin is Perry Saint George, with an address in Freeport, Bahamas. He has identification on his person with the same name. He gave his base as Freeport, Bahamas and said he was returning from a fishing trip. Standard fishing gear is aboard, but there is no indication it has recently been used, and negative fish in the coolers. The boat has substantial damage to its interior hardware and electronics equipment, but the captain is at a loss for words as to how and why the damage occurred. His explanation for not stopping was his fear of being hijacked and that the bright lights from the *Hatteras* made it impossible to see who was chasing him.

Suddenly, an excited voice from the lead searcher crackled over the *Hatteras's* radio, "We've made a closer body search, and one male is carrying a substantial amount of American money still in their bank wrappers. Request an officer and additional help in making a more detailed search before she sinks."

As they examined every inch of the boat, expecting to find a cache of cleverly hidden drugs, an unusual piece of equipment was noticed in the engine room. The young recruit, puzzled because of its compact shape and weight, asked for advice.

When the chief shone his light on the object, the words, 'Property of USMC' got his attention. The tool or instrument didn't appear old or used, virtually ruling out the likelihood that it was surplus military stock. Baffled, he radioed for the officer on board to take a look. It was lifted onto the deck, and the captain of the *Andros Angelica* was quizzed about its purpose and where he'd obtained it. His answers changed twice, and neither made sense. The information was radioed to the *Hatteras,* along with a serial number and that it smelled of fuel.

Commander Wilser shot back in an excited tone, "Verify that it's stamped 'property of the USMC.'"

"That's affirmative, sir."

"Okay, standby while we check this out with Charleston. And keep your weapons handy. This is starting to take on an ominous tone."

"Roger that, sir."

"*Hatteras* to Wolfman."

"Go ahead, *Hatteras.*"

"Wolfman, ah, this is the captain, Commander Wilser. I need some advice. My search crew hasn't found any drugs or illegals so far, but one male passenger is in possession of a fairly large amount of one hundred dollar bills still in their bank wrapping paper. I suppose that could be accounted for or they could be counterfeit, but the most troubling thing is a heavy tool or instrument found in the power room. The boarding crew says it looks new, smells of fuel, and is stamped property of the U.S. Marine Corps. They estimate it weighs about ninety pounds and mike charlie one-four-four is inscribed on its side, presumably a serial number. So far the captain's explanation as to where he obtained this thing and what he uses it for has been evasive and ambiguous, over."

"We copied that, sir, stand by please."

Shortly afterwards, Wolfman at Charleston transmitted the following instructions: "*Hatteras*, Wolfman, come up on MBS encrypted channel two."

"Roger, Wolfman, switching."

Seconds later: "Wolfman, *Hatteras* on channel two, over."

"Captain, I want you to seize that instrument, photograph, and forward immediately."

"Wilco, Wolfman."

After a short pause, Wolfman operations at Charleston provided the following: "The information given by the captain, his license and boat registration, are confirmed correct and current by the Bahamian authorities. He has no serious offenses on record. At least that's what they tell us. No confirmation on the crew member or passengers."

Shortly, Wolfman received several pictures of the fuel pump taken from various angles, including a close up of the inscription and serial number. An immediate classified message was forwarded to all Naval and Marine Corps Air Stations requesting help in identifying their find.

40

While the boarding party was conducting their search of the *Andros Angelica*, Scott returned to the Pentagon's war room to brief the officer-in-charge while his Snake was being retrofitted with an Anti-SAID for test purposes. The Phoenix team, and Scott, had been working in shifts around the clock, taking short rest periods only when fatigue and hunger overcame them. Through their perseverance and teamwork, a breakthrough had occurred. The team had successfully activated the firing mechanism of a dormant SAID when standby power was turned on by tricking its computer into opening its gateway and bypassing its security system. But, this was a laboratory test conducted under ideal conditions and at close range. The real test would come within hours, as soon as the Anti-SAID equipment was installed in Scott's Snake.

Scott was escorted to the fox den where he met the officer-in-charge, General Wainright. "I wanted to personally brief you on this exciting development, sir."

After quickly briefing the general of the good news he said, "I'll be returning to Patuxent River to conduct operational testing in my F-35. If successful, I'll proceed directly to Knoxville and commence surveillance. Obviously, I'll need some help. I can't remain on-station continuously. An E-3 would be an ideal platform for long endurance surveillance. I highly recommend we position one at Pax River. If the Anti-SAID test is successful, the E-3 could be retrofitted immediately."

"That's fantastic news, Commander. Let's pray your idea works. Who knows when that mad dog will strike. It's been several days since he disappeared."

"Yes sir. Ten days to be exact."

"Good idea to get an E-3, possibly two, involved for continuous coverage. We'll get to work on that project immediately."

General Wainright turned to an Air Force Colonel, who was listening to the conversation, and said, "Colonel Elmont, let's start the coordination process and station two E-3s to Pax River for possible conversion. If you run into any stonewalling let me know."

"Yes, sir. I'll get right on it."

"Seems like an eternity since this nightmare started instead of ten days," the general added. "By the way, I sense and agree with your urgency, but I want to take a moment of your time to get your thoughts on a rather unusual request from the Coast Guard."

General Wainright glanced at an army captain and pointed at the console. The young captain, who had been attentively listening without saying a word, nodded, then touched a screen. Several pictures appeared.

Scott immediately recognized the fuel pump used by the Marine Corps and explained, "That's a fuel pump the Marines use to refuel their Stove aircraft in forward operating areas. Have any idea as to why the Coast Guard is interested in a marine fuel pump?"

"Not the faintest, but we'll find out if you're interested or think it's relevant."

Scott didn't respond. His brain was almost overloaded with data.

The general turned to an army major and said, "Andy, get Wolfman on the MBS secure link for the commander."

While the major made the connections, thoughts flashed through Scott's mind. Ideas and data flowed similar to a gargantuan computer. He churned the related and discarded the unrelated. Then he began struggling to sort, assemble, and re-arrange this data into a logical format. Several vague but seemingly important and related pieces of information confounded his innermost thought processes.

Let's see if there's some dots I can attach. McGruder's phone call to the Bahamas…radar track toward the Bahamas…fuel pump on a Bahamian boat. I wonder…

"Wolfman on, Captain Anderson speaking."

Scott touched the talk button and said, "Captain Anderson, I'm Commander Scott Wallace at Alpine. General Wainright and several other officers are present. I'm looking at your pictures of a Marine PFP, marine slang for portable fuel pump. Tell me what you know about it please."

"Okay, Alpine, about thirty minutes ago, our cutter *Hatteras* intercepted and disabled a suspect boat near the Bahamas bearing the name of *Andros Angelica.* They found this instrument or tool—I believe you referred to it as a fuel pump—on this boat. One passenger had a fairly large amount of American money on his person. They all have a bad case of what looks like insect bites and sunburn. Their clothes, including the captain's, are torn and muddy. The boat interior is trashed. The radio and radar power supply is ripped out. Most of the cabinets are either damaged or completely gone, as if someone was searching for ah—drugs for instance. The captain didn't provide adequate answers to our questions, and we were duly concerned because of the Marine Corps inscription."

Scott, face glowing with excitement, glanced at General Wainright and said, "Captain, there might be a link between this pump and another event currently unfolding. Sir, what I'm about to request from you could possibly help solve a national security emergency. I request you transfer all members of that seized vessel to the *Hatteras* immediately. I want to interview the captain and possibly others."

"Commander, I'm afraid we might break our treaty with the Bahamian government and possibly break some international law. I suggest—"

General Wainright interrupted. "Captain, this is General Wainright, officer in charge here at Alpine. Maybe you missed it when Commander Wallace said this incident could be the thread that links us to an ongoing national emergency, which I don't care to discuss with you at this time. Now I'm giving you a direct order to proceed immediately and call me on this secure line when you're ready for the interview. In the event this goes sour, keep in mind for your own protection that all of this conversation is recorded, and I'll take full responsibility for this action."

"Thank you, General Wainright. I was concerned about the interrogation, not the removal. The seized boat is slowly sinking, and we're already in the process of removing the crew and all passengers. As soon as the search is complete, we intend to sink her."

"Captain, do *not*, repeat, do *not* destroy that boat until we have a chance to interrogate the captain," Scott said, in an urgent tone of voice. "In fact, it's imperative that you keep it afloat as long as possible. Additional evidence could be aboard."

"Understood, and will comply, Commander."

Shortly thereafter, Commander Wilser transmitted, "*Hatteras* copied and we'll keep her afloat as long as safety permits. Captain Saint, ah, George is here with me. He doesn't look very happy but says he has some questions he wants answered."

"Captain, my name is Commander Scott Wallace, United States Navy. Are you the owner or operator of the vessel seized by the U.S. Coast Guard named *Andros Angelica*?"

"My name is Perry Saint George, Captain of the once beautiful *Andros Angelica.* I do not own her completely. I own shares of the Windjammer Company, and I am employed full time as her captain. She and several other boats are owned and operated by our company in Freeport.

I am fully licensed with my government to operate this boat, and I have complied with all safety regulations, both international as well as Bahamian. I employ one other crewmember. We were returning from a fishing trip. Why did your Coast Guard attack an unarmed vessel, endangering my passengers in international waters?"

"Captain Saint George, let's get something straight. You're not in a position to ask questions. I'll ask questions, and considering the potential trouble you're in, I suggest you cooperate to the fullest. Do you understand?"

"Perhaps. Keep in mind your government has destroyed private property without probable cause. Rest assured my government will be asking some very critical questions concerning this matter. I haven't committed a crime. I've lost my livelihood, and I just wanna go home and forget this nightmare."

"Captain, one of the individuals on your boat is in possession of a fairly large sum of American cash. Normally that kind of money is not needed on an ordinary fishing trip. And cautious captains cancel fishing trips when dangerous weather conditions exist. Captain, where did that money come from?"

The captain paused, a distraught look on his face. "I…can't answer for my clients," he said, choosing his words carefully, "except to say they are fairly wealthy for Bahamians."

"I see…Captain Saint George, we found property on your boat that belongs to the United States Marine Corps. Any idea of how it just happened to be on your boat?"

"Sir, I am not knowledgeable about Marine Corps pumps or stuff like that."

He's tipped his hand. Spilled the beans. Gotta finish him off, thought Scott.

"I was never in the military and know very little about military things. It could have been inadvertently left aboard from my last trip. I carried a full load of cargo, and some of the dock workers don't like to lift heavy objects. They probably left it on my boat. Too lazy to remove it. Happens frequently."

"Captain Saint George, how did your boat sustain the interior damage? The radios and radar? The woodwork?"

Captain Saint George paused, pushed his cap backwards, and scratched his head, grappling for a quick, plausible answer. Finally, he said, "Happened a few weeks ago. The police report said it was hoodlums looking for drugs. It happened while my boat was being serviced in Freeport."

"I see…Captain, where and when did your group use the Marine Corps pump to transfer jet fuel?"

A long silence ensued.

Captain Saint George suddenly realized he had inadvertently mentioned a critical piece of information that linked him to a possible crime against the U.S. Government.

Up to this point, he had been responding in a confident and authoritative voice. His reply to Scott's last question took on a totally different tone. His voice quavered. He removed his cap, nervously glanced at Commander Wilser and the other officers who were observing his interrogation, and wiped small beads of perspiration from his forehead.

"Captain, you should consider the fact that under American law, an individual that cooperates fully will be looked at very favorably by our courts."

"Yes sir. Because I haven't committed a crime, I will tell you everything I know."

"Go ahead, Captain, and quickly as possible."

"Several weeks ago, a gentleman from England contracted with Windjammer for transportation to a small island."

"What's his name?"

"His name's Arnold Goodwin. From England. At least that's what he told us and that's the name on the rental contract. Said his company was considering the possibility of developing some small islands…similar to the construction they're doing overseas in the Gulf…Dubai I believe. Wanted to visit one of them to evaluate that possibility. He requested and I promised him I would keep this information confidential, but I doubt that it matters now. After walking around the island for quite some time, he returned to my boat and said some sand and small shrubs must be removed before he could completely evaluate the land. He contracted with our company on the spot to transport four workers, a tractor, and other small equipment to the site. He rented my boat for six days and paid the full amount in American cash, plus a bonus to guarantee that we would be available anytime his workers called."

"What are the names of the workers?"

"The leader is Robello. I don't know the name of the others. I believe they are relatives of Robello."

Scott interjected, "Did you say Robello?"

"Yes sir. It's Robello. Robello Martinez. He's in charge and the one that coordinates with me."

"What business is Martinez in?"

"Owns a taxi."

Another dot connected, thought Scott.

"As I recall, I transported a tractor, two wheelbarrows, several machetes, and shovels. Food and water of course. Robello said the area he was clearing was for fuel drums. Sounded crazy to me, but I wasn't asking any questions and didn't care as long as the cash kept flowing. By that I mean…I didn't care as long as a crime wasn't being committed."

"Captain, did you say fuel drums?"

"Yes, sir."

"Captain, could you describe them?"

"Standard size, metal barrels. They were painted green with a lot of black numbers and letters stenciled on them."

"Where did you first see these barrels?"

"When I supervised the loading in Freeport. Robello and his relatives delivered the barrels to the marina in a covered truck. I thought it was odd they made the delivery about 3 AM. They used a company truck, so I assumed it was just normal company business. As I said, the pay was good, and so I didn't ask questions. My job was to transport, not ask our customers questions. That is, of course, if it's legitimate business."

"What was the size of this area they cleaned?" Scott asked.

"I'd say, probably ninety to a hundred yards square—

anyhow, I transported the barrels to this small island or sand bar, I believe it was twelve or fifteen days ago. They tried to use their tractor to move the barrels to the site, but it kept bogging down. Eventually they rolled the barrels through the marshy ground to the concrete platform."

"Concrete? Did you say concrete?" Scott exclaimed.

"Yes sir, concrete. We were supposed to return to this location last Friday to transfer fuel from the barrels and pick up the final payment."

"Transfer the fuel to what?"

"I didn't know at the time. I didn't realize what was happening until we anchored. I could see the top of a plane."

"A plane?"

"Yes sir. I'm positive. It was a military jet."

More dots connected.

"Continue, Captain, but make it snappy. I want only the important details."

"Yes sir. I'll do my best. Even though the seas were still very rough, the weather improved somewhat and we returned Tuesday. I couldn't believe my eyes when we went ashore. That large military looking plane was parked in the clearing made by Robello and his relatives. Only one person in flying overalls stood guard outside that jet. His head was covered with a mosquito net and he had a pistol in his hand, which he kept pointed at us. I could see his thick, black beard through the net. I still can't figure how he managed to get that jet on that tiny speck of land. But there it was, bigger than life. Then he called Robello and me by our first name. Robello looked stunned, and I was speechless. How did this strange, dirty man know our names? And why was he pointing that pistol at us? He hobbled over to where Robello was standing and shoved him so hard Robello stumbled backwards. He demanded to know why he hadn't delivered the pump with the fuel. Robello was finally able to speak. He tried to explain that the pump was on my boat, but he forgot to remove it the previous trip. The man pressed the pistol against Robello's forehead and told him the next mistake would be his last. He was extremely angry, and smelled like a dead fish."

Scott interrupted the captain again and ordered him to get to the point and skip the useless garbage. Captain Saint George continued, apparently unable to distinguish exactly what was unimportant, while Scott became more impatient as the minutes ticked by.

"He raved and cursed in a shrieking voice, threatening to shoot us for being late. I tried to convince him the weather had been too dangerous and that it had only slightly improved, but he just yelled louder. I didn't mention the weather again. He said he'd eaten the last of his survival food and water and that he was tired of eating filthy bugs and lizards. I don't care to admit, I was scared, really scared. All of us were scared. And why not? This was not what we expected. Didn't expect a screaming maniac waving a pistol at us. Finally I convinced him to let me get some food off of my boat. He told me to do so but made me toss the boat keys to him. He looked like an ape-man, but I could tell he was intelligent. He was thinking faster than all of us put together.

"I cautiously approached him and gave him the food and water. That's when I recognized who that mad man was. How could I forget those cold, devious eyes? Those huge, hairy hands? It was Arnold Goodwin from England.

"After gulping down a sandwich, two bananas, and a bottle of water, he calmed down a bit. But he had a big problem with that plane—"

"What kind of problem, Captain?" Scott asked, becoming more impatient with each question.

"One of its wheels, the back wheel, was sitting down in a hole. I think the concrete broke from the weight of that metal plane. Anyhow, he told us we were going to help him free the jet, refuel it, and then he would pay us. He asked me if I had a jack or any type of heavy metal that could be used for leverage to pry the wheel upward. I told him the truth. I didn't have anything like that. He wanted to know if any of us knew where a large jack and heavy piece of steel could be located. Robello cautiously volunteered that he could find a heavy-duty jack at a railroad maintenance shop but wasn't sure of a steel plate. Then that pilot, Arnold Goodwin, used a rope ladder and pulled himself up into that plane. He reached inside, removed some money, and waved it at us. He told us the plane was half-full of money and it was ours under one condition. We had to locate and deliver a large jack, two shovels, and a steel plate. He suggested finding a steel plate used to cover holes during road repair. He said it must be very strong—strong enough to support that plane's wheel. Once the aircraft was freed and gassed up, he would pay us and the contract would be fulfilled.

"He tossed my keys to me. We all headed for my boat, but he ordered Tabatha to stay with him. For company, he said. I believed it was for insurance. To ensure we would return. But before we had a chance to depart, he changed his mind and limped out to my boat. He ordered Robello and his brother to remove the pump. Then he ordered me and Robello to rip out the power supply cables to the radar and radio and place them near the barrels of fuel. More insurance. We were his captives."

Scott again interrupted the captain and said, "Captain, I haven't got time to listen to your life history; just give me the meat of your involvement in this debacle."

"Yes, sir, I'm doing my best. But each time you interrupt me I slow down."

Scott released the transmitter button and spoke to the others. "He's using too much valuable time. Could be intentionally stalling. If I could get my hands on him I'd—"

The captain continued. "We returned to the island Friday, much later than planned, due to the rough seas. We were fortunate. We located everything he wanted. He had no respect for me as a captain, and I didn't ask for any. I worked alongside my deck hand and everybody else. He instructed us to take turns digging out enough mud to slide the steel plate under the wheel. It all began to make sense. But it took a long time. We worked in mud and water up to our knees. Most of us had large blood blisters on our hands. It was very hot and those bugs nearly ate us alive. And Robello found some leeches on his legs."

"Captain, did that pilot ever mention his name?"

"No sir. But, as I said before, it was definitely Arnold Goodwin."

"Was there any writing on his uniform?"

"I believe so. But I can't remember what it said."

"He didn't have an English accent as he did before, but I recognized those piercing eyes and his weird hands. It was the same Goodwin that was on my boat for almost a full day. We all worked as hard as we could under the circumstances, except for Goodwin. He didn't point his pistol directly at us, but he always had it strapped over his shoulder where he could easily reach it. That night he confiscated the keys to my boat, climbed up into that plane, lowered the plastic top, and went to sleep. We slept on my boat. Or at least we tried to. Actually the bugs chewed on us so much that normal sleep was impossible.

"Yesterday at daybreak, we were able to drag the steel plate from the boat to that plane and slide it under the tire. He told us to set the jack on the steel plate and raise the tire level with the other rear tire. I could see the problem. Metal rods were tangled with the rim on both sides."

"What kind of metal rods?"

"Rods they put in concrete to make it stick together. Make it stronger. Then he motioned for us to keep moving the jack handle. The steel plate began sinking in the mud, and the wheel didn't budge one bit. After the jack was fully extended without moving the wheel, he cursed and ordered us to lower the jack and remove the steel plate. He limped toward my boat and said to me and Robello, 'Come with me and bring the jack handle.' Robello and I climbed aboard my boat. Then came the order I detested the most, 'Dismantle anything that will fit under that metal plate. Cabinets, tool boxes, anything you can pry loose.' Down deep, I began to despise him for damaging my boat, but I didn't dare complain or let my anger show.

"We ripped out anything we could, threw it overboard, and the others carried the pieces to the plane. We placed most of the stuff from my boat into the sunken area, then replaced the plate. We reinserted the jack and started putting pressure on that wheel again. It started making a moaning sound, almost like when you tune a guitar. Just when the jack was almost extended, one of the bars broke, followed by two or three more, and the plane jumped up with a loud bang. He was happier than at any time before. Even told us we did a good job. Next he ordered us to begin pumping gas out of the barrels into the plane. He watched us very closely and cautioned us to be careful not to let any sand or dirt mix with the fuel."

"Captain Saint George, did the pilot use a hand-held radio or cell phone?"

"Not to my knowledge, sir.

"I believed he might shoot all of us once the fuel was pumped into that plane. As I saw it, he wouldn't have any use for us after the fuel was pumped. I wanted to run, but there was no place to go on that speck of land."

"Were you able to pump the fuel into the jet?"

"Yes sir. He instructed and watched every move we made. It was a very slow process. We all wanted to high tail it out of there as quickly as possible. After we finished, about 2100, he removed some money from the airplane and tossed it all to Robello. Gave me the boat keys. I was astonished, very happy, but at the same time shaking inside with fear. Any moment I expected to hear a popping sound from his pistol. We loaded my radar and radio parts and left in a big hurry. Most likely in the confusion the pump was put aboard by Robello and stored in the engine room. I didn't care. I just wanted to get out of there. So you see, I was just an innocent victim in all this. Just trying to earn a decent living for my family."

Scott cleared his voice and said, "Captain Saint George, you have been very helpful. You said you got under way as soon as the fuel was transferred. Did you see or hear that jet take off?"

"No sir, I did not. And I'm glad it didn't. I kept looking over my shoulder for that plane. I was afraid he might sink my boat. I thought the Coast Guard was somebody Goodwin had ordered to kill us, take my boat and the money Robello was carrying. And now you know why I didn't answer my radio. I didn't hear the Coast Guard calling because I didn't have a radio."

"You're starting to make sense, Captain," Scott said, in a less aggressive manner. "What time did you leave the island?"

"I estimate it was about, ah, 2130. I normally log my arrival and departure times, but I didn't tonight."

"Captain, I want you to re-board your boat before it sinks. Give the Coast Guard boarding party the GPS coordinates of the jet's position, the location of that island."

"No sir, my boat is going down fast. They shot a hole in

the aft, and she's taking on water. I would be in great danger, great peril, especially in this weather."

"You'll be in greater danger if you don't. Now get moving."

Captain Saint George removed a piece of Sandollar stationary from the inside roof of his cap, gave it to Commander Switzer, nodded, and said, "These are the coordinates you're looking for. The coordinates for the island with that jet."

The Pentagon
Sunday, March 27, 2015
0300 Hours

Scott contacted Development of Special Operations at Patuxent River to obtain a progress report. The Phoenix team had completed the installation and ground testing of the black box, now dubbed the Anti-SAID. Extensive flight-testing should have been the next step, and certainly would have under normal circumstances, but this was anything but normal circumstances. The ultimate test of the Anti-SAID was imminent.

His original mission of testing the Anti-SAID had dramatically changed. So he exercised SecDef priority and ordered base operations to mount a GAU-22/A Gatling Gun Pod with a full drum of ammo and two AIM-120C AMRAAM missiles. Next, he instructed them to file a flight plan with the FAA for direct Knoxville exercising top priority handling by order of the SecDef.

Before leaving the war room, Scott requested Commander Wisler, Captain of the *Hatteras,* to proceed directly to the coordinates obtained from Captain Saint George, at maximum speed. General Wainright ordered Commander Wisler to use whatever force necessary, including deadly force, to prevent the Stove from departing. But in his mind, as well as Scott's and others closely involved, it was highly unlikely McGruder would remain a sitting duck longer than necessary. And they were right. While Scott's helicopter was en route from the Pentagon to Patuxent River, McGruder had been airborne almost thirty minutes. Forty minutes later, he slipped through the intensive radar net searching for him.

The sheriff's office at Saint Simons Island, Georgia received several noise complaints concerning a low-flying jet. The crucial information was logged in a computer by a very tired and sleepy deputy as just another routine report from rich whiners, and no further action was taken.

Scott's Snake, heavily guarded by the FBI, marines, and under surveillance by the CIA, had been in an obscure building near the combat aircraft loading area during the modification. Civilian and military personnel had scurried in and out of the area all day carrying small packages and briefcases bulging with documents. When the hangar doors were opened and the tug pulled the Snake outside for refueling, a retinue of civilian and military personnel accompanied it like bees attending to their queen.

At Patuxent River, Scott jumped off the helicopter the

moment it touched down and vaulted a short distance through turbulent air churned up by two F-22 Raptors fast-taxiing to the departure runway. He would not perform his normal preflight. Time was of the essence, and his goal was to get in the air as quickly as possible. Sam Croswell, lead Phoenix SAID representative, gave Scott a quick show-and-tell briefing on the installation and operation of the Anti-SAID.

When Croswell completed his briefing, Scott asked him to move slightly away from the Snake, out of earshot of the others, and said, "Sam, this is not a test. I'm proceeding to Knoxville at full speed. We believe McGruder will fly to Norris Dam tonight. He's refueled his Stove. No doubt he's itching to destroy that dam. He might be en route as we speak. This thing must work the first try. If not… Well, I think you've got the picture."

"Let's pray it does, Scott. We'll be monitoring in our test room and standby on the test frequency in case you need us. Good luck, Commander."

As the crew chief assisted the strap-in, Scott verified that a detailed pre-flight was conducted while the Snake was in the hangar, the missiles were stowed in the bay, and a full supply of ammo for the cannon was onboard. Not all of the ground crew were privy to the unfolding mystery but sensed that something big was under way. However, they hadn't connected the dots between the Snake and the situation at Norris Dam. That information was on a strict need-to-know basis.

Scott contacted clearance delivery for his IFR clearance and started the checklist at the same time. Clearance delivery was aware of the time-critical situation and had already obtained the necessary clearance. The young controller rattled off a clearance. "Cleared to Knoxville via direct, maintain flight level 510, squawk mode 3 code 1424, altimeter 2987, winds 230 at 8."

As the Snake's engine came alive, Scott began taxiing and transmitted, "Son, just slow down a bit and say again the assigned flight level."

"Rifle 1, maintain flight level 510. Believe I forgot to mention you're categorized as priority two."

"Outstanding. Great. Unrestricted climb to flight level 510. In that case, revise my speed with center to mach one-point-two. We'll worry about any broken windows later. And cancel my schedule in restricted area 4006. I won't be using it tonight."

As Scott began a fast taxi, he advised ground control, "Rifle 1's in a big hurry, need to expedite, will depart runway 14 with a right turn out."

"Rifle 1 roger, cleared for take off runway 14; departure frequency is 281.80. Good hunting, sir."

"Thanks, we need it."

Shortly after becoming airborne, Scott received an update from Alpine. The kind of report that hits you in the chest. Hard. Like a young mule kick. Not unexpected news, but nevertheless disheartening and nauseating. The *Hatteras* confirmed the story of Captain Saint George. The evidence was complete and overwhelming. Empty fuel barrels, wrappers from U.S. emergency food rations, water bottles, broken concrete and jack, just as the captain described it. But McGruder and his Stove had escaped again. However, one part of the report was encouraging. The search party reported that the concrete in and around the blast area was still fairly hot, indicating a recent departure by McGruder. But, even that report was stale. The million-dollar question remained: Where's McGruder?

Delayed satellite images verified all of the reports but didn't help solve the current problem. Imagery experts poured over the satellite data, scrambling to see if earlier images would provide a better departure estimate, or if they got lucky a satellite photo of the actual lift off. They weren't lucky. They only had images before and after the lift off.

After receiving this information, the Pentagon advised Homeland Security, who immediately raised the alert level to Juniper, the maximum for peacetime. Scott had inadvertently become the key player in possibly the largest and most spectacular manhunt in U.S. history.

He made a mental calculation of a worst-case scenario; i.e., if McGruder departed shortly after refueling and flew directly toward Norris Dam at maximum speed.

He most likely would have already arrived at his target. McGruder could easily travel the approximately seven hundred nautical miles in an hour and a half. Hopefully, he stayed hunkered down in his lair. Just waiting for that magic hour. Probably using the old philosophy of attacking around 4 AM, when man's metabolism is at its lowest, guard's down, most vulnerable…I'm afraid there's a distinct chance that McGruder has out-foxed the most technologically advanced military machine in history.

How far he had progressed depended on several factors. Among the most important for Scott to consider was the route and altitude chosen by the elusive and cunning

McGruder. He might try a circuitous route in an attempt to confuse and throw his assumed aggressors off his scent, thereby reducing the possibility of radar detection. But a circuitous route would take longer and use more fuel than a direct route.

Leaving Flight Level 200, Rifle 1 entered clear and smooth air with only a thin, scattered layer of clouds below and a first quarter moon above. Passing abeam of the Brooke VORTAC, and clear of the Washington, D.C. area, Scott thumbed the power lever forward and the air speed left mach .93 for mach 1.2.

Better advise ATC.

"Washington Center, Rifle 1 increasing speed to mach 1.2."

Probably going to annoy some folks on the ground with a sonic boom, but that's much better than a boom from a SAID.

Sam Croswell advised Scott that all components of the Anti-SAID were monitoring normal. Alpine confirmed that all SAIDs nationwide had been deactivated to prevent their unintended detonation. Under normal circumstances, such an undertaking to design and build an Anti-SAID would not have evolved out of research and development for possibly months, or more likely years. But sometimes desperate humans can perform Herculean tasks well beyond their perceived capabilities, and this was one of those performances. Now it was a race between man, time, and technology. One highly sophisticated computer trying to dupe another, each the brainchild of the U.S. Navy.

As Scott reached Flight Level 510, the optimum altitude

calculated by Phoenix to provide maximum Anti-SAID coverage, a faint and unnoticed shadow made by a Stove flickered across the shimmering water of Lake Hartwell, 120 miles southwest of Kings Mountain. An irrational and determined pilot with a lethal weapon on board thundered directly toward Norris Dam. The onboard INS/GPS mileage had shrunk to a mere 150 nautical miles southeast of the target, Norris Dam.

A pact made almost 66 years ago was only thirty-seven minutes from execution. That is, unless Scott's Anti-SAID was successful in the early demise of Major McGruder.

The majority of Oak Ridge and Knoxville residents had recently returned home, adding to the potentially calamitous situation. Most people could not be absent from their jobs, schools, and homes indefinitely. The realities of life simply overcame their fear, and so they returned in droves. Most were in their homes asleep on this early Sunday morning, oblivious to the grave danger just minutes away.

And then, what had been feared could happen, happened—a basic problem yet a significant one. Murphy's law at work? Or perhaps Gremlins? The Anti-SAID overheat light illuminated in Scott's cockpit. Croswell and his engineers received the over-heat indication simultaneously, and immediately asked Scott to verify the condition of the heat sensor.

"It's in the red. Suggestions?" Scott replied in a somber voice.

"Stand by, Commander. Are there any other problems, such as excessive heat in the cockpit?"

"Negative, Sam. All other instruments are normal."

"Frankly I didn't believe we would have a heating problem," Sam responded, as if he was talking to himself. "Okay, Commander. Here's what we must do initially. Turn the Anti-SAID power completely off for now. We realize this is a critical time to do so. But, my engineers have come to the conclusion that the heat could ruin some sensitive components. When the heat has sufficiently dissipated, you can power up again. I know very little about the F-35 air conditioning system, but if possible, suggest selecting a cooler temperature."

"Roger that. Main power switch is off and reducing cockpit temp. Sam, I don't consider this a satisfactory solution. We won't know if and when it's cooled down enough to be turned on again. After we turn power back on, we'll have to repeat this process. In the meantime, that dam could be wasted."

"Understand, Commander. The best brains in the world are swarming over this problem as we speak. Unfortunately we didn't have time to design a cooling system and install it."

"Roger that, Sam. Keep me posted."

There's gotta be a better way, Scott thought. *Just inches away, the outside temperature is sixty degrees below zero yet we can't use it for cooling…or can we?*

He punched up the emergency checklist displayed on his PCD, then touched the screen for Rapid Decompression.

>PROBABLE CATASTROPHIC STRUCTURE FAILURE ABOVE FL450.

>RECOMMEND EJECTION OR EMERGENCY DESCENT.

I'm taking this baby down to a lower altitude and utilize some of that cold air.

Scott flipped his mode 3 transponder to emergency, checked the PCD ACID and AESA radar for traffic, reduced power slightly, and pushed the nose of the Snake almost straight down. If he cracked some walls, he hoped the good folks in Roanoke would understand.

He transmitted on his radio: "Washington Center, Rifle 1

emergency descent. I'll miss the northeast-bound FedEx air bus at 1 o'clock, flight level 350."

After a slight pause, Washington Center transmitted in a startled voice: "Roger, Rifle 1. When able, advise nature of problem and intentions. Out. FedEx 1420 traffic, F-35 two o'clock eight miles southwest bound in emergency descent."

"Ahh, FedEx 1420, got 'em on the metal detector 2 o'clock. Passing clear. Thanks center."

Seconds later, reaching flight level 200, Scott leveled the Snake and punched up the emergency checklist for rapid decompression at flight level 200.

RAPID DECOMPRESSION

>OXYGEN 100%

>GLOVES ON

>ADJUST COCKPIT TEMP

>DESCEND TO LOWER ALTITUDE IF NECESSARY

>ANALYZE REASON FOR DECOMPRESSION

"Washington Center, Rifle 1 leveling at flight level 200. Keep you advised."

"Rifle 1, roger. Maintain flight level 200. When able contact Atlanta Center 257. 90. They're aware of your emergency descent."

Scott replied, "Rifle 1, wilco." He tuned his radio to the new frequency for the Atlanta Air Route Control Center and lowered the volume. Didn't check in. He had more important things to chew on.

Don't wanna go lower than flight level 200. The lower I descend, the less coverage, warmer air, and less likelihood of snagging McGruder. Better inform Phoenix.

"Phoenix, Commander Wallace."

"Go ahead, Commander," Sam Croswell replied in a determined voice.

"I may have a solution to our overheating problem. I've descended to flight level 200 and plan to decompress my cockpit and let the colder air inside. This will, hopefully, cool the overheated components of our Anti-SAID. Do you have any problems with this idea?"

"Standby a second, Commander."

Less than a minute later Croswell replied, "No problem, Commander. The Anti-SAID components are not pressure sensitive and shouldn't be affected. But the attenuation will be reduced substantially at the lower altitude."

"Roger that, Phoenix. I'm decompressing now."

Scott touched Emergency Decompress and heard the air howl through the emergency porthole as the air pressure stabilized. The outside temperature measured minus 10 degrees Fahrenheit, and he immediately felt the cold air as it rushed into the cockpit.

Five minutes later Scott transmitted, "Phoenix, the cold air is rapidly cooling the cockpit. See any problems if we power up again?"

"Negative, Commander. Give it a try. We'll monitor."

Scott turned the main power switch of the Anti-SAID to the "on" position. The overheat red light momentarily flickered, then disappeared.

"Looks like you've got a winner, Commander Wallace. Congratulations," Sam yelled from Phoenix operations.

"And congratulations from Alpine also," boomed a

euphoric voice Scott recognized as General Wainright.

Scott didn't reply.

This is a lot easier for them than for me. Possibly the most difficult thing I've ever done. If this works, I'll destroy one of my best friends. But unfortunately, I've got to do it. Life has lots of strange twists and turns.

He shrugged his shoulders, turned the volume up, and monitored Atlanta Center before checking in on the new assigned radio frequency.

"Centurion seven six one victor echo Atlanta Center, radar contact ten south Jacksboro, climb and maintain one four thousand."

Scott overheard the controller talking to civilian pilots because the controller transmitted on both VHF and UHF frequencies. But, he couldn't hear civilian pilots because he normally did not use his VHF radio.

"Atlanta, Rifle 1 flight level 200. We've got our problem resolved."

"Rifle 1, roger, squawk 1426."

"Rifle 1, roger."

43

The nose of McGruder's Stove pointed down at a steep angle as it hugged the north side of the Smoky Mountains. Two AWACs aircraft and several ground radars searched in vain for the Stove. They had been alerted that McGruder was probably en route to Norris Dam and to be extra vigilant. Occasionally, a tiny portion of the radar energy reflected from the Stove. But neither the AWACs' onboard computers nor the intercept controllers were able to discern the small and infrequent bits of data that briefly flickered on their radar screen. The controllers used all their skills to locate the bandit that was surely headed their way. They adjusted the MTI range and power differently on various radar displays, hoping they would get lucky and snare McGruder.

The shimmering lights from the charming city of Gatlinburg slid under McGruder's port wing. Thoughts of happier times flashed through his mind.

It seems like only yesterday when we vacationed at Gatlinburg. Abby was about five, and Melanie three. And Deborah, ahhh. Especially in those white shorts. Man. So much fun to be with. Always happy and smiling. Outgoing and full of energy. What a great time we had, camping, hiking, and just being together at our cabin. Lord, if I could only go back in time. If only that awful day in Iran had never happened. Why was I flying the only aircraft that had just refueled and had the correct weapon on board? A dozen other aircraft were on CAP. Why me? What will they think of their dad after this? They'll be scorned everywhere they go. I love them so much. Maybe I should stop while I have the opportunity…I could put this thing down anywhere and pretend I lost my mind, or blacked out. Pretend I couldn't remember anything since the ORE. But if I carry out the Pact, I can return the land taken by the TVA to its former state. At least for a while. I might awaken the people of this country, our leaders might be forced to return to the principles upon which our nation was founded. That's the greater good. Hopefully stop this insane killing. Yes, I must carry out my blood commitment as specified in the Pact. I must…and I will.

Several aircraft navigation lights appeared in his peripheral vision. He glanced up from scanning his instruments and peered through the canopy in a frigid stare.

Hmm. Wonder why so many aircraft are in the Knoxville area this time of night? Not normal.

McGruder touched his glass cockpit PCD and selected ACID.

Dummy! The ACID should have been on all the time, he chided himself.

Immediately a complete picture appeared on his PCD of all aircraft in the Knoxville area tracked by the military and FAA radars, including the identification, altitude, direction of flight and ground speed of each aircraft.

What the…? AWACs, tankers, and Raptors. Somehow they've discovered my plan. But my aircraft's not being tracked. They can't find me. All that fancy radar and I'm invisible. Ha! Uh-oh. There's a Snake…call sign of Rifle 1. How could this be? That's Scott Wallace's call sign.

McGruder touched the communications buttons and selected Command and Control, then Search. The computer searched military frequencies in use within a selected radius of Knoxville. It stopped at an active frequency. McGruder listened intently. But something of greater importance distracted him. The red light in the PCD weapons window blinked twice, then stayed on indicating power was being sent to his SAID.

"Looks like you've got a winner, Commander Wallace. Congratulations."

"And congratulations from Alpine also."

Puzzled and distracted, McGruder stared straight ahead and slowly turned the volume down.

That's Wallace all right…My old bosom buddy, Commander Scott Wallace. Who's Alpine?… Why would Wallace be here…and how? He should be on that flat top. I don't like this. But they can't destroy what they can't see. He bit his lower lip, sneering to himself, and uttered a series of obscenities. *I'll not let him stop me now. I've got too much time and energy invested. No way. Never!*

McGruder stared outside the cockpit, gritting his teeth in

frustration, then his attention returned to the PCD.

I've got to think rationally. Not let that brown-noser control my actions. Can't let him get inside my head and cloud my thinking. Use my training...I'm a Marine officer...I must have inadvertently turned the power on to my SAID. But how?

McGruder selected SAID POWER OVERRIDE on the PCD.

No change.

His brain had difficulty rationalizing and accepting data that seemed completely illogical. Completely irrational. Data a hundred and eighty degrees out of sync from all his training. Opposite to all of his intimate knowledge of the SAID's complicated system. Its guts. He'd programmed it with detailed knowledge of Norris Dam—its dimensions, trashrack structure, and its most vulnerable part, the penstocks. He was familiar with every circuit, transistor, and computer chip inside the SAID. He was its master. Its creator. So why wasn't it responding to his commands?

He punched up the PCD checklist to deactivate the SAID, touched the screen, and completed the simple procedure to neutralize it. The red light remained on. He thumped the screen lightly with his index finger.

No change.

What's happening? This is impossible.

While McGruder was trying to analyze his SAID problem, Scott noticed something in his peripheral vision that startled him. His PCD acquired a SAID symbol at ten o'clock and a hundred miles. He stared at the symbol. It was moving northwest at a ground speed of 310 knots. On a track directly toward Norris Dam.

"Alpine, Rifle 1."

"Stand by, Rifle 1."

Seconds later, Alpine inquired, "Rifle 1, Alpine. We're receiving a classified symbol about ninety miles southwest of your position. Tracking to the northwest. Anything on your PCD?"

"Affirmative Alpine. And my AESA radar is painting a bogey at the same location as the symbol. You thinking what I am?" retorted Scott, excited.

"Probably. We've come to the conclusion it's our man, McGruder. We've verified again, using serial and manufacture numbers, that all SAIDs are in the power off mode. Except for one. Gotta be him."

A startled controller in the AWAC's aircraft stepped on her floor pedal and transmitted, "Sentry 7 confirms a classified symbol at that location. We're also painting an occasional primary bogie at the same location that matches the symbol."

A colonel in Alpine shot back, "Roger that Sentry 7. Stand by for possible assistance to Rifle 1."

Scott replied, "Concur with your analysis, Alpine. But McGruder's too intelligent and careful to accidentally turn the power on. And he's too far from the dam to intentionally activate it."

"Concur. Check it out, Rifle 1, but proceed with caution. Could be a decoy or trap. You're cleared weapons tight. Engage with deadly force, your discretion."

"Rifle 1, understand, weapons tight, deadly force authorized."

McGruder's eyes narrowed. A hot sensation boiled up in his stomach. He bit his lip as he contemplated what he had just overheard. *Weapons tight, deadly force authorized by Alpine. They mean business. My SAID power is on and the whole world can see me. Gotta knock that power off, and quick.*

Let's see…Can't turn the main power off. I'll lose my navigational system, PCD lights. No control. Possibly crash into a ridge without them…Don't want to climb to a higher altitude and lose some of my stealth…

Scott transmitted to Atlanta Center, "Atlanta, Rifle 1 emergency descent. Cancel my IFR leaving flight level 180."

McGruder's INS/GPS indicated sixteen minutes before launch and eighteen minutes before impact.

Leaving flight level 180, Scott touched his PCD screen and turned off his IFF and AESA radar. This was unusual, not standard operating procedure, so the onboard computer instructed him to verify that he actually meant to turn them off. He did. When he turned the IFF off, his ACID disappeared from all PCD screens, including McGruder's. Now Scott's PCD was tracking what he believed to be McGruder. But McGruder couldn't track Scott. Neither was Alpine.

"Rifle 1, Alpine."

"Go ahead, Alpine."

"Okay, we were concerned. Not tracking you. Verify IFF status."

"All modes killed."

"Roger that, Rifle 1."

In a short time, McGruder would only have an educated guess as to the location of Scott and his Snake. He was flying blindfolded.

Scott doused his navigational lights and dimmed the cockpit lights as much as possible.

"Sam, you overhear our last conversation?" Scott inquired.

"Affirmative, Rifle 1. We're stumped here at Phoenix. That SAID should have exploded when it received power. For reasons we don't yet fully understand, we believe our Anti-SAID somehow turned the power on and the over-ride switch is ineffective. I've got my people working on it as we speak."

"Thanks, Sam. If your analysis is correct, and I believe it is, we should be able to eliminate this problem. If your engineers start tinkering with my Anti-SAID, there's always the possibility that it will discontinue doing whatever it's currently doing. Research and analyze after this incident's over."

"Rifle 1, I concur. We'll discontinue. Good hunting."

The SAID symbol was now at eleven o'clock and twelve miles. Scott slowed to 400 knots indicated airspeed and selected the starboard AIM-120C missile. The Snake shuddered slightly, yawed starboard, and wind noise increased substantially in the cockpit as the 335-pound missile swung downward into firing position. Seconds later, the PCD confirmed the missile was in launch position.

The SAID symbol on Scott's PCD had moved to twelve o'clock and five miles moving left to right with a ground speed of 310 knots. Scott began a right turn.

44

McGruder, frustrated, angry, and out of ideas, continuously moved his head up, down, back and forth searching in the darkness for an F-35. Scott's F-35. He touched the PCD screen and activated his AESA radar just long enough to make a few scans, then turned it off. Negative contact. Either no targets were within range or he hadn't left it on long enough. Leaving the radar on for an extended period of time would be a dead giveaway. Almost like painting a bull's eye on the nose of an aircraft and inviting all takers to take a pot shot.

Better get prepared. Use the only weapon available, my gatling gun. And it may not fire due to the damage I did at Lobster. Better test it, thought McGruder. He selected GAU-22/A Gatling Gun on the PCD. Almost immediately, a PCD message confirmed the gatling gun was loaded and ready for action. He squeezed the firing button for an instant. The Stove vibrated when the cannon spit out several rounds. McGruder smiled and said, "Yes!"

A faint reflection from the quarter moon glimmered in McGruder's peripheral vision simultaneously with an image of an F-35 in his HMDS. He turned his head right and squinted.

There he is. Now the real battle begins!

A Snake whizzed by his starboard wing. Slightly higher. McGruder's heart rate jumped. Fear or excitement before the kill? Only McGruder knew.

Scott Wallace. My old buddy. So, finally comes down to the two of us. I've had a gut feeling for some time that we would duke-it-out some day. This is the day. Got to outsmart him… somehow.

After Scott completed a steep right turn, the SAID symbol on his PCD was at twelve o'clock and two miles. His HMDS confirmed the presence of an F-35. He reduced his speed to be compatible with the symbol's speed. Nothing in sight. He touched the PCD screen for terrain minimums and started a descent from 4,000 feet to 2,300 feet, the minimum altitude to remain slightly above the terrain. Reaching 3,000, he briefly saw the outline of an aircraft at twelve o'clock and below his altitude. He continued a slow descent.

McGruder noted the time Scott's Snake flashed by his starboard side. The fact that Scott had located his stealthy Stove in darkness confirmed to McGruder that his SAID was transmitting.

Telling the entire military my exact location, speed, and direction of flight. That's the only logical way he could have found me.

McGruder made some quick mental calculations based on assumptions—but valid and intelligent assumptions. Assumptions carved from many hours inside a jet cockpit.

Should have completed his turn by now. Directly behind me, and closing. I'm a sitting duck. Can't see him. He can see me on his HMDS…probably has visual contact. Apparently doesn't have any ordinance on board or else I would have a missile up my tailpipe by now. So…what's he going to do, ram me? RAM! That's it!

Without further thought or hesitation, McGruder reduced power to idle, lowered the gear, and extended full flaps. The Stove practically stopped in mid-air.

Gotta get a visual confirmation before I attack, Scott thought. He touched his PCD and selected landing lights.

McGruder's Stove lit up like Times Square on New Year's Eve.

McGruder's Stove was practically sitting in Scott's cockpit. Scott winced, slammed the power to burner, turned hard to the right, and climbed. The Stove flashed beneath his port side. Close. Very close. Too close. Missed by mere inches.

The Snake's jet engine screamed, belched a plume of fire as burner kicked in. A second later, McGruder's Stove shuddered when it entered the Snake's wake turbulence and the disturbed air from the forty thousand pounds of thrust spewing from Scott's Snake.

McGruder jammed the power to burner and raised the gear, flaps, and speed brakes in a split second, honed from years of training. As the speed quickly increased, he turned twenty degrees right, climbed, and switched on his landing lights. But, he didn't need the illumination. The flame emitting from Scott's Snake resembled a torch. A dead giveaway.

"Got the bastard," McGruder yelled.

He increased the rate of turn and pitch attitude until Scott's Snake was in the crosshairs of his GAU-22/A

Gatling Gun. He pressed the red firing button on top of the stick with his thumb—held it down with ten times the pressure needed, his teeth gritted and his jaw muscles flexed.

Sensing what was imminent, Scott abruptly broke hard left and dove at a steep angle. He utilized every ounce of his air combat knowledge, skill and technique. A solid line of orange tracers passed within yards of his Snake. McGruder mimicked the Snake's jinks. He ignored the pain in his ankle and caressed the rudders until the crosshairs aligned perfectly with the Snake, then pressed the cannon's firing button. The four-barrel gatling gun purred, spitting out 67 rounds per second. Hundreds of tracers left their orange telltale signatures as they penetrated the darkness. Pieces of aluminum and composite broke away from Scott's Snake and whizzed by McGruder's canopy.

"Take that, old buddy!" McGruder snarled.

Scott's Snake shuddered. A 25-mm projectile passed through the port vertical stabilizer, skipped along the top of the fuselage, then ripped through the port side of the canopy. Wind noise screamed through the three by eight inch gash. Three projectiles found one of the support levers cradling the AIM-120C, ripped through it, and continued on to destroy a rear missile fin and damage another. With nothing to support the rear end of the missile, it sagged and began to wobble violently. The missing and damaged fins made the missile aerodynamically unstable. Occasionally it slammed against the bottom of the Snake's fuselage.

I'm hit. Gotta get behind him. Fly the aircraft! Fly the aircraft! What's that noise…and vibration?

Scott scanned the PCD to determine the damage. The outline of an F-35C popped-up on his PCD. Inside the F-35's symbol, an AIM-120C symbol flashed in red followed by a calm-voice, "Missile disengaged. Missile disengaged."

Scott glanced at his airspeed. Approaching Mach 1.

Got to lose him and get rid of that missile.

He pulled the control stick fully back. The Snake went from level flight to vertical almost instantaneously. It happened so abruptly that McGruder lost visual and HMDS contact simultaneously. Scott struggled to breathe as the g-force pulled on his entire body. He strained and grunted like a stuck pig, forcing blood upward toward his brain. The bladders in his g-suit sensed the force and exerted pressure on his lower body. His eyeballs wanted to leave their sockets. A casual voice from the PCD gave a dire warning of high g-forces. His head felt as though it weighed a ton. The colors in his PCD turned black and darkness encroached into his peripheral vision, brain screaming for oxygen.

Keep the stick back. Breathe hard…tighten legs and stomach…

His physical conditioning was paying off.

Don't black out. Be over in a second.

Tunnel vision. Hang on.

Completing a vertical loop, Scott leveled and reduced power. Blood flowed to his starved brain. Normal eyesight returned. But, the AIM-120C didn't rip off. It hung on like a fish shadowing a shark.

Don't make the same mistake twice. Keep a close eye on McGruder's speed.

Scott touched the PCD and released the safety on his

GAU-22/A Gatling Gun. *Hopefully that missile hasn't damaged the cannon.*

A voice announced that the cannon was ready for firing, and confirmed by a message on the PCD. McGruder's Stove was on Scott's nose less than a mile but jinking violently. The tables had quickly turned against McGruder. Now it was Scott's turn. He maneuvered until McGruder's Stove was perfectly aligned with his four-barrel cannon. He pushed the trigger button down and held it down. McGruder didn't repeat his ram trick but began jinking to the extreme. The missile on Scott's Snake twitched like a bucking bull as he maneuvered. But, he stayed on McGruder's tail, increased power and eased in closer. Tracers, sparks, then fire lit up the sky. McGruder maneuvered violently, trying to shake Scott. It didn't work. Pieces of composite material, titanium, and aluminum erupted from the Stove. McGruder went into a steep climbing turn. Scott stayed with him and continued firing, pausing momentarily to let the barrels cool.

Suddenly, a long plume of fire erupted from the Stove. Fumes and smoke from burning jet fuel entered the gash in Scott's canopy and seeped inside his mask. He selected one hundred percent oxygen, tightened his mask, and selected emergency vent. The Stove's wings wobbled back and forth. But not from jinking. McGruder was losing control.

A voice from McGruder's PCD calmly announced what he already knew. "Fuel leak, fire, smoke in cockpit, turbo fan out of balance, rudders damaged."

"Fuel leak, fire, smoke in…"

He slammed the PCD with his large fist. It fluttered, came back up, then turned black.

Could explode any second. Time to exit stage left. Hit the silk, thought McGruder.

Scott climbed to a higher altitude and reduced speed. Backed away. Then, just for good measure, he pushed the nose over slightly and hammered the Stove with another ten second burst from his cannon.

Gonna see an explosion shortly. If that SAID explodes, it'll shake the countryside. Back off. Don't need any more damage from flying parts.

At that instant, McGruder pulled the overhead ejection handle. The canopy departed first, tumbled through the slipstream, and vanished. A loud explosion was followed immediately by rockets that slammed his seat up the rails and propelled him into the dark night. Seconds later, his chute opened, and the heavy seat automatically separated and fell away.

The Stove rolled over on its side, nose pitched straight down. Seconds later, it went into a flat spin. Scott circled the area watching for an explosion and possibly a parachute. A bright flash temporarily blinded him followed by buffeting from a shock wave. The SAID explosion and jet fuel erupted into an inferno. Ground fire lit up the entire area.

When his vision returned, he saw a parachute at ten o'clock drifting lazily toward terra firma.

There it is. Take a look before it gets too low… Careful. Watch the terrain.

Scott pulled the power to idle, pushed the nose over, and

started a left turn. Thud! One of the four Beretta 9 millimeter bullets found the hole in Scott's canopy, ricocheted, then entered his shoulder. Scott winced, grabbed his shoulder and unknowingly banked the Snake hard to the left, directly toward McGruder's chute.

He's firing a pistol at me!

Thump! Scott looked up. A parachute canopy fluttered from the nose of the Snake and covered part of the canopy.

The PCD came alive with a dire warning. "Terrain, Terrain, Pull Up, Pull Up."

Scott slammed the power to burner, pulled the stick back, and leveled the wings. When the nose came up, the parachute canopy broke lose and vanished.

He pressed the AWACS command frequency on the PCD and transmitted, "Mayday, Mayday. This is Rifle 1, Mayday."

Almost immediately, Sentry 7 replied, "Rifle 1, this is Sentry 7, go ahead."

"Rifle 1, low on fuel, have a damaged canopy…ah, and a missile dangling beneath me. Possible fuselage damage, and I've been hit in my shoulder…with small arms fire, probably a pistol… over."

"Rifle 1, Sentry 7 copied. Say position and squawk mayday."

"Ah, roger, Sentry 7. IFF was off. Coming on now, emergency squawk. Vector an aircraft to intercept, assess damage…and help me solve the missile problem. I'm currently forty miles northeast of McGhee Tyson Airport. Can't land with that missile hanging loose. Need a restricted area in case we figure out how to release it. Also, I only have about thirty minutes of fuel. Need a tanker…now."

"Rifle 1, roger. Have you on radar. Smoky 4, a three-holer ten was orbiting in AR 633A. We're vectoring him toward you now. Will come up shortly on refuel frequency. Rifle 1, if able, change to refuel freq."

"Rifle 1, switching."

Seconds later, "Rifle 1, Sentry 7."

"Go ahead, Sentry 7."

"If you have time, I repeat, if you have time and can do so without comprising your safety, advise status of the other aircraft."

"Roger, Sentry 7. Scratch one F-35 Stove. Large explosion, either on the ground or just prior to impact. Large ground fire. Confirmed successful ejection but the parachute became entangled in the nose of my Snake. Suggest immediate ground search. They won't have any trouble locating the search area. That fire's huge. The area is mostly uninhabited…but emergency and rescue crews should check it out for possible casualties and extinguish that ground fire."

"Roger that, Rifle 1. We saw the explosion and fireball; have visual on the ground fire even from this distance. Picked up his emergency IFF squawk for a few seconds. Striker 5, a flight of two F-16 Falcons is twenty miles west of you. Will come up this freq shortly. Rifle 1, say your angels."

"Rifle 1 is anywhere between ten and eleven angels. I have the Falcons on the PCD. Is that my tanker forty west?"

"Affirmative, Rifle 1. We're vectoring both flights to

intercept you. They'll come in at an altitude above you. Striker 5 will be first. When they have visual contact with you, they'll switch to this frequency. Give you a good examination. Rifle 1, the nearest restricted areas are Redstone in Huntsville, Alabama and Fort Campbell, Kentucky. They're about equidistance, 180 miles."

"That's too far without extra fuel."

Seconds later, he added, "I'm not going to chance air refueling. You can call off the tanker. I'm really having a difficult time controlling this beast. I may eject at any time."

"Roger that, Rifle 1. Striker 5 has a visual on you, switching to this freq."

Seconds later, "Rifle 1, Striker 5, how do you read?"

"Loud and clear."

"Welcome to Knoxville, Rifle 1. We're about a mile behind you. My wingman will pull along your starboard side and I'll take the port."

"Roger that, Striker 5. I'm indicating 230 knots, which seems to be the optimum speed to reduce the missile flutter. Angels and heading varies."

"Roger, Rifle 1. I'm at your eight o'clock now. I'm going to shine a bright light on you, take a look at that missile. Suggest looking away from the light."

Seconds later. "Rifle 1, that missile is dangling beneath just like you said. It's swaying back and forth for two or three cycles then up and down. Probably explains why you can't hold a steady heading or altitude. You have considerable damage to the fuselage. It's severely bent with some skin missing. There's a round hole in your port, vertical stabilizer large enough for Larry Byrd to throw a basketball through. A mist is streaming from beneath. Probably a small fuel leak."

"Roger, Striker 5. I've only got about 20 minutes of fuel left. I can't refuel with this thing bucking around like a young mule in the springtime. How does the starboard side look?"

"Six lead, give him a report."

"Roger lead. Rifle 1, this is Striker 6. I doubt very seriously if your gear would extend even if you weren't carrying that missile. Lots of damage to your underside."

Got to make a quick decision. If I land with that missile, it could explode, which would cause the other missile to explode. Fifty-fifty chance it would. Too risky. Kill myself and probably others.

Scott stared at the twinkling lights of Knoxville at two o'clock and Maryville at ten o'clock. The faint outline of the Smokies on his port side announced the breaking of dawn.

Be daylight soon. If I was a boy back on the farm I'd be up tending to my chores…Farm! That's it. My dad's farm is large enough…I hope.

"Striker 5, tune in the Volunteer TACAN 231 at 015 and take me to that fix, over."

"Ah… roger. 231 at ah, verify at one-five miles, Rifle 1."

"That's correct. Two-three-one at fifteen."

"Roger, Rifle 1. I've got it tuned in. Need about a fifteen-degree port. I'm turning now. I'll pull in front of you and then keep my speed on 230. Follow me."

"Roger, turning port."

"Rifle 1, what's the plan?"

"The fix I gave you is my parents' farm. Its size is about

a mile and a half square. Nothing out there except a possible herd of cattle. Should be large enough. Gotta be. I'm going to slow as much as possible and eject from 5,000 feet. That'll be approximately 4,000 feet above ground. Say distance from the fix."

"Understand, Rifle 1. Your farm is twelve o'clock and eight miles."

"Roger, eight miles."

"How's your shoulder?"

After a short pause, Scott replied, "Throbbing pain. Blotch of blood on my flight suit."

"Roger that, Rifle 1.

"Six, back off some, call ops, and scramble a medevac helicopter."

"Wilco, lead. Switching."

"Striker 5, let's start descent to angels five and slow to 200 knots."

"Roger that, Rifle 1, five angels, 200 indicated."

"Okay, Striker 5. I'm practically burning fumes now. Let's make this work the first pass. I want you to count down each mile starting at three miles. The last mile, count down each tenth."

"Roger, Rifle 1. We're slightly over five miles from the fix."

Okay, cowboy. Review your eject procedures; get it right the first time. May not be a second chance, thought Scott.

He selected NACES on his PCD and scanned ejection procedures, as he had done in a simulator many times. But this was the first time for real.

Two hundred knots. Over the farm, power off, gear and flaps down, eject.

"Three miles, two hundred knots."

"Two miles. Turn 4 degrees port."

"Roger, two miles, four port."

"Wind's calm."

"One mile."

"Roger."

"Ten, niner…two, one, zero, mark. Good luck, Commander."

The last thing Scott heard a split second before he pulled the face curtain down was a voice calmly announcing, "Stall warning, stall warn…" Instantaneously, he was blown out of the cockpit.

The wounded Snake shuddered, pitched up at a twenty-five degree angle, stalled, seemed to momentarily hang in mid-air, then rolled over on its back and pointed straight down. When the chute deployed, it jerked Scott around and separated the seat. Seconds later, he heard a loud crunching sound when the Snake met its fate on a hillside.

Rocks, red dirt, and pieces of the Snake mushroomed upward then settled back to earth. No fire. No explosion. Not yet. He tugged on his parachute shroud line to put as much distance between himself and the crash site as possible.

The countryside was very familiar—hadn't changed a bit since he'd left home. He'd been over all the fields at one time or another, either driving a tractor or hunting for quail. His parent's farmhouse was visible in the distance. The steeple of the white church where the Wallace family attended stood majestically over the small community.

The ground was coming up fast. A Black Angus bull bellowed in the far distance, challenging and defending his harem against all takers. Wham! The seat hit, bounced twice, and stopped.

Feet together and slightly bend knees. Hit the ground feet first and roll into a ball. Nothing but open pasture. No trees. No barbed-wire fences. Fairly level. No wind. Pure luck.

The early morning stillness was broken when Striker 5 abruptly emerged from behind a ridge and circled overhead at a low altitude. Foom! He hit the ground, fell sideways, and rolled twice. The chute fluttered to the ground. The young blue grass and clover smelled good. The ground felt good. He lay on his back momentarily, gazing up at the fading stars to the west. *Thank you, Lord.*

Got to move it, that missile might explode any second.

He stood up, unsnapped the chute, and ran toward his parent's house, discarding his helmet and mask. When he was a safe distance from the crash site, he stopped, gathered his breath, and pulled the emergency radio from his vest.

"I'm on the deck, Striker 5," he said. "No broken bones."

"Roger, have a visual. That was a great job. That thirty-five went straight down. We'll orbit overhead until the copter arrives. A vehicle is approaching from the southeast. This place will be swarming with the news media shortly."

Scott looked up, continuing to move toward his parents' house.

"Roger that," he said, "and thanks for your help."

A red Ford pick-up approached, driving as fast as conditions allowed. As the truck drew nearer, he recognized his parents. The Ford slid to a halt in front of Scott. Both doors flung open. His mother screamed his name. The three embraced for what seemed like an eternity. The Falcons slowed, made a low pass, and dipped their wings as Scott looked up and returned a sharp salute. He sat between his perplexed parents as they drove to the emergency room, trying to explain what had transpired in the last few days.

I can't believe what's happened. Better call home. I need to hear their voices. He chuckled to himself and mused, *I'd love to see the expression on the kids' faces when I tell them I just dropped in on their grandparents.*

ACRONYMS/ABBREVIATIONS

ACETEF – Air Combat Environment Test and Evaluation Facility, Naval Air Station Patuxent River, Maryland

ACID – Aircraft Identification. Used in flight plans to identify a particular aircraft such as Air Force One, which would be displayed on a radar data block as AF1. Southwest Airlines flight 2214 would be displayed as SWA2214.

ADF – Automatic Direction Finder. Ground based navigational aid operated by the FAA and occasionally by city or state aviation agencies. ADF is old technology that is being phased out of service in the U.S.

AESA – Active Electronically Steered Array Airborne Radar. On-board AN/APG-81 radar utilizing gallium arsenide and monolithic microwave integrated circuits for superior performance.

AIM-120C AMRAAM – Advanced Medium-Range Air-to-Air Missile. All-weather, beyond-visual-range capability. Aircrew navigates the missile using an aircraft data link guidance system until close-in to the target where the missile's radar turns on to complete the intercept.

ARTCC – Air Route Traffic Control Center. A facility established by the FAA to provide air traffic control service to aircraft operating on IFR flight plans within controlled airspace and principally during the en route phase of flight. When equipment capabilities and controller workload permit, certain advisory/assistance services may be provided to VFR aircraft.

AWACS – Airborne Warning and Control System. United States Air Force E-3 aircraft equipped with long-range radar. Carries sufficient personnel to carry out the primary duties of surveillance, command and control, and battle management.

CAG – Carrier Air Group. Commanding officer of a Carrier Air Wing based aboard an aircraft carrier is known as the CAG.

CAP – Combat Air Patrol. Fighter aircraft in a defensive mission to protect military or civilian assets from enemy attackers.

CATCC – Carrier Air Traffic Control Center. Located on an aircraft carrier and has responsibility to provide separation and flight advisories to naval aircraft operating from an aircraft carrier.

CDC – Combat Direction Center. Located on an aircraft carrier. Acts as the ship's defensive and offensive nerve center utilizing computer-enhanced radar and communication systems.

CERAP – Combined Center/Rapcon. A Federal Aviation Administration Air Route Traffic Control Center that controls en route air traffic from one airport to another and is located in the same building with an FAA Rapcon, which controls air traffic in the vicinity of an airport.

COD – Carry On Delivery. A C-2 turboprop aircraft used by the US Navy to deliver personnel, food, mail, and the like to and from aircraft carriers while at sea. Affectionately known as a greyhound.

CVN-77 – Carrier Vessel Nuclear - Nuclear powered Nimitz class aircraft carrier. Utilizes some stealth through a rounded flight deck edge and superstructure that scatters a percentage of radar energy instead of reflecting it back to a radar antenna.

DSN – Defense Switch Network. A military communications system. DSN has several layers of precedent, allowing authorized users to pre-empt other users with a lower precedent.

FAA – Federal Aviation Administration. An agency of the Department of Transportation charged with responsibility and authority to regulate all aspects of civil aviation in the U.S. Most notable and visible of these functions are the vast National Airspace System air traffic control system conducted in Air Route Traffic Control Centers (Centers) and Control Towers.

GAU-22/A – A four-barrel, electric gatling gun cannon that shoots a .98 inch diameter shell. It can deliver 67 shells per second at a very high muzzle velocity. This cannon is mounted on an external pod on the F-35B and F-35C.

HMDS – Helmet Mounted Display System. System built into pilot helmet. Provides video with virtual heads-up display in day or night conditions combined with precision symbology for improved situational awareness and tactical capability. Technology is based on the measurements of the thermal energy of an object against its background by distinguishing small variations in thermal radiation. This enables a pilot to see in total darkness, through fog, and in other low visibility settings.

ICAO – International Civil Aviation Organization. A specialized agency of the United Nations whose objective is to develop the principles and techniques of international air navigation and to foster planning and development of international civil air transport.

IFF – Identification Friend or Foe. Used by military to identify their own aircraft on radar displays by assigning classified transponder codes to be used by pilots on a daily basis. In a hostile environment, any aircraft not transmitting on the correct code would be considered hostile. Prevents or reduces mistakes from friendly fire.

IFR – Instrument Flight Rules. Rules governing the procedures for conducting instrument flight. Allows pilots to conduct flight in low visibility conditions. Separation from other aircraft is provided by air traffic controllers.

INS/GPS – Inertial Navigation/Global Positioning System. INS is a navigational system totally contained in an aircraft. It does not require information from external sources. Provides aircrews information derived from inertial effects on components within the system. GPS is a space-base radio positioning, navigation, and time-transfer system.

MBS – Military Briefing System. Worldwide encrypted briefing system using audio or audio and video if equipped (fictional).

MINOT – Military Alert Notice. Used by military to search for unreported or overdue military aircraft (fictional).

MTI – Moving Target Indicator. An electronic device, which displays radar presentations from targets that are in motion. A minimum speed and range can be selected in which moving objects will be displayed or discarded. MTI partially eliminates ground clutter but at the same time reduces the effectiveness of radar to depict a moving object, such as an aircraft.

NACES – Navy aircrew common ejection seat.

NORAD – North American Aerospace Defense Command. A United States/Canadian organization charged with the missions of aerospace warning and control for North America. These responsibilities are the monitoring of man-made objects in space, detection, validation, and warning of attack by aircraft, missiles, or space vehicles. Ensures air sovereignty and air defense of the Canadian and United States air space.

ORE – Operational Readiness Exercise. Military exercise to evaluate combat readiness.

OSD – Office of Secretary of Defense.

PCD – Panoramic Cockpit Display. A liquid crystal display located at the top of the instrument panel. The PCD displays all major functions of the F-35, including flight and sensor displays, communications, navigation, identification, and a worldwide mosaic display of all aircraft tracked by FAA and military radars (partially fictional).

SAID – Submarine Acquisition Identification and Destroy. Ultra secret Naval weapon capable of locating, identifying, and if ordered, attacking a submarine with conventional or nuclear weapons (fictional).

SCAT – Security Control of Air Traffic. A procedure implemented by appropriate military authority during a national emergency. Requires all air traffic to obtain an authorization before departing and have an operational radio and transponder set on an appropriate mode and code (fictional).

SecDef – Secretary of Defense

STOVL – Short Take-Off and Vertical Landing. Aircraft capable of vertical climbs and descents.

TVA – Tennessee Valley Authority. A quasi-governmental corporation charged with flood control, river navigation, and electrical power generation.

UTC – Universal Coordinated Time. Occasionally referred to as "Zulu time" or Greenwich Mean Time (GMT). Reference is located at Greenwich England. Thus all clocks in the world using UTC time have the same time regardless of where they are located.

VAL – Vertical Approach Lights. Lights on STOVL aircraft that illuminate the surface directly below a landing aircraft during hours of darkness (fictional).

VFR – Visual Flight Rules. Weather conditions authorizing pilots to fly without FAA clearance utilizing the see and be seen concept.

VOR – Very High Frequency Omni Directional Range. A ground based navigation aid operated by the FAA. Aircraft navigate along airways and jet routes using VORs.

VORTAC – A Co-Located VOR and Military Tactical Air Navigation aid called Tacan. The Tacan is used by civilian aircraft to determine distance and by military aircraft for lateral and distance navigation.

Printed in the United States
147633LV00002B/17/P

9 780978 951009